THE HANGING GALE

Captain William Townsend was not a man
to look back, once he'd embarked on a
project. He'd been warned of the dangers
here, and though his predecessor in the post
he was about to take up had been marked
down as missing, believed drowned, he knew
full well what the truth behind the man's
disappearance must be. More and more, the
newspapers at home had spoken of the
unrest among the Irish, and the
ungratefulness of the people towards their
English rulers and benefactors. As he rose,
he considered some of the opinions he had
heard and read: 'There is a degree of truth i
the sarcasm that the only secret an Irishmar
keeps is the whereabouts of a fugitive from
justice'; 'All Irish seditions are branded with
the foulest murder and most diabolical
savagery. There is always the pretence of a
constitutional aim; there is always murder
and savagery'. 'There are few who have not
heard of the Ribbon Societies of Ireland;
those dark and mysterious confederacies
which, springing up from time to time in
different localities, have spread terror and
dismay into the breasts of both rich and
poor; which have done so much to
discourage the influx of capital into Ireland;
and to promote the absenteeism of hundreds
of wealthy proprietors who would be only
too glad to be allowed to reside upon their
Irish estates, and in the midst of their Irish
tenantry, could they do so in peace and
safety.' Well, he would see for himself now.

RAY EVANS

has written scripts for several different television series, as well as books such as this one. He is unmarried and lives in London.

THE HANGING GALE

Ray Evans

BBC BOOKS

This book is published to accompany the television series entitled
The Hanging Gale which was first broadcast in May 1995.
The series was produced by Little Bird in association with Kensington
Fields for BBC Northern Ireland in association with RTE.
Executive Producers: Robert Cooper, James Mitchell and
David Blake-Knox
Screenplay by Allan Cubitt
Producer: Jonathan Cavendish
Director: Diarmuid Lawrence

Published by BBC Books,
an imprint of BBC Worldwide Publishing
BBC Worldwide Limited, Woodlands,
80 Wood Lane, London W12 0TT

First published 1995
Screenplay © Little Bird/BBC, 1995
Novelization © Ray Evans, 1995
The moral right of the author has been asserted

ISBN 0 563 37193 5

Designed by Tim Higgins
Typeset in Adobe Caslon by Nick Morley
Printed and bound in Great Britain by
Richard Clays Ltd., St Ives plc
Cover printed by Richard Clays Ltd., St Ives plc

In many cases the landlord refused a lease because he had the tenant more completely under his control; in others, the tenant declined because recent legislation had so greatly increased the cost of a stamp on a lease that he could not find the necessary £10 or so.

In most cases, however, even a lease did not give security, owing to a deplorable and 'very prevalent' Irish practice known as the 'hanging gale' — 'gale' being the term used for a periodical payment of rent. The hanging gale allowed an incoming tenant to leave his rent in arrear, that is 'hanging', for six, twelve, or fifteen months. Tenants were almost invariably without capital, land was let bare, frequently even a dwelling had to be erected, and it was useless for the landlord to look for his rent until at least one harvest had given the tenant a chance to gain something.

But, once the tenant owed rent, any security his lease might give vanished.

Cecil Woodham-Smith, The Great Hunger

Acknowledgements

The author would like to thank
Proinsias Ó Drisceoil of the Coiste
Gairmoideachais Cho. Chill Chainnigh for
his help with translations from Irish,
and for his book *Culture in Ireland – Regions:
Identity and Power*; John Percival for allowing
him to read the manuscript of *The Great
Famine*; Allan Cubitt; Jonathan Curling;
and Heather Holden-Brown for her
sympathetic support during the
writing of this book.

The Phelan and Dolan Families and the Galready Townspeople

James Phelan *father of the family, cottier*
Sean *head of the family, cottier*
Maeve *his wife (née Dolan)*
Joseph, Molly and Hannah *their children*
Conor *second son, cottier*
Daniel *third son, national schoolmaster*
Liam *fourth son, parish priest*

Patrick Dolan *head of the family, cottier*
Sarah *his wife*
Michael *their son, cottier*
Mary *their daughter, betrothed to Daniel Phelan*

Lord Hawksborough *absentee landlord*
Captain William Townsend *his agent*
Mr McBride *his chief clerk*
Mr Curran and Mr Harkin *his bailiffs*
Mrs Brogan *housekeeper to Captain Townsend*
Sub-inspector McCafferty *policeman*
Reverend and Mrs Denny *the Protestant minister and his wife*
Dr Davis *the doctor*
Mr Coulter *proprietor of Coulter's Stores*

ONE

It was already spring. But you would not have known it from the grey land, greyer than ever now in the dawn light as a fierce wind blew in off the restless sea, strong enough to ruffle the heavy skirts of the barefoot figure walking along the path at the top of the cliff. Below, the same wind whipped the water into angry foam among the black rocks, and you could hear the roar of the water above the sighing air.

Turning her back to the gusts, the woman reached out a lean hand to draw her dark shawl more closely about her hidden face and paused, waiting as another figure rounded the shoulder of the low treeless hill above the path and made its way down to join her, bare black feet tracing a hard route through the scattered rocks on the slope. Far behind her, dark shadows in front of the first sunlight, the cold mountains rose.

No sooner had the second woman joined the first than they fell into step together, dark red petticoats brushing the stones on the track. They had not exchanged a greeting and they walked in silence, shawls over their heads, their faces in darkness. There was a purpose to their walk, but they did not hurry. You could not imagine where they were going at that time of day, on the bleak hillside above the cliff. But now, from nowhere as it seemed, two others joined them. Tall women, with a long stride. Still no-one said a word and the only sounds close by were those the wind made in the tough tussock-grass, and the soft tramp of their naked feet on the cold land.

At a point on the path they turned inland and spread out, walking loosely in line abreast, making for a road which meandered across the hill. They were tenser now, and cautious. Little more than a glimmer of movement ahead showed them where the carriage was, but the light was getting brighter by the minute and soon the carriage was close enough for them to hear the noises of the horses and the wheels. They stood and waited. One squatted down, picked up a large stone, and weighed it in her hand.

The road had been a good one, one of the many that crisscrossed Ireland, the result of relief works brought in by the Government in London to help the poor in the years when the potato failed; but despite new works in the year just gone, this road had not been kept up. It chiefly benefited Lord Hawksborough's estate here at Galready, and the Government in its wisdom had decreed that no relief works should benefit one individual, but the people as a whole. Still, roads had seemed a good idea, and a man might think now that the country had enough of them. What it needed, many said, was food. A new disease had struck the potatoes the year before, and although this year the crop bid fair to be good, far less had been available for sowing than the people would need.

But the rents had to be collected, and so Lord Hawksborough's agent jolted along over the rain-ruined road in his carriage on one more of his interminable journeys of assessment across the estate. Henry Jenkins had been in his lordship's service for just over thirty years, starting as a boot-black at the town house in Eaton Square – a job he'd been glad enough to get following his demobilisation from the army with the rank of lance-corporal after we'd seen off Boney once and for all at Waterloo. Then there'd been the Derbyshire estate, where he'd been under-gamekeeper. That'd been best.

Jenkins glared through the window at the bare land, whose unforgiving look the watery light of the rising sun did little to mitigate. He shuddered and reached into his coat for his flask. The one thing they could do properly in Ireland was make good whiskey. And they needed it. Nothing but cold and rain. Still, it was a pity his lordship never came here. The crumbling Irish mansion stood in five hundred of the lushest, most beautiful hunting acres Jenkins had ever seen. It was a shame they were going to waste. On the other hand, this was a damned country, and it had been getting worse in the years since Emancipation and the rise of O'Connell. That slippery lawyer might have been in favour of political solutions but he was still a nationalist, and these were days in which an Englishman had to look out for himself.

Gingerly he raised the flask to his lips, but just then, they hit a pothole and the driver reined in. The bottle hit his mouth, bruising it, and alcohol splashed on to his lapel. This early in the morning it smelt unpleasant. He leant out of the window and looked ahead, then up at the driver, swaddled in a black overcoat, hat and scarf. The driver had the horses walking now. The slow progress of the carriage made it lurch the more. With that and the smell of the spilt whiskey, Jenkins felt ill.

'What is it?' he shouted up at the man, irritably.

The driver half-turned in his seat to look down. His heavy clothes made his movement stiff. 'People up ahead, your honour.'

Jenkins immediately pulled his head in and reached across to open the pistol-box on the seat opposite him. Both guns were ready primed. He took one out and cocked it, checking that the percussion cap was in place over the nipple. He leaned out again, squeezing his eyes up to see better. The light was still dim and made things shimmer, but he could see the figures by the side of the road all right as the carriage approached them slowly.

He relaxed and sat back, lowering the hammer of his pistol. He hit the roof with the butt of the gun and shouted, 'What's wrong with you, Shanahan? It's only a bunch of women. Drive on!'

But the driver didn't obey, and Jenkins felt the carriage lurch as the man clambered hurriedly down from his seat. Looking out, he saw that the women were running towards him, scattering their wraps as they did so and drawing thick sticks from the folds of their skirts. A fine rain had started to fall and it streaked the soot with which they had covered their faces, but even without its help Jenkins would have recognised the four big men who now made for the carriage, freed of their disguises, in shirtsleeves and homespun trousers. He knew what was about to happen, but he saw everything clearly, unfolding slowly. He saw Shanahan stumble off over the field, and he saw one of the men break from the group to chase him and grab him easily by the neck, dragging him back. Another made for the horses, to take hold of their harness.

Jenkins raised his gun and fired, but the shot went wide. He spun round and threw himself on to his second pistol but as he did so he heard the carriage door torn open behind him. Strong hands seized his coat and pulled him outside, sending him sprawling on to the rocky ground. He grazed his hands and the guns scattered from them. Arms pulled him upright, face to face with one of the men, a man from Brannocktown, Martin Ferry.

Ferry looked at him with blank eyes. 'On his knees,' he ordered.

The other man, Bryan Meagher, grappled Jenkins into a half-nelson and forced him down. As he did so, the agent could see Ferry walk unhurriedly over to where the pistols had fallen and pick them up. The man was unused to handling guns, he could see that, but that did not stop the fear.

'Please,' he said.

'Hold him fast,' said Ferry.

The horses were nervous, but stilled. The two other men stood a little way off, with Shanahan, head bowed, between them. The taller of the two was Daniel Phelan. The other, whose face was gentler, was ironically the one out of the four whom Jenkins knew to be a troublemaker: Michael Dolan, whose good-for-nothing father was already two years behind with his rent.

Behind and above him, Meagher was talking. He was speaking formally and his tongue got round the words awkwardly.

'Henry Jenkins. Land agent for the estate of Galready. You have been tried and found guilty of crimes against the people of Ireland.'

'What crimes?' said Jenkins, anger for one moment getting the better of his fear. What a damned people. Lazy and arrogant. This is what you got for being too soft with them.

'Houses tumbled,' Daniel said, his voice high with rage. 'Families turned out on to the road.'

'You have been sentenced to death,' said Meagher.

Jenkins was still looking at Ferry. The heavy shoulders. The huge bald head with its fringe of lank grey hair. Those blank eyes. Ferry was cocking one of the pistols. The land agent sought desperately to gather his wits.

'How have I been "tried"? Who spoke in my defence?'

'I did,' replied Ferry, levelling the gun at Jenkins's head. 'I wasn't very convincing.'

'And were you judge and jury too?'

Ferry looked amused, and as if he were on the point of answering, but if so he was interrupted by the driver suddenly babbling to Michael, who was holding him:

'Please, Michael, for the love of God. I've seen nothing. Heard nothing. Let me go.'

'Shut up,' said Michael. He was nervous. He did not like the look which had come over Ferry's face. Ferry was turning towards the driver. He had not lowered the pistol.

'Shanahan,' Ferry said gently. 'Do you like working for the English?'

The driver's eyes were wild. 'For God's sake,' he said. 'I've a wife and children.' He turned his face to Michael. 'Please Michael. Mikeen.'

Then Ferry came up close and shot Shanahan in the head. Michael and Daniel had been holding his arms, one on either side. Now it was as if he'd been wrenched away from them and thrown to the ground, his head a bloody mess on the stones. The pistol had twisted in Ferry's hand as it had gone off, and the ball had slewed in Shanahan's head. Michael felt it brush his shoulder as it flew past him, taking the side of the driver's skull with it. Daniel was looking at his own hands, then looking at the body. Michael turned to Ferry in horror.

'Jesus God, man, we said the agent!'

'The man couldn't have kept his mouth shut,' said Ferry, meeting his eye.

Jenkins looked from one of the men to the other. A desperate hope grew in him.

'Don't be part of this, Michael,' he said. 'I'm sure that whatever it is you want, we can talk about it. After all, I'm only doing my job.'

Ferry was cocking the other pistol. Now, without haste, he crossed back to where Jenkins knelt and placed its muzzle to the agent's ear. It felt cold. Ferry held the gun roughly and it bruised the flesh. Michael said nothing.

'For the love of God,' Jenkins implored.

Ferry pulled the trigger. The gun did not fire.

Jenkins's head swam with relief. He opened his eyes. 'It's God's will,' he gibbered. 'God's will that I live!'

Ferry turned the gun round in his hand and hit him with the butt. Blood spurted from his ear. He hit him again, across the eye, then again, full in the mouth. Ferry's blows were deliberate, as if he were hammering a nail into a plank. Meagher turned his face away, but continued to hold the man. At last Jenkins slumped forward, like a puppet whose strings are cut. Ferry leant over him and hit him twice more.

'The man is dead for Christ's sake!' said Michael. He looked at Daniel, but Daniel wouldn't look at him.

Ferry straightened and stretched his shoulders. Something like relief came over the four men. For better or worse, it was done. They started to look at each other, almost to smile. Then Jenkins shifted on the ground, and groaned.

'Did you say dead?' Ferry leaned over to his work again. He took the man under the arms and started to drag him away from the road, downhill to a bog pool. He was up to his knees in water when Jenkins began to struggle. Ferry seized his hair and with both hands forced his head under. Jenkins's struggle became frenzied. Ferry could hardly keep his balance in the water. The other three watched the messy killing. Jenkins's head came up, the mouth gasping.

'Will somebody help me here?' yelled Ferry.

After a moment, Daniel moved forward.

'Daniel, don't,' said Michael. But he could not raise his voice above a whisper. Instead, he watched as Daniel waded into the pool and helped Ferry drown Jenkins. It seemed to take a long time, but at last it was over. The two men did not have any strength left to pull the body out of the pool, but left it there, floating on its face, sluggish in the muddy water. Meagher had to brace himself on the bank and lean forward to haul them out. They threw themselves on to the turf and lay there, panting and exhausted. When Daniel had recovered sufficiently to look around him, he saw that Meagher had collected their women's clothes together to hide them among the rocks. Michael still sat with Shanahan's body. Daniel called to him, but Michael ignored him.

'These'll come in handy, at least,' said Ferry. Daniel turned and saw that he had got hold of Jenkins's pistols. He passed one of them to Daniel. Daniel cradled it in his hand. He thought of what he had just done, and looked at Ferry. What kind of thoughts were passing through Ferry's mind? He looked into his heart and wished he could find more feelings there than he did. He had just helped kill a man. Surely the moment should seem more important.

Ferry became aware of his gaze. 'Put it behind you,' he said. 'We did what we set out to do. Jenkins had it coming.'

'There'll be another agent,' said Daniel.

TWO

James Phelan stood in the May sunshine and looked back from the edge of the bogland to his distant farmhouse, freshly whitewashed in defiance of the hard times just behind them, and sparkling among the dark green fields of potatoes that surrounded it. This year had to be better, he told himself. God would not visit such a pest on a suffering nation twice.

He closed his mind to the thought of the possibility, and turned his gaze toward Michael Dolan, sitting a short way off on a mound, looking away across the sea. Miles away, as usual, thought James, glad that his daughter-in-law Maeve was of a more practical bent than her brother. He screwed up his eyes against the sun and turned them now to the bogland, where his eldest son, Sean, was inspecting the wall of peat from which the men were about to cut turfs. As he watched, Sean bent down to pick something up from the ground. James saw that Sean was holding the slane – *his* slane – the peat-cutting tool his own father had had made for him by the blacksmith in Brannocktown when he was twenty, forty-one years ago. James's father had been a sailor in the British navy as a youth, before he'd come back to the family farm, and the slane had been a present to celebrate and mark Admiral Nelson's victory at Trafalgar. Sean was a big strong man, like all James's sons, and still just on the right side of thirty. But he was not about to start using the slane without so much as a by-your-leave.

'Put that thing down,' James shouted as he strode across the moor to where Sean stood. He put his own strong hands around the shaft of the slane, but Sean did not loosen his grip.

'Is it not time to cut, Father?'

'The strongest man does the cutting,' replied James, twisting the shaft of the slane upwards to shake his son's grip on it.

For a moment Sean was angry. He was the stronger man and they both knew it. With his father cutting, the job would take an hour longer. But he accepted before he started to struggle with James for possession of the slane that he would have to give way. He could not hurt the old man's pride that much. He glanced across at Michael, saw him watching them. He tightened his hold on the slane, grasping it near its heavy iron head, and met his father's eye. He could see that James found even this token resistance hard, so he did not keep it up for long. It grieved him to see his father grow weaker with age; but as he let go of the slane and saw his father's grin of triumph and relief, he acknowledged to himself that the man had plenty of life in him yet, and had every right, as long as he ate his twelve pounds of potatoes a day with the rest of the men, to remain head of the family. He looked around over the farm himself now: at nearly twenty acres, one of the best in the parish, and they'd been able to withstand last year's blight the better for it. On the other hand, the rent would soon have to be paid, and word was that a new agent was due any day, following the disappearance of the last one. One thing the English didn't drag their feet over was collecting money.

Michael came up to him as he moved the turf-barrow into place by the cutting face. Michael was not so strong. His father Patrick was a cottier and had a tiny holding. But Patrick had fathered two fine daughters – hadn't Sean married one of them himself? And his brother Daniel looked certain to marry the other. With the two families linked, the future might be brighter. Though of course there'd only be the same amount of land for a greater number of people, and Sean and Maeve already had three children. If only there was more land to go round. Not for the first time, Sean thought of the acreage of Lord Hawksborough's unused parkland.

His father's voice interrupted his thoughts. 'Where's Conor? Mikeen, do you know?'

'I don't.'

'How about you, Sean?'

'Am I my brother's keeper?' Sean sounded more irritable than he had meant to and caught the look in his father's eye, but then they smiled at each other. It was a fine day, at last the rain seemed to have abated and the air from the sea was fresh.

'You'll have to take Conor's place,' James said to

Michael, and turned without another word to wield the slane against the peat face. Michael was nothing like Conor's size and started to protest, but James had already sliced down with the slane and cut a turf, which he pitched to Michael without more ado. It struck the young man hard on the chest and almost knocked him over, but he recovered his balance and heaved it on to the turf-barrow, turning back just in time to catch the next. But the barrow had jolted and Sean had to steady it. Sean knew that his father couldn't keep up the pace he'd set himself, that he was showing off, as much to himself as to prove to the younger men that he was still as good as they were. In fact he was stronger than Michael, and Sean could see that this barrow at least would be untidily loaded, and more time wasted. Ah well, perhaps it didn't matter all that much. But he would have liked to know where Conor had got to. Not that he didn't have a pretty shrewd idea.

And indeed he would have been right. Conor, a year his junior, was not far from them at that moment. If Sean had walked across the land to the edge of the cliff that dropped sheer to the black rocks of the seashore below, he would have seen his brother by looking down. Conor was pressed against the cliff-face, digging in with toes and fingers and knees, edging across it from nest to nest, ignoring the angry, frightened seabirds that mobbed him. From each nest he could reach he took one egg, reaching precariously behind him every time to place it gently in a pouch he had slung round his shoulders.

At last he was satisfied, and, taking care that he kept his body between the pouch and the rock, started to climb upward, heaving himself at last round the overhang and on to the grass at the top. Once there he rested, getting his breath back. His brown linen shirt was scuffed and stained, and his homespun breeches torn just above the left knee, but that was nothing. He dipped into the bag and looked at the eggs with pride. Then he stood up and made his way to join the others.

By the time he came in sight of the peat face the first barrow was loaded full and he could see Sean wheeling it over to the spread-field where he began to pitch out the turfs to dry. His father and Michael had paused to rest and sat, heads bowed, dripping with sweat, on a slope nearby. The two of them had not seen him yet, though Sean had glanced in his direction. Con hastened his pace as he saw his father pick up the slane and stand again, followed reluctantly by Michael.

'The blessings of God be upon your work,' Conor said to his brother as he passed him.

'The same blessing on you,' replied Sean, not pausing.

James was cutting again by the time Conor came up to him. Michael had loaded two or three turfs on to the second barrow, but he tottered as each sod was pitched into his arms and he stopped the moment he saw Conor. James stopped too, and glared at his second son.

'Where have you been?'

Con shrugged. 'Nowhere.'

'What?' snapped James.

'I forgot – about the cutting,' said Con lamely.

James leant forward and swiped him hard across the head. 'Don't forget your father again,' he said angrily. But he knew that his son was too old to put up with being hit like that, and he watched Con for a moment. Con stared at the old man, then lowered his eyes and took his place where Michael had stood, ready to catch the turfs. He barely had time to brace himself before James slung him the first one. He caught it neatly, turned, and in one movement had placed it tidily in the barrow and placed himself in readiness to catch the next. Michael, in a job that required more dexterity than strength, used a wooden blade to flatten the peat face in preparation for the slane's cut.

They did not stop until the sun was near its zenith, their only rest coming in the pauses when Sean replaced the full barrow with an empty one. By then the mechanical pace at which they worked had slowed, and Con had begun to look more and more frequently towards the farmhouse from where he knew Maeve would emerge with their dinner. Soon she did, a brown shawl over her shoulders, her long red Connacht frieze skirt a bright point of light in the sun. On one hip she held her youngest child, Hannah, born three months ago when things had been bad, and still a small baby. On the other, she balanced a flat wooden tray with a cloth on it, earthenware crocks and a big dish made of willow rods. Her feet were bare and grimy, her face and hands weatherbeaten; but her neck was as white as milk.

She made her way to them without hurry or fuss, and, putting down her things, spread out the cloth and laid the baby on a corner of it. She arranged the crocks and placed a large jug of buttermilk by them. The dish contained big potatoes from the side field, now replanted, boiled in their skins. Amidst them was a wooden bowl of salt water. Not until she was finished and called them did the men give over their work, taking their lead from James. They walked heavily over to the food and sat down to it, drawing pointed knives from their belts to peel them – all except James, who used a long thumbnail. Michael served himself, but did not eat.

'What's the matter?' Maeve teased him. 'Is your sister's food not good enough?'

Sean was the last to arrive, dumping the empty barrow and wiping his hands on his corduroy trousers.

'Look who's here,' said Maeve to Hannah, picking the baby up and holding her out to him. Sean smiled and nuzzled his little girl, then kissed his wife on the cheek and glanced across at Con.

'Con,' he said slyly, 'have you got something for Maeve?'

'And what might that be?' said his brother, defensively.

'In your bag.'

Conor looked away, moving slightly to conceal the pouch which lay beside him, and concentrated on peeling another potato before dipping it in the salt water and putting it into his mouth. But Maeve was interested now. And it wasn't the first time they'd played this little game.

'What've you got for me, Conor?' she asked.

Shyly, almost brusquely, Conor handed her the pouch. He'd have preferred to have given it to her later, in private. She took it from him and placed it before her on the ground. She reached her hand in and from it drew the first egg, laying it down carefully.

'Kittiwake,' she said. She drew out another and placed it beside the first. 'Guillemot.'

'You've been busy, brother,' said Sean, loosening his hobnail boots with a grunt of relief.

'Why risk your life for a few eggs?' asked James, gruffly.

'You mean you won't eat your share?' retorted Con. James was silent. The family kept a few chickens, but their eggs were reserved to be sold, except for one or two now and then for the children.

'Eight eggs,' said Maeve, emptying the pouch. 'I think they're beauties, Conor. Thank you.'

The tension was broken. Con looked at his sister-in-law and gave her a simple, affectionate smile.

At the end of the day the men made their way back home by way of the coast path before striking across the land. Their route passed the point where Shanahan's body had been found, and at that spot a cairn was beginning to grow as passers-by placed their stones. As James came up to it he stopped and stooped for a stone, placing it and removing his battered wideawake hat as he did so. He stood for a moment as Sean and Conor placed stones in their turn.

'How many children did the poor man have?' asked James. 'Was it four, or five?'

He had noticed that Michael had not placed a stone and directed the question at him. The whole parish knew about Michael's Young Irelander sympathies.

'Four, I think,' replied Michael, and after a moment's hesitation, he placed a stone too. Then he walked off alone, without waiting for the others.

'Why are you so sympathetic to Shanahan, Father?' asked Conor. 'He worked for the agent.'

James looked at his son. 'All the man did was drive a carriage!'

'He worked for the agent.'

'What do you know, boy? You've never had to feed a wife and children.'

Sean, listening to them, watched Michael in silence as the distance between them lengthened. Then he saw Michael take the turning that led to his father's smallholding.

The sombre mood which had settled on Michael since the killing had deepened after passing the cairn. He made his way home slowly, glad of the respite of solitude and yet looking forward to escaping from his feelings in company. The prosperous, healthy Phelans made him uneasy sometimes, especially the grizzled old yeoman of a father. As far as James Phelan was concerned, this was the way it always had been and always would be, but to Michael's way of thinking even if Lord Hawksborough had been a good landlord, like Lord Mounteagle, for example, there would be little enough excuse for his ownership of Irish land.

Nevertheless, the murder of the agent and especially of his driver seemed wrong, seemed more than anything to pinpoint the desperate futility of their struggle. To the English, the Ribbonmen's attacks were nothing more than isolated acts of terrorism. The Ribbonmen, small groups of Irish freedom fighters, did indeed work alone and their actions didn't represent the will of an organised movement. If only Daniel O'Connell, the Catholic lawyer-turned-politician, whose pressure on the Government in London had gone some way to serve the interests of Irish independence, could have kept a hold on power! But the younger men were growing impatient with him. There seemed to be no way out of the trap. But Michael would not give up. There had to be a way.

The sun hung low and dirty-red over the lake by which Patrick Dolan's modest farmhouse stood. Michael looked down at the single-storey building, still needing this year's coat of whitewash, huddled under its turf roof from whose single stack a thin wisp of smoke was rising. By the door stood bundles of reeds cut from the lakeside, which his father would use to weave the mats, baskets and toys he sold in the market to supplement the wretched income the smallholding provided. Somehow this year the rent would have to be paid. But the potato had been hit so hard by the new blight last year that it would take a miracle for them to have food for themselves and money for the rent by collection day. Michael found himself thinking the very thought that he wished to be free of; he found himself praying that the land agent sent to succeed Jenkins would be less severe, more reasonable, than his predecessor. But the hope was a slender one. Agents were not a breed renowned for their humanity.

The surface of the lake became dull pewter as the light went off it, and Michael shivered. The sweat of the working day had cooled on his body, and his physical discomfort did nothing to improve his mood. As he approached the farm, he saw his younger sister, Mary, sitting by the lakeside with Daniel Phelan. He knew they were looking at him, but refused to return their gaze. He entered the house and crossed the earthen floor to the kitchen and the niche where the poteen was kept. He filled a flask from the barrel and went outside again, walking away from the couple and selecting a place where he could sit alone. He wondered vaguely where his parents might be. Perhaps they were off on another futile jaunt around the parish trying to sell some rushwork. As if anybody here had the money for such things! And the traders in Brannocktown only dealt in saleable commodities – things which could be eaten or drunk. Not that Patrick Dolan would have got much more than a penny piece out of any of them for his work, even in good times.

Michael took a swig from the flask and felt better, fleetingly, as the alcohol burnt its way down his throat and warmed his stomach. From the corner of his eye he could see Daniel and Mary. He knew they would have noticed his mood, and he knew they were talking about him. Dear Mary. So gentle, and yet the toughest of the three Dolan children, did she but know it. He saw Daniel get up and start making his way towards him. Well, there was nothing he could do about that. He took another pull at the flask. How could Daniel, whom he had thought to be so close to him, who was the local schoolmaster, for the love of God, have lent himself to such an act? Was violence the only way to gain freedom?

Too soon, he heard Daniel approach, but he did not look round. His friend sat down beside him, but his tone when he spoke was harsh.

'For Christ's sake, Michael. You have everybody wondering what is wrong with you.'

Michael stood up and moved away to the water's edge. Daniel followed him. Both men were fully aware that Mary was watching them.

'Have you told my sister?' asked Michael, not looking at him. 'Have you told Mary she's betrothed to a murderer?'

Daniel sighed. 'No.'

Michael turned on him. 'I think you should. Sure she'd be proud of you.' He took another long pull at his flask.

'What else could we do, Michael?' asked Daniel. 'We'd already watched him turn five families off their land. Him and people like him have got to be stopped. Look, they turned three hundred people out of Ballinglass last March, so that the land could be made over to grazing. We can't let them go on treating us like this. We're all supposed to be British citizens. They treat us worse than they would their cattle.'

'But we killed the driver, too,' said Michael, unable

now to stop the tears from coming to his eyes. 'We shouldn't have killed the driver.'

Daniel was silent for a moment. He, too, had been shocked by Ferry's shooting of Shanahan. But he controlled himself. 'For Christ's sake, Michael, there'll soon be an eviction order sitting on your own table. What'll you do if the new agent carries on where Jenkins left off and sets about clearing the estate? What will you do then?'

'I don't know,' said Michael, bitterly. He saw that Mary had risen. She'd noticed something beyond their line of vision. It had to be something important, for she had started to run towards them.

'Do you want to watch your family set on the road, crawling in the dirt, split up in the poorhouse?' persisted Daniel. 'Isn't it just as violent, what they are doing to us?'

Mary had reached them. 'The fires are burning,' she said, triumphantly, out of breath. 'Come and look.'

She took both the men's hands to lead them up to the brow of the slope above the lake.

'You go on ahead,' said Michael.

'Oh, Michael!'

'Go on.'

'But you'll come later?'

'Yes – now, you go on.'

The sun had dipped below the sea. The sky had darkened, and as he watched them mount the brow, Michael fancied he could see the glow of the fires beyond them. But he did not follow.

By the time Daniel and Mary had reached the top of

the valley, it was almost dark, but fires had been lit on almost all of the hilltops. Below them, they could see the neat lazy beds of the Phelan farm's potato crop, and on the hills to either side smaller farms clung, eking a living from poorer soil. The country was crowded. They could see the lights in the Phelan house, and they ran down the slope to it.

Inside, the form was drawn up to the table. This was a well-to-do household, and James Phelan even had his own chair at the head of it, a chair made by his father in the better days. His grandchildren Joseph and Molly, who'd gladdened his days for the past seven and five years, sat near him on high stools that he had made for them. If only his own dear Molly had lived to see them. On the table stood two wicker baskets full to the brim with steaming boiled potatoes and the big jug of buttermilk was at his elbow. Around him sat his family. The uneasiness which had come over him after his difference with Con had passed, but he still eyed his second son cautiously.

Suddenly, the front door opened and Daniel stood there, Mary close behind.

'The fires are lit – the new agent's coming,' said Daniel.

Immediately Con was on his feet, taking a smouldering turf from the fire with a pair of tongs.

'Finish your food,' said James.

'Come on,' said Daniel.

'D'you think a grown man's going to be disturbed by a few fires?' James said, trying to exert his authority.

But no-one was listening to him. Con and Daniel

were already leaving the house with the glowing turf and the others were quick to follow. Outside, Mary was standing by the huge pile of driftwood stacked to be lit.

'Quickly,' said Mary. Con thrust the turf in among the timber, but it didn't catch, only smouldered.

'Oh, God,' said Mary, anxiously and impatiently. She got to her knees, leant forward and blew on the turf. It glowed fiercely, then the first kindling flared. Mary stood, her face red and happy. Maeve hugged her.

'He'll be coming along the road over there,' said Con.

'Yes,' said James, who had joined them. 'Past the spot where they found Shanahan.' In the silence that followed, he looked from one of them to the other, then at the bonfire. 'It's a waste of good wood,' he said, and turned back to the house.

In the distance, they could just hear the jangle of harness and there was enough light left for them to see the dark shapes of a group of horsemen and a wagon travelling hurriedly down the road.

'There they are,' said Con.

'Which one is he?' said Mary urgently. 'Which one is the agent?'

'There, at the centre,' said Daniel. 'That must be him.'

The little boy, Joseph, produced a penny whistle and started to play. The others watched the horsemen pass by in silence.

The man who rode in their midst was the only one not in the black uniform of the constabulary. He was on his own white horse, brought from England, the last luxury he allowed himself since the death of his wife and the only reminder of his days as an officer in the Hussars. He wore a black suit with riding boots, a white shirt with a black stock, and a black stovepipe hat. He looked at the fires burning in the bleak countryside around him with cold eyes. They did not intimidate him, but he felt safe surrounded by these men. The police here, he knew, received full military training, knew how to ride, and carried the short-barrelled carbine muskets he'd already seen Irish soldiers in the British army use to great effect in India, where he'd spent the greater part of his now-ended military career. What's more, many of these men were from Ulster, and Protestants. The Catholics were an unknown quantity, and the advice he had got was to treat them with suspicion.

He half turned in his saddle to see if his traps and trunk, lashed to the wagon which danced across the wretched road behind him, were still aboard. They were, but he did not hold out much hope for the breakables among his luggage. He was tired. He had been four days on the road since his arrival at Dublin, and England and home seemed a prospect ever more remote. But Captain William Townsend was not a man to look back once he'd embarked on a project. He'd been warned of the dangers here, and though his predecessor in the post he was about to take up had been marked down as missing, believed drowned, he knew full well what the truth behind the man's disappearance must be. More and more, the newspapers at home had spoken of the unrest among the Irish and the ungratefulness of the people towards their English rulers and benefactors. As he rode, he considered some of the opinions he had heard and read: 'There is a degree of truth in the sarcasm that the only secret an Irishman keeps is the whereabouts of a fugitive from justice'; 'All Irish seditions are branded with the foulest murder and most diabolical savagery. There is always the pretence of a constitutional aim; there is always murder and savagery'. 'There are few who have not heard of the Ribbon Societies of Ireland; those dark and mysterious confederacies which, springing up from time to time in different localities, have spread terror and dismay into the breasts of both rich and poor; which have done so much to discourage the influx of capital into Ireland; and to promote the absenteeism of hundreds of wealthy proprietors who would be only too glad to be allowed to reside upon their Irish estates, and in the midst of their Irish tenantry, could they do so in peace and safety.' Well, he would see for himself now.

He turned again in his saddle to address the sub-inspector who led his escort. 'McCafferty, what is the meaning of these bonfires?'

'To celebrate the arrival of the new agent, sir,' replied the officer.

'And the departure of his predecessor, perhaps?'

They rode on in silence. Townsend was beginning to wonder if the journey would ever end. They had left the fires behind them and ridden through grand gates, though from what he could see, old and rusty, down a broad but neglected drive to a grey house of imposing proportions, built in the style of a hundred years before. In front of it, Townsend saw the dusk-blurred shapes of sheep grazing in an overgrown topiary garden. The house had an air of neglect, even of decay, which was mitigated slightly by the warm light which spilled from the hall as the front door was opened to reveal a stout couple in their late middle age.

Townsend had reined in his horse. 'This is Lord Hawksborough's house,' he said crisply.

'Yes, sir,' answered McCafferty. 'This is Galready House. But his lordship is never here. All your predecessors have used it.'

'I will not,' said Townsend. 'There must be a proper agent's house.'

'There is, sir. In Brannocktown.'

'Then take me there.'

McCafferty was taken aback. 'But it is much smaller. It has not been made ready for you.'

'I do not need so large a house as this. This is his lordship's house, not mine. I prefer to be in the town. Let us go there now.'

'As you wish.' McCafferty looked at his men, then dismounted and exchanged a few words with the couple at the door. He returned to Townsend. He made no attempt to disguise his feelings.

'If you insist, sir. Mr Brogan will have to stay on the estate to see after the house, but Mrs Brogan will wait on you by the day. Tonight all we can do is get someone to make up a fire for you and remove the dust-sheets from some of the furniture down there. The agent's house has not been used for years. Are you sure you won't change your mind?'

'Perfectly.'

'Very well.' McCafferty remounted and wheeled his horse around without another word.

It seemed an age before he was alone, but at last the fire had been lit in the parlour of the square Queen Anne house that stood in its own walled garden at the end of the town, and his bags unloaded and bundled into the hallway. A bedroom had hastily been made ready, but when Townsend went to touch the curtains in the room, the fabric crumbled in his hand. Still wrapped in his riding coat, he drew an armchair to the fire and uncorked a bottle of brandy that had miraculously survived the journey. The fire and the brandy soon warmed him and he began to doze.

Two miles away, at the Phelan's farm, the only ones still sitting by the fire there were Mary and Daniel. The night was well advanced, and the fire all but dead.

'It's cold now,' said Mary. 'I'd better go.'

She stood up and Daniel wrapped his own coat around her.

'Michael never came,' she said.

'No.' Daniel stooped and drew a smouldering stick from the fire. He handed it to her. 'Here,' he said. 'This will bring you luck for the rest of the year.'

She took the stick and kissed him briefly, without speaking.

'Safe home to you,' he said.

He watched her out of sight, then turned and set off

towards Brannocktown, and his room adjoining the schoolhouse.

In the grey light of dawn, Townsend awoke with a start. He had been dreaming of Bombay, and now for a moment, he could not get his bearings. The fire was out, and through the window he could see that yesterday's fine weather had given place to a sky heavy with rain. He rubbed his face and eyes and stood up. The start of his first day at work. He had better exercise some authority from the outset. He could hear movements in another room and set off to investigate. In the dining room across the hall he found breakfast laid and a fire lit. The breakfast was bacon and potatoes. He was inspecting it when Mrs Brogan, looking younger than she had the night before, but no less solid, entered.

'Welcome to Ireland, sir,' she said. 'I'll have someone take your luggage up to the best bedroom and I'll get the place seen to while you're at the office. Sure and it's a wise choice you've made. The big house is a nasty, draughty place, but you'll be as snug as a bug here in no time.'

Townsend ate his breakfast, as it was ready. Then he washed, changed and shaved, ready to meet the day. His horse, saddled and groomed, was brought round from the stable, and to his slight surprise he found Sub-Inspector McCafferty and an escort waiting to ride with him to the office, which, as far as he knew, was only at the other end of the town's main, and indeed only, street. He was looking forward to seeing the town. He knew it was tucked into a little natural harbour but that was the extent of his knowledge, and it had been too dark to see much the previous night.

The potato was Ireland's blessing and Ireland's curse. It was an easy crop to cultivate, requiring little management between planting and harvesting. In the first half of the century, its cultivation had spread to such an extent that a third of the rural poor now depended on it entirely for food. The population of the overwhelmingly Catholic country had exploded as a result of this bountiful staple food – for you only needed a small plot to produce enough potatoes to feed a family. But now the very size of the population was choking the land – rents were insanely high in comparison with those in England and the landlords took full advantage of the fact. But you could not blame all the landlords either – some ran their estates at a loss because of the dues they owed to the poor rate, designed to underpin the poor in days of shortage and famine, such as those experienced in the year 1845. The losses, though, made landlords want to get the people off the land: the land was lush and good for grazing. Cattle-rearing was simpler, needed fewer people to do it, and was more profitable. One option open to landlords was to pay emigration passage to America for their tenants – a small once-and-for-all outlay that rid them of responsibility and cost for good.

In 1845, the potato had proved what a dangerous food it was to depend on. You could not store it over seasons; it did not keep, and indeed the summer months, when the old supply had finished and the new was not yet come in, were always the thin times.

Plenty of grain was grown, but that was sold to pay the rent, never used as food. If you couldn't pay the rent, you lost your land, and you and your family would be out on the road. Most preferred to sell their grain and starve, rather than have that happen to them. A few farmers grew a handful of other crops, like turnips and cabbages, but as often as not such eccentricity was laughed at – the potato was the most efficient thing. The people were used to a hard life. If the crop fluctuated, that was no more of a problem than bad weather. But in 1845 came the blight, which destroyed the potato, and the people began to starve to death.

The English had brought in Indian corn from America early in 1846 – Peel's brimstone – the people had called it, after its colour and the name of the English Prime Minister. But the maize didn't fill a man's belly or give him the vitamins that are in a potato, and the distribution was botched and insufficient. The population was reeling. In a country of over eight million souls, eighty per cent were poor and only half a million lived in towns. The urban poverty in Dublin was likened to that of Bombay. Yet the tax rate on Indians was five shillings a head. In Ireland it was twelve shillings and twopence. The poorest two million in Ireland had virtually no milk. Throughout the land there were only 123 workhouses with 42,000 inmates in 1845. There was no poor relief outside the workhouse, and if you went in, your family was split up. That was how it was.

On the morning that William Townsend was

preparing himself for his first day in his new job, James Phelan was up early, walking between the lazy beds of his potatoes: trenches were dug and the earth from them piled on the potato sets laid out between them. The young plants were glossy and healthy, crowding each other already and promising a good crop, provided God sent some more sunshine along with the rain. But at least it was mild, and by this time of year they could put any fear of frost behind them. James, a tight and much-patched waistcoat buttoned over his woollen shirt and his barrel chest, walked slowly between the beds, muttering a prayer for the good of the crop and dipping his hand into a small wooden bowl of holy water he had with him, sprinkling the young leaves with it at regular intervals. To either side of him, Sean and Con were hoeing the trenches clear of stones and waste that the rain had sluiced into them, and earthing over the young shoots to protect them.

James had reached the edge of the beds when he saw Michael Dolan coming towards him with a purposeful stride. Troublemaker, he thought, and would have turned away but for his natural sense of courtesy and duty towards a neighbour. As the younger man approached, James thought he could discern a hint of desperation behind the young man's set expression.

'James, I'm going into Brannocktown to talk to Lord Hawksborough's new man,' said Michael, after they had exchanged greetings.

James merely stared at him.

'Will you come with me?'

'I will not,' replied James. Michael glanced across to

where Sean and Conor had looked up from their work, but he seemed to think better of addressing them and went on his way without another word. James turned back and worked his way along two more sets of lazy beds, sprinkling on them what was left of the holy water in his bowl.

As he rode along the main street with his escort of police, Townsend felt faintly self-conscious. For a time there were houses on both sides, some of them imposing, though almost all now were fallen into decay to some degree. There were shops, too, though none of them looked particularly busy. As they approached the quayside, only the harbour was on his right hand. There was a handful of boats tied up, but the men idling on them looked tired and resentful, and from the look of the craft there had been little fishing in a while. Along from them, a freighter was unloading stores from England, and another was being filled with sacks of grain. Nostalgically, Townsend wondered if the cargo's final destination would be India. But it was the centre of the town that made the greatest impression on him. Among the grey, flinty façades, which seemed to share the same blankness as that in the eyes of the people, there was a black gibbet. The wooden platform on which it stood was scrubbed clean and there were no marks of rust on its ironwork.

The people slunk along the sides of the buildings, or simply sat in the dirt road resting their backs against walls. One in five was shod, most were dressed in rags. Townsend's look was returned with a weary stare, though one man turned away, cursing. Children with large eyes, pencil-thin arms and legs and swollen joints, stared too, leaving it almost too late to get out of the way of the horses. Townsend noticed that the police made no attempt to slow their pace for these waifs, who appeared to be sleepwalking in the middle of the road. A large shop-cum-warehouse in the corner of the quayside square where Townsend's office was also situated looked like the only centre of real activity. As he dismounted, Townsend read the name in faded paint on its wall: Coulter.

No sooner had the little troop stopped, than a small crowd gathered round it, but at a respectful distance. Townsend thought he had never seen such emptiness in people's faces.

Dismissing McCafferty, Townsend entered the office. The outer room, on to which the door from the square gave directly, was a bare room dominated by a large plain chimney-piece, a big standing-desk and a bench. There was also another desk, behind which a small, round, bald man sat in a buff jacket that was too tight for him. Two younger men, in riding boots, lounged as far as they could on ladder-back chairs either side of the chimney-piece. All three rose to greet him, and the little man's hands fluttered to his lapels in a tidying movement.

'Is it Captain Townsend, sir?' he said.

'It is.'

The man took a step forward. 'McBride is my name. Your chief clerk. And these two gentlemen are your bailiffs, Mr Curran and Mr Harkin.'

Townsend nodded at them.

'I received your communication, sir,' continued McBride, coming from behind his desk and crossing the room to a door at the back. 'According to your instructions, I have made ready for your inspection all the documents you requested.' He opened the door to reveal another room, with its own chimney-piece, desk and chairs. On the desk Townsend could see two ledgers and one pile of bound papers. He looked interrogatively at McBride, whose expression became apologetic. 'Insofar as they exist,' concluded the clerk.

'I daresay you have business to attend to, gentlemen,' Townsend told the bailiffs. 'We will speak later. My first duty must be to advise myself of the state of affairs here.' The men nodded and rose. As they left, Townsend noticed the two thick sticks resting by the door which each of them picked up. Townsend entered the inner office and seated himself at the desk, first drawing towards him a dusty map of the estate which had been spread out in a shaft of watery sunlight which came through the tall window to his left. Motioning McBride to close the door, he settled down to his work.

By the time an hour had passed, marked by the dull ticking of the wooden clock that hung over the mantle, his brow was furrowed. He had spent twenty-five years in the army and was used to order, to matters performed on time and without question. A swift perusal of the few papers at his disposal made him almost glad there were not more. A mess of uncollected rents, of payments in dribs and drabs, and finally, a thick packet of eviction orders waiting to be served. He had taken this job partly as a challenge; more, if he was honest with himself, because there were few jobs available to a former military man, who at forty-five had not got beyond the rank of captain. London was too expensive a place for him to live after the death of his wife, and her loss had provided him with the excuse he needed to quit an occupation which had become increasingly difficult for him to tolerate, particularly after his service in India had been terminated and he had been seconded to barracks in Lincolnshire. Still, what he confronted here bid fair to put him more than on his mettle.

But he had accepted the job, and he meant to make a go of it. If he failed, his prospects at home later would be even gloomier than they were now.

A knock at the door interrupted his musing. He looked up irritably to see McBride standing there. Behind him, Townsend noticed two or three people, poorly dressed, jostling one another. He fancied he could smell them, too. It was not an unpleasant smell: they smelt of the earth.

'What is it?'

'Some of the tenants would like to talk with you, sir, begging your pardon.' His hands were at his lapels again.

'Tell them I'm busy,' said Townsend. 'And see to it that I'm not disturbed again.'

He bent his head to his work once more, aware of the muffled noise of conversation in Irish behind the door which McBride had just closed. The tone of the talk was not friendly, but it was perhaps more urgent than angry. Then he heard the glass pane of the outer door rattle as it, too, closed.

He sought to regain his concentration, but he'd hardly turned another page before a great crash marred the silence of the room and a shower of glass from the window covered him, followed by the stone which had broken it, which bounced across his desk, knocking papers to the floor. His hands had gone to his face instinctively and the left one was nicked with a tiny cut which, however, bled hard. The stone had scored the surface of the desk.

'What in God's name?!' he shouted. Seizing the stone, he rose quickly and stormed into the outer office, pushing McBride aside despite his protests and flinging open the door to the quay. Going outside, he found himself confronting a large crowd of men. He had had experience of this kind of situation in India, and he knew what to do. He quickly identified the ringleader, a slight, good-looking young man with reddish-brown hair, and held his eye with his own.

'What is the meaning of this?' he asked, keeping his voice loud but level. As he had expected, the crowd drew back a pace. But the young man stood firm.

'We've come to see Lord Hawksborough's agent.'

'And this is your calling card?' Townsend held out the stone.

'In a manner of speaking. Are you the agent?'

'I am.'

The man's expression became less sure. Had he expected Townsend to deny it? 'Then I tell you we are pressed and ground down, and we must have a removal of our grievances.'

Remembering all the unpaid rents, Townsend wondered for a moment if it was not Lord Hawksborough who had a right to grievances; but as he scanned the crowd he could not deny to himself that there was genuine despair in some of the faces he saw before him.

'What is your name?' he asked.

'Michael Dolan.'

Townsend placed his feet apart, his hands behind his back. 'I have been in Galready twelve hours; I have barely taken up my post in this office. What can I yet know of your grievances, Michael Dolan? Or of the grievances of any other man here?'

There was a murmur from the crowd.

'You only have to look around you,' said Michael, his voice rising. 'Or talk to any man here.'

'I intend to,' replied Townsend.

The murmur was louder this time.

'I intend to make a thorough study of the situation,' he continued. 'I intend to visit personally as many tenants as I can. But until I have done so I am in no position to discuss your demands.'

'When will you discuss our demands?' Michael came back at him quickly. 'Name the day.'

The crowd took this up fast, and the bolder amongst them, or those standing well to the rear, shouted: 'Name the day!'

Townsend's glance flickered over them. They had to be answered. 'On Monday,' he said loudly.

'On Monday,' repeated Michael, turning to the

crowd and raising his arms.

Townsend was taken aback by their cheering. It was as if they had won some kind of victory already. He wished he could have talked to his predecessor, or anyone with more experience of this kind of work. Again, he was reminded of India. And yet this was a part of the United Kingdom and these were British citizens, living two days' journey from London.

'Dolan,' he cried, shouting to make himself heard. 'Limit yourself to a respectable deputation. Three men – no more. I will not talk to a mob.'

Michael looked at him seriously, then nodded. 'Three men,' he said.

It was late by the time Townsend was ready to return to his house. The broken window had been boarded up – he'd given strict instructions to have it re-glazed by lunchtime the next day – and as night fell he had an oil-lamp brought in to work by. The bailiffs had returned but he had dismissed them after only a brief word – he needed above all to get the estate papers in order. Clearly that had been a task with which Mr Jenkins had not unduly troubled himself , and from his manner McBride, who had been agitating feebly to be off home since five, was not one for hard work either. By exerting pressure, Townsend had got the chief clerk – though chief of what, as there seemed to be no evidence of other clerks, Townsend was at a loss to know – to unearth several more packets of papers from cupboards and shelves. Almost all, as he opened and read them, revealed themselves to be notices of eviction.

Evicting tenants appeared to be not just the principal, but the sole function of Lord Hawksborough's agent. On the other hand, the books confirmed that the vast majority of the rents due remained unpaid. It was a situation which Townsend was determined not to tolerate. If he could turn this estate around and make it function well, then his lordship would be bound to look favourably upon him. But he did not allow himself to daydream about a rosy future in England.

At last he knew that he could work no more. He stretched and rubbed his eyes, and called to McBride to send for his horse.

The night air was balmy and the sky still primrose with the last streaks of day. The threatened rain had held off, and Townsend filled his lungs with the keen smell of the sea, which at this time of day overrode the more mundane odours of the town. He heard a clattering of hooves and looked across the square to see McCafferty leading his horse at the head of a small escort of mounted police.

'Sub-Inspector,' he greeted McCafferty cautiously. 'There is no need of this. I will ride alone. You can see I have saddle-pistols.'

'Our orders are to stay with you at all times, sir,' replied McCafferty, who was by now having some difficulty in disguising his exasperation with the new agent.

'I am land agent of this estate,' said Townsend, 'and I intend to go about my business without unnecessary encumbrances. I will ride alone.' He mounted his horse with an easy, practised movement, turned him and rode briskly in the direction of the agent's house. McBride, locking up, and McCafferty watched him go. The two men exchanged a glance.

Townsend did not stop at his house, but rode on, up and along the clifftops in the dying light. He did not know if he was looking for anything in particular, perhaps just a sensation of the place he had come to. The evening felt gentle and even the treeless hills had a wild beauty at this time of day.

Before long he saw what seemed to be a rocky outcrop ahead of him, but as he approached he realised that it was a group of cottages which had been pulled down when their tenants had been thrown out. He dismounted and walked among the tumbled ruins. Clearly this was the result of a recent eviction: there were still signs of the people who'd been here. In one roofless room he found a broken stool by the hearth; in another a baby's rattle, woven from rush. He shook the rattle, but he did not ask himself where the baby was now. Looking up from it, and slightly inland, his attention was drawn by a wisp of smoke from a peat fire that appeared to be rising from the edge of the bogland. On impulse he remounted and rode towards it.

Within a few minutes he had arrived at the source of the fire. He could hardly identify the mound from which the smoke rose as a dwelling at first, but in the lessening light he could see that a circle of stones had been roofed with turf. A gap in the circle was the only door. Nearby, a man hoeing a small bed of potatoes paused to look at him. Townsend dismounted. He could not remember any record of a tenancy registered here.

'Good evening,' he said to the man, who continued to stare at him. The man was dressed in the remains of a shirt and waistcoat, and much-patched moleskin trousers tied round the waist with a strap of leather. The clothes were too big for him and hung loosely about him. His feet were bare and black. 'I am William Townsend,' he continued. 'Land agent for this estate.'

The man looked blankly at him. Townsend cast a quick look behind him to reassure himself that he was within reach of his saddle-holsters. There was a scuffling from inside the hovel then, and from it emerged two thin children, their skin grey in the dusk, and a woman. All were barefoot and dressed in the merest rags. A rancid smell came from these people. They fixed him with an empty gaze.

Townsend addressed himself to the man again. 'You are squatting on Lord Hawksborough's land,' he said stiffly. His remark met with no reaction and he knew then that they spoke no word of English. Nevertheless, he persisted. 'May I look inside your …' He was at a loss to know what to call it. 'May I look inside?'

None of the people made any movement to stop or encourage him, so he stooped to look through the hole in the stones. It was close inside. The turfs of the roof were supported with driftwood. The peat fire gave scant illumination, but there was nothing to light. Some bracken along one wall must have served as a bed. There was a small pile of berries and nettle-leaves as well. And that was all.

Townsend withdrew. No-one had moved. He glanced at the potato patch. It looked as if it would yield a good crop come harvest-time. He remounted and rode off without another word. After he had ridden a hundred yards he reined in and turned in his saddle. The woman and children were no more to be seen. The man had returned to his desultory hoeing. His movements might even have looked lazy to a casual observer.

Back at his house, Townsend dined quickly on the mutton stew Mrs Brogan had prepared for him. He had tasted better, but it was warm and nourishing, and he realised as he ate how hungry the day's events had made him. There was beer, or rather the dark stout of the country, to drink, and the agent drank it *faute de mieux*, making a note to tell Mrs Brogan to buy a supply of wine the next day. Coulter's Stores had looked prosperous enough to run to such things, he supposed.

After he had eaten, he explored his new home and was pleased to find it warm and aired. He would, perhaps, have to look about for a servant or two more in due course, for it was apparent that Mrs Brogan's own abilities were limited. But she had made a good job of preparing the three rooms which principally concerned him – the parlour, the dining-room, and the bedroom. The curtains which had crumbled had been replaced, the linen was fresh and clean.

His clothes had been unpacked and hung away, so that there only remained the contents of his personal valise to deal with. Among the few books and mementos he carried with him were the two daguerreotypes he could not bring himself to part with, and which he placed now on the chimney-piece with a reverence due to the lares and penates of the house. One showed him as a slightly younger man, the William Townsend of a few years earlier, resplendent in the dark uniform of his regiment. The other was of a severe but beautiful woman, whose regal gaze was fixed on a point just beyond the photographer's shoulder. This picture Townsend draped with a small piece of black crêpe. He looked at it for a moment. It hardly seemed as if his late wife had ever belonged to the world now. She was a figure in a half-remembered dream. And yet so much of his life had been spent with her, spent for her; and it had all appeared so real then.

There was little leisure for reflection in the few days that followed, for Townsend had only given himself a short time to prepare himself to meet the deputation, as he had rashly promised Michael Dolan. But by Sunday he had brought matters into a kind of order. He attended Matins at the neat little Protestant church at his end of the town, and found the congregation matched it completely – small, but prosperous.

The Reverend Denny did not mince words in his sermon, during which he attacked those who had made away with Henry Jenkins – though the former agent's body had never been recovered, it was clear to everyone what had happened to him – and damned them to hellfire for all eternity. Townsend listened coldly to his diatribe, and found himself wishing that he had an excuse not to take luncheon with the vicar and his wife after the service. But it would have been impossible to refuse. There did seem to be at least one sympathetic face among those in the other pews – that of Dr Davis. Townsend promised himself that he would cultivate the doctor's acquaintance when leisure permitted. The man had a humorous, sardonic expression which suggested a less provincial outlook than the rest of them.

At lunch, it quickly became clear to Townsend that Denny regarded himself as a soldier on the front line. A few questions elicited the information that the parson had been born towards the end of the last century in Dublin. His parents were English, and since his ordination there he'd held three livings successively in the depths of rural Ireland, all the time watching his hopes of preferment to the capital fade. Embittered and too intelligent to be ignorant of the dislike in which he was held by the Catholics, upon whom tithes were levied to support him, though here in Brannocktown at least they had no priest of their own, he held that all Papists were children of the devil, people you should never lower your guard against.

'Calculations done in Devonshire,' Townsend was saying, 'show that a family of five needs a minimum of ten-and-a-half acres to survive. Yet here, families are subsisting on plots scarcely sufficient to feed a goat.'

'It's the potato,' Reverend Denny interrupted him eagerly, forking beef from his plate to his mouth and washing it down with half a glass of red wine.

'Without that gift from the New World they couldn't feed such families, or their livestock. A woman out at Black Ridge has just given birth to her twenty-first child. The potato. That's the cause of it all.'

'In Devonshire, every family has a kitchen garden,' said Townsend. 'Cabbages, onions, lettuces.'

'Devonshire is such a lovely county, I understand,' put in Mrs Denny. Both the Dennys affected an English accent, but Mrs Denny's was so good that Townsend wondered if she had in fact been born there.

'It is indeed, Mrs Denny,' said Townsend. 'The soil is fertile, not peaty and unproductive like much of the land I see here. Yet tenants here are paying twice as much as his lordship's tenants in England.'

'Understand this, Captain Townsend,' said Denny, gesticulating with his fork. 'This is not England. These people are no better than heathens and they must be ruled. Moses set the law before the Children of Israel. The Ten Commandments. And he warned them what would happen if they disobeyed God's law: "The Lord shall bring a nation against thee; a nation whose tongue thou shalt not understand; a nation of fierce countenance. And he shall eat the fruit of thy cattle and the fruit of thy land until thou be destroyed." He speared another piece of beef. 'They must be ruled,' he repeated.

Townsend, surprised by the violence of this out-burst, looked down at his plate. Placidly, Mrs Denny continued to eat.

Sleep would not come to Townsend that night. The covers of the bed were too hot for him and he tossed and turned, finally rising at four to pour himself a half tumbler of brandy. The result was that he was not as alert or as calm as he might have wished to be when he confronted Michael Dolan and the two men he had brought with him – strong, good-looking, fit men – in his office the following morning. He sat at his paper-strewn desk and wished that the faint headache which lurked behind his eyes would go away. What were the names of the other two men? Sean and Conor Phelan. They looked like leaders in the community. Well, it was good that he was meeting such people immediately. *Aequo animo*, he told himself. That was the best way to deal with the situation. Neither of the Phelans looked to be in dire straits, at least. But he could not get the image of the man hoeing potatoes out of his mind. And there was a further distraction. Outside the office, a huge group of tenants had gathered. They made a noise like the murmur of the sea. They had a fiddler with them, and occasionally he could hear the snatch of a tune. But mostly the men and women sounded surly.

'Your honour,' Michael was saying, 'your tenants feel oppressed and ground down. They are looking to you for relief. In the last few years, whenever a lease has come up for renewal the rent has been increased – as much as fourfold. Your tenants cannot pay that sort of money. Now, eviction orders have been served on all tenants in arrears, and more are threatened. Five families already have been turned out on to the road. We ask you to revoke all eviction orders. We ask you to reduce the rents.'

'Gentlemen,' said Townsend, placing his fingertips on the desk and pressing down, his eye momentarily catching the scratch mark made by the stone only four days earlier, 'it would seem to me that the cause of the misery I see about me is the pernicious system of sub-division and sub-letting of the land.' He turned to one of the ledgers before him. 'One farmer here, holding a good-sized farm, gives his eldest son five acres, two other sons four acres and his daughter three – all holdings now too small. Another man here has four families of squatters living on his land and paying their rent not to Lord Hawksborough but to him. That contravenes all estate regulations.'

'What else can they do?' Conor, the larger of the two brothers, said. 'Growing a few potatoes on a patch of land is the only way they can put food on the table.'

'And what if those potatoes should fail?' added Michael, the memory of the last season fresh in his mind.

'Praise be to God, the potatoes are growing well,' put in Sean, more mildly.

'Quite so,' said Townsend. 'The potato murrain that destroyed crops in Waterford, Clare, Monaghan and Antrim left Donegal completely unscathed.'

'Here in the valley maybe,' replied Con. 'But in the uplands the late crop was lost, and the people faced starvation.'

The noise of the crowd outside was growing.

'The people are at their wits' end, sir,' said Michael. 'Many of them have come in from the uplands to hear what you have to say.' Townsend did not reply, but rose, crossed to the window and looked out. 'We ask you again,' continued Michael, 'apply to his lordship for a reduction in rents; remove the threat of eviction that hangs over us all.'

Townsend paused before replying, then turned on his heel and faced them again. He was not eager to say what he had to, but the matter had to be made clear: 'I'll be frank with you, gentlemen. It is Lord Hawksborough's opinion that the present distress has not been caused by high rents but by poor management and husbandry. Therefore, although he is both willing and anxious to relieve the really distressed, he does not feel bound at present to make either a temporary or permanent reduction in rents.'

Outside, the noise grew ever louder. Townsend crossed to the window again. The broken pane was still boarded. McBride had merely spread his hands when Townsend had questioned him about it.

'I asked you to limit yourselves to a respectable deputation,' he said severely.

'And we have done so,' replied Michael. 'You cannot blame the tenantry for coming here. They are without hope.'

He was interrupted by a crashing noise from outside, as if a cart had been overturned.

'We must be able to tell them something,' said Michael. 'Present them with some sign of good faith.'

But Townsend had had enough. 'I am sorry,' he said. 'I cannot continue against this uproar.' He strode from the room, leaving the others to follow him. From the outer office, McBride watched him nervously.

The square was full and the crowd far greater than Townsend had imagined. A small group of policemen on foot were attempting to move men on, but to no avail. The agent was worried, but once people had caught sight of him, there was a buzz of anticipation and the noise abated. Townsend climbed on to the wooden platform built above the muddy street in front of the office. Raising his voice, he began to address the crowd angrily. Who were these people to try to put him under pressure? His head was pounding now.

'I am sorry, but I cannot continue my meeting with your representatives. I want this area cleared now. Go back to your homes, go back to your work. The meeting is at an end.'

His words spread quickly through the crowd. Michael, Sean and Conor had emerged behind Townsend and stood at his elbow. Suddenly a large man with pale eyes came forward and knelt at the agent's feet. Michael recognised him immediately and bit his lip. It was Martin Ferry.

'Your honour,' said Ferry. 'We ask you on our knees to get us a reduction on our rents.' Despite his words, his tone was far from pleading.

'Please get up,' said Townsend. But more men knelt. The whole crowd knelt, though they did not bow their heads or remove their hats, nor did they let go of the sticks which most of them carried, and Townsend knew that there was as much defiance as supplication in the people. This was not a time for weakness.

'I have nothing more to say,' he told them crisply, and turned to go back inside. As he did so, Ferry leapt up with a great cry and dealt the agent a double-handed blow across the back with his stick. He threw the stick aside and grabbed Townsend's collar, hauling him back. The rest of the crowd was up now, taking its lead from Ferry, turning into a mob in the space of a breath. Another man dealt the agent a crack over the head with a stick and blood flooded from the wound. A hundred hands tore at him as he was bundled over men's heads. His jacket was ripped off his back and then his waistcoat and shirt. He flailed like a drowning man on the surface of a stormy sea.

The Phelans and Michael watched transfixed for what seemed like minutes. Then Michael plunged after Townsend and Sean and Conor had to follow. 'Oh, God, no,' Michael was crying, clawing his way through the mob. Ahead, Townsend, stripped all but naked, was thrown to the ground and kicked and punched.

'Reduce the rents,' roared the men and women in the crowd. Out of the corner of his eye, Michael could see the policemen running. They were going to get help. Would they be in time? Ahead, he could see that they had got Townsend upright. He was still conscious and looking about him defiantly. No mistaking an English army officer, thought Michael, clenching his own jaw. He felt more than saw that Sean and Conor were still with him. Indeed, he would not have got this far on his own.

'We've got to save him,' he gasped. 'Kill him like this and we'll all be damned. They'll call in the troops.'

But as he spoke, Bryan Meagher appeared from nowhere with a rope. It had already been tied into a noose, and now Ferry was cramming it over Townsend's head, his hands slipping on the blood. That done, Meagher threw the loose end over a derrick.

'Haul him up!' roared the mob.

Across the square, Sean could see the faces of the children pressed to the windows of the schoolroom. Behind them, he could just make out his brother Daniel. He looked calm. Was he bidding them back to their desks? Among the faces he could see those of Joseph and Molly. They looked curious, excited and frightened all at once.

'Come on,' shouted Con, throwing himself at Meagher and bringing him down. The rope's end flew free of the derrick. Con got to his knees and drew his knife to cut the rope from Townsend. It had pulled tight round his neck and the man's face was blue. Sean was just in time to prevent Ferry from aiming a kick with his hobnailed boot at Con's head, grabbing the man's leg and pushing him violently away, off balance. Ferry smashed into a bollard, cursing. He was about to come back at Sean when another cry went up:

'Police!'

And at the same time there was the crackle of carbines as McCafferty and his men rode into the crowd. Screaming women clutched toddlers to them and tried to flee, but Michael saw one fall under a horse's hooves, and neither she nor the child with her moved afterwards. The crowd scattered. Ferry and Meagher had disappeared into it. Con, Sean and Michael remained with Townsend, holding him up. His breathing was harsh and ragged, and his head was a bloody mess, but his eyes were bright.

In moments McCafferty was up to them. A dozen policemen dismounted and seized the three men, forcing them away from Townsend, kicking them and beating them to the ground with the butts of their guns.

'Release them,' gasped Townsend.

McCafferty couldn't believe his ears. 'What?'

'Those men tried to save me.'

'I won't release them until I've questioned them. Two minutes more and you'd've been dead, sir.'

Townsend looked at him. 'McCafferty, I will not press charges against these men. Now, release them.'

McCafferty was silent for a moment, then growled an order. The police dragged the men to their feet and shoved them away. They started to run. Townsend watched them go. One of the policemen brought him a blanket and placed it round his shoulders.

Sean, Con and Michael didn't stop until they were beyond the town. By a stream, they sat down to bathe their faces and rest. Their clothes were filthy and ruined. But they had hardly had time to draw breath before they were showered with stones. Looking up, they saw half-a-dozen youths on the ridge above them.

'Brave Irish heroes! Bloody traitors!' taunted the youths repeatedly.

Michael was furious. He picked up some of the stones and hurled them wildly back at the children. 'Get away from here. What do you know? Get away!'

They ran away laughing. Michael sat with his head in his hands. What a mess. Townsend would turn against them for sure. And what could be done to save them from ruin now?

THREE

Townsend winced as Dr Davis put two stitches into the cut above his eye, washed it with brandy and dabbed it clean with a linen pad. He was sitting upright in a leather armchair in a corner of his parlour, his shirt loose over the thick bandages which Davis had strapped round his ribs. He stretched his neck and massaged his throat gently. There was a fierce rash on it.

'There,' said Davis. 'You'll be able to ride again in a day or two.'

'You might have warned me about the stitches; I'd've had a glass or two more of brandy.' Townsend's voice was thick.

'It wouldn't have helped you sleep – and that's what you need now.'

Sub-Inspector McCafferty eyed him with scarcely concealed disapproval from where he stood by the door.

'Do you think that attack was organised? That the Ribbonmen were involved?' Townsend asked him.

'That's what I intended to find out by questioning those men,' replied McCafferty evenly. 'Still, perhaps now you will realise that police guards are something more than "unnecessary encumbrances".'

'We'll see about that, McCafferty,' said Townsend, carefully, aware how foolish it would be to antagonise the Sub-Inspector unduly.

McCafferty grunted, nodded at the doctor, placed his cap on his head and left.

Davis was applying a thick ointment which smelt of eucalyptus to Townsend's neck. 'You're going to be very, very sore,' said the doctor, 'and you should get as much rest as possible.' He stood up and stepped back to survey his work.

Townsend struggled into his smoking jacket. 'Well, one thing is certain. The tenants, rightly or wrongly, have a firm conviction that they were not treated fairly by the late agent.'

Davis laughed out loud. Townsend looked at him, smiling at the naivety of his own remark.

'Are you an Irishman, doctor?'

Davis laughed again. 'Good God I hope so, Mister Townsend. I hope so.'

'Then will an Irishman have a drink with me before he goes?'

Davis looked at him. 'He will.'

Townsend levered himself out of the chair, but the effort of standing was too much for him. He smiled again, weakly, and indicated the walnut table where the decanters stood. Davis put down his bag and crossed to it, pulling the stoppers and sniffing the contents. The agent resumed his seat.

'I see you've had some whiskey brought in. Are you developing a taste for it yet?'

'For the moment I'll keep to brandy.'

Davis poured the drinks. 'What will you do now?' he asked.

'I'll tell you one thing,' replied the agent, taking his glass and drinking. 'I won't be intimidated.'

As soon as the doctor had left, Townsend forced himself to rise from the chair again. He paused for a moment to find his feet, then made his way slowly upstairs, where he changed into a fresh shirt, waistcoat and jacket. He tied a loose stock round his throat and looked at himself in the glass. He felt better for being properly dressed, though despite the looseness of his cravat his neck chafed against the linen of his collar. He eyed the ship's decanter on the military chest that stood near the bed, but thought better of another drink. Then another thought struck him and he crossed the room to the chest, removing the decanter from it and raising its lid. From its interior he withdrew a long morocco box, whose leather was badly rubbed at the corners. The box contained one of his most prized and useful possessions – one of the five-chamber American revolvers that had been invented by Mr Colt eleven years previously, though few had yet crossed the Atlantic. A brother officer who had gone to work for a telegraph agency in New York had sent it to him upon his leaving the Indian service, and even in the most needy times since he had resisted selling it. He checked the well-oiled pistol carefully and from a heavy board box loaded five bullets into it. 'If they want trouble,' he said to himself grimly. He would not forget the face of that grey-eyed, bald brute in a long time.

It took him a while to get into town, walking slowly and stiffly as he did, and he attracted not a few curious stares. But with the revolver in the belt beneath his greatcoat he felt confident. A fine rain had begun to fall, the kind of soft rain that hardly makes itself felt until you realise it has soaked you, and his hat and outer clothes were dripping by the time he reached his office. It was empty except for McBride, who sat at his desk dozing over an open accounts book. The clerk started when he saw Townsend enter.

'Captain! Surely it's some rest you'll be needing after this morning's excitement.'

Townsend looked at him. 'You work for us, Mr McBride. Doesn't the sort of outburst you saw this morning bother you?'

McBride did not meet his eye. 'I live here in the town. We keep ourselves to ourselves. If it wasn't me, someone else would do the job, and we know what side our bread's buttered. Besides, whoever's on top, they always need clerks.'

Townsend let it go. 'Get your pen and some paper, Mr McBride. I've a proclamation to dictate, and I want it ready for Curran and Harkin to make known to the tenantry tomorrow morning.'

It did not take long for McBride to take the dictation, but later in the day Townsend felt more tired than he had expected, for he had made himself stay, learning the map of the estate, until late afternoon. He asked for a wagon to be fetched to take him back to his house, and accepted McBride's offer to send a boy to the police barracks to ask for an escort. He would need to humour McCafferty as much as possible in the coming days.

When Townsend arrived back at the agent's house, he was bidden to dinner immediately by Mrs Brogan. Mutton stew. He sat down wondering how he could ask her to vary her repertoire. He watched her pour him a glass of claret. It was a large glass, but she clearly meant to fill it as full as possible.

'Thank you,' he said, meaning her to stop.

But she went on pouring until the glass was too full to raise without spilling. All this in silence. Was this a kind of protest? Or was her English that limited?

'Leave the bottle,' he said.

But she ignored him, bearing it away on a tray. He looked at his glass. Then, with a sigh, he leant forward to drink the wine free of the brim, so that he could raise it.

McBride had worked quickly, toiling late to make copies in Irish and English. The following morning the two bailiffs rode out together, carrying their long sticks tied to their saddles. They had an escort of six policemen. The Phelans had breakfasted and were getting ready to continue their morning's work when they heard the horses approaching the farm. None of the men on horseback dismounted. Harkin drew the proclamation out of his leather pouch with thin grey fingers, unfolded the paper and, without looking at James, Sean or Con, began to read. As he did so, Maeve, Hannah balanced on her hip, emerged from the house and stood on the threshold. It had rained all night and the leaves in the fields were still dripping, though it was still mild and the sun was a ghostly presence behind the clouds.

'The tenantry on Lord Hawksborough's estate,' read Harkin, 'residing in the manor of Galready, are requested to pay into the Land Agent's office, on the first of June, all rent and arrears of rent due up to the thirty-first of May. Otherwise, the most summary steps will be taken to recover the same. Signed, Captain William Townsend, on the fifteenth of May, 1846, at Brannocktown.' When he had finished, Curran motioned his horse forward, and, leaning down from the saddle, handed James a copy of what had been read. Then, without a word, the party rode off. Sean, seeing the expression on Maeve's face, went over to her and put his arm round her waist, drawing her to him. She did not relax in his arms.

They worked distractedly that day, all minds on the family meeting they would have in the evening. Soon after the bailiffs had left Michael came over and Conor went off with him, to James's silent anger. Michael had come to Con in the far field and James hadn't known about it until later, or he'd have had something to say.

Con still wasn't back by the time the potato bowl was cleared away and the oil lamp brought to the centre of the table. Joseph and Molly were tucked up in their cot at the foot of the wooden bed Sean had made for him and Maeve and which now stood in the main bedroom off the living room – James had the small room under the eaves, and Conor slept on a palliasse in the room that adjoined the byre.

What little cash the family had was counted out in piles at one end of the table. James sat by them, a thick, worn book open at his elbow. From time to time he wrote laboriously in it, using a goosequill and a stone pot of ink.

'We'll need to sell some butter and cheese,' he said heavily, 'and as many eggs as we can. Some of the chickens, too. They're good birds and should fetch sixpence each.' He looked up from his work. 'If we're to pay the whole of the arrear as well, we'll have to sell the calf.'

'If everyone's selling at the same time, the prices will be low,' said Maeve. She glanced out at the night. The rain had already begun to fall by late afternoon and showed no sign of letting up. 'I don't like to think what'll happen if the potatoes should fail.'

James looked up sharply. 'Hold your tongue, woman!' But his voice was weary.

'Don't speak to her in that way,' said Sean.

'Praise be to God, the potatoes are fine,' said James, deflecting the argument. There was enough trouble without squabbling. In the silence that followed he made another entry in his book.

As he was doing so, the door from the yard opened noisily and Con came in, a sack round his shoulders to protect him from the wet, followed by Michael. Both men were pretty well drenched, but in a high good mood. Con dipped into his wallet and carefully produced a sheet of paper. With due ceremony and making sure he had got everyone's attention, he unfolded it and began to read:

'Bryan Meagher, Boyle, McFadden, Pat Gallagher, Joe Gallagher, the O'Donnells, John Duffy, Shane Kenny, Friel, Loughrey, the Kellys at Greallach ...'

'What is this?' said James, impatiently.

'They've all agreed,' said Con, showing him the paper.

'What? What have they agreed?'

'That on the first day of June the one place they will not be is standing in line outside Townsend's office.'

'By Gale Day we'll have talked to everyone from here to Brannocktown,' added Michael triumphantly.

'Now, can I add our name, Father?'

James snatched the paper from Con's grasp. 'Jesus Christ, you cannot!' he shouted, enraged. He stood up, shoving his heavy chair back violently, and crossed to the blazing fire, screwing up the paper and pushing it into the flames. 'Do you want to see these people evicted?'

Con was on his knees, rescuing the list. 'No.'

'Nor do we want to see them bled dry by an English landlord,' said Michael.

'Can he evict an entire estate?' said Con, emboldened by his friend's stand against his father.

'Yes,' replied James slowly. 'He can.'

Sean had not spoken. Now he silently took the list from Conor and studied it.

'He has the law on his side,' continued James.

'English law, not God's law,' said Michael.

'God's law won't keep a roof over your head.' James paused. 'People must pay what they can and hope he will be merciful.'

'Who? God, or Hawksborough?'

'What good will hoping do us?' said Maeve.

Sean spoke at last, 'And all these people have agreed?'

'Yes,' said Conor. 'They won't pay a penny, Sean.'

James looked from one to the other of them. What were they, he wondered. Dreamers? Had they really expected the new agent to act any differently after they had rescued him the previous morning? But above all, what did they know of the land? Wasn't it bred into their bones, as it was into his? Didn't this house smell of it and didn't their food smell of it, and the air, and their bodies? Didn't it fill their lives? What did they think they would do, without the land? Wasn't their fear of losing it as great as his?

'I shall pay in full,' he said firmly. 'I won't be turned off.'

The days passed uneasily, but there were no more evictions and the people went on with their work, getting the stones out of the ground, cutting peat, keeping an anxious eye on the potato plants as they grew, weeding and thinning, and wishing that God would send some sunshine along with the rain. But at last the morning of the first of June – Gale Day – dawned. Townsend, fully recovered, in a newly-laundered shirt with a high stiff collar and a black satin stock, was in his office by half-past eight. An hour later he was sitting with McBride at the big table in the outer office, the paying-in ledger open in front of them. McBride had by him a stock of newly-sharpened quills. The bailiffs sat on their ladderback chairs near the chimney-piece. The door to the square stood open. The day was overcast, but dry.

The men sat in silence. Not a sound was heard but the ticking of the clock. Not a man was to be seen in the square.

At the Phelans's farm, you could cut the atmosphere with a knife. James was already dressed in his market-day clothes, the grey frieze coat three years old now, but good for another season or two. He looked good in it, not at all like farmers are supposed to in their Sunday best. There was a bit of looking-glass that had belonged to his Molly but that he'd given Maeve. He was looking in it, tying his stock, now. He, too, had a freshly-laundered linen shirt on. Maeve, Sean and Con were in the room with him, but there was silence between them. Maeve stood by the fire, arms folded over her chest, watching the peat smoke rise. Con sat at the table, hands folded before him, looking down at them. Sean stood uneasily by the door, watching his father.

James finished tying his stock, bent to adjust his top-boots, then straightened. From a stool by the fire he picked up his leather purse and his stick. He looked at Sean. Would his son try to block his way?

Reading his thought, Sean moved from the door, but he said: 'Father, please.'

James made for the door.

'If Conor is right.'

'I am right,' said Con.

'If Conor is right, and everyone's agreed, we can't be the only ones to pay.'

Without a word, James pushed past him and went out into the yard.

'Father!' Sean called after him.

'All our money,' said Maeve, bitterly, looking at her husband.

'What can I do?' he asked her.

There was no mistaking the contempt in her eyes. 'All our money,' she repeated.

James was already mounted on the thick-backed cob, riding him easily along the track that wound the length of the valley. The sun had peeped out reluctantly and his back felt warm under the heavy material of his coat. People were watching him as he rode by and none of the stares were friendly, but he did not return them. He paid no heed to the muttered words he heard in snatches either. But when someone flung a clod of turf, that hit him in the back, his pent-up anger burst its banks. Eyes blazing, he dismounted and turned to face whoever had thrown it. There was a gaggle of people he knew, and two or three youths. It must have been one of them. Then he saw his son Sean coming along the track towards him.

He turned away, back to his horse, and he had one foot in the stirrup when he felt a hand on his shoulder. He knew whose it was and tried hard to shake it off.

'Don't do it, Father,' said Sean.

James made to mount. The hand restrained him.

'Don't.'

'Take your hand off me!'

He tried to remount again, but this time the hand was less gentle, pulling him back and round with a force that made James start. He faced his son, furious.

'What the devil do you think you're at?'

'Father, don't do it.' Sean's voice was no longer asking him, but telling him. James hit him across the chest with his stick and turned again, but felt himself grabbed from behind and thrown to the ground. For a moment the shock was too much. He thought back to the day he'd wrestled his son for the slane. He got quickly to his feet and faced Sean, breathing hard. Somehow he'd let go of his stick. Well, so be it. His fists were still good enough. He let fly with his right. Sean held his wrist and twisted it. James fell into the mud by the side of the track. Winded and humiliated, he felt a hand at his belt, loosening the purse. Sean stood back from him. He was holding the purse. James struggled to get up, reaching for the purse. It was his. He had worked for it. He would not let them put his land at risk. Let the others do what they liked! But his son pushed him back again.

'Stay down, Father. Stay down.'

The father's pride made him try to get up again. Three times. The third time Sean pushed him back, he lay still. Both men had tears in their eyes.

A crowd had gathered. Sean wanted to help his father, but he knew he could not. After a moment he turned and walked back to the farm, holding the purse. A few people cheered. One or two clapped. The cob looked round from where he'd been grazing and followed Sean. James lay there, looking at the sky.

Returning to the farmhouse, Sean needed no words to tell them what had happened. Maeve took the purse from him, embraced him. He stood in her arms as if made of wood. Conor looked at him with unwonted admiration and read the appeal in his eyes.

'I'll go to him,' he said.

The rain had started by the time Conor found his father, sitting on a hillock at the end of the far field, looking out over the lazy beds and the sea. The potato plants were glossy in the rain, a rich healthy green that glistened as the crowding leaves rustled in a light breeze. James's suit was crumpled and muddy. There was blood on his face and a lost look in his eyes that Conor had not seen before and which made him obscurely frightened. But when the sky-blue eyes turned on Conor they hardened.

James began to speak. 'My great-grandfather made this farm out of a patch of stones,' he said. 'Cleared it and dug it with his own naked hands and bought his first spade out of his first crop of potatoes. Soon he had oats growing where not even furze had grown before.'

Con reached out to his father but James angrily brushed his hand away. 'Leave me be! It's your fault, with your lists and stupidity. We'll lose this land and it will be your fault!'

The day wore on. In Brannocktown, Townsend stood side by side with McCafferty outside the door of the office, watching the activity in the square. Across it, in the vicinity of Coulter's Stores, a fiddler had started to play despite the drizzle, and a good number of men were dancing an untidy jig, jeering and crowing, for they were drunk as lords. Watching them, Townsend felt nothing but disgust.

'It would seem that word has been spread quite effectively,' said McCafferty, drily.

'And whose word would that be, Mister McCafferty?'

McCafferty looked at him seriously. 'Michael Dolan's. He might have saved you that day they tried to hang you, but he's the one you've got to watch out for, all the same. There are troublemakers and violent men around here – they won't change and they won't change anything. But Michael Dolan is a politician.'

The rain had got inside Townsend's collar and water trickled down his back. What a godforsaken country. He turned back to the office where McBride and the bailiffs sat, McBride before the still virgin pages of the ledger. Townsend looked at the men. What were they thinking?

'Close the office,' he said.

McBride made a token gesture with his hands. 'There's still two hours.'

'Close the office.'

Wrapping himself in his greatcoat, which protected him from the rain but overheated him in the mild weather, he walked down the street to his house, away from the square, whence whoops and yells followed him which he tried to ignore.

By nightfall, Sean came in and sat by the fire with Maeve and the children to dry himself. There was silence between them, and Joseph and Molly were cowed by it. Maeve stirred the cabbage stew in the pot on the fire. She'd found a scrap of smoked bacon in the larder to liven it up, but she was beginning to have to eke out the remaining store of potatoes. Conor had come in earlier to say he'd found their father but that the old man wouldn't come back with him. He'd waited with Sean and Maeve for a space, then left again to see Michael. Now the family waited alone.

At last the door swung open and James entered his house. Drenched and bedraggled, it seemed to him that he was entering it as a stranger. He glanced over at his son, the usurper. Sean rose immediately.

'Come and sit by the fire, Father.'

The old man shook his head and did not reply. He longed to be dry and warm in his bed, and a word or a gesture would have let him be so. But he could not yield his authority yet. In his discomfort lay his pride. He struggled to prevent himself from shivering. He could not look at his daughter-in-law. A strong woman was stronger than the strongest man, he thought. He did not even sit in his chair. He sat on a three-legged stool in the farthest corner.

Maeve swung the cauldron out from the fire and ladled soup into a bowl. She gave the full bowl to her daughter, gesturing towards James with her eyes. The old man would accept the soup from the child. Molly took the bowl with all the seriousness of responsibility and trotted across the room to her grandfather, where she held it out to him. He looked at her earnest face and allowed himself to smile at her. God protect this little innocent from the life she had coming. Molly reached out hesitantly and touched the mud that begrimed his clothes.

'Did you fall over?'

'Yes, my darling,' he replied. 'I fell over.'

Townsend had not been idle on the day following the abortive Gale Day, and the next morning he awoke as keen and excited as if he were about to go on a hunt. He'd laid careful plans with McCafferty, who'd gone off secretly to recruit some roughnecks in Letterkenny, the policeman pleased at the thought of some positive action at last. He rose quickly and washed, dressing in riding clothes and boots, not forgetting his revolver and a whip. Waving aside breakfast, he drank a cup of tea with brandy in it and then rode hastily down to police barracks, where he found all in readiness. The police had been equipped with bayonets for their carbines. Harkin and Curran on their bays were surrounded by a motley mob of men who looked hardly better fed than the inhabitants of Brannocktown, but armed with clubs and with the promise of a shilling apiece for their day's work, they were ready to break the head of anyone Townsend wished. He rode up to the Resident Magistrate, Brady, who looked uncomfortable straddling a low-slung mare that was almost as fat as he was himself.

'Are you ready Mr Brady?'

'Yes.' Brady was pasty and nervous. There were liver-coloured bags under his eyes.

'I am glad you could make yourself available at such short notice, but this must be done according to the letter of the law.'

'Indeed. Though I would have preferred to have made the new agent's acquaintance over a glass of punch.'

'Time for that later, Mr Brady.' Townsend wheeled his horse round and addressed the men, rising in his stirrups as he did so. His horse sensed his excitement, and he kept him on a tight rein.

'The law allows us to drive to the pound the cattle of any tenant who owes any rent whatever. The cattle so impounded can be kept until the rent is paid. But we have no legal right to break open any door or take livestock out of any house. We may only seize what we find on the open fields and upon the land of the defaulting tenants. Mr Harkin there has a list of those in arrears. The gentlemen with him are responsible for driving the livestock to the pound. Mr Brady is here to see that everything is done by the book. The task of the police is to protect the bailiffs and their drivers as they go about the lawful execution of their duty. Now, is everything clear?'

There was a general murmur of assent.

'Very well. Here's to a successful day's work!'

McCafferty signalled to his men and, led by Townsend, the troop streamed out of the barracks gates. Watching from the hill above the town, boys turned and ran towards the farms, yelling the news.

It was Michael who came running to the Phelan's farm: 'Townsend is driving for rent!'

Sean and Conor, earthing up in the potato beds, leapt from the trenches and ran towards the house. 'Get the cows into the byre,' Sean shouted to Maeve as he came.

She was in the yard. 'What?'

'The animals! Shut in everything that you can!'

79

Molly and Joseph had been collecting eggs. Together they hustled as many chickens as they could into the coop. James, mending a hoe in the yard, dropped his work and helped Maeve drive the two milch cows and the calf back to the byre. By luck the pigs had not yet been turned loose from the sty. They were just in time. They'd hardly closed the yard gate when Townsend's posse galloped into their part of the valley. The drivers spread out, yelling, waving their sticks, ducking the stones that the tenants hurled at them.

The drivers had arrived at a farm on the opposite side of the track from the Phelans'. The people there had not been so quick to round up their livestock, though Michael and Sean and Con had hurried across to help them. People were everywhere, and the air was filled with shouts and yells. A child was hit by a stone and fell into a ditch where he lay inert. Four cows, panicked from their grazing, their eyes rolling, galloped aimlessly in their field as Harkin and Curran helped the drivers smash down the gate to get at them. Behind them, Townsend and the police formed a line to prevent any rescue. From away on the hill came the cries of those who had managed to drive their livestock to a safe distance.

Seeing Townsend, Michael called to him, 'Don't do this!'

Townsend was exhilarated. His horse was handling well on the difficult ground and his mind was stimulated by the operation. It was going well. He had misjudged McCafferty, it seemed. With luck, they would soon be able to launch an almost military offensive against these recalcitrant people. And here was this Michael Dolan again.

'I am legally entitled to impound these animals,' he shouted angrily.

'Don't do this, Mister Townsend,' Michael called back to him.

'Drive them this way,' Townsend ordered Harkin, ignoring Michael's pleas. But then his horse shied, hit under the eye by a stone. Townsend raised his right arm as a volley of stones thudded around him. He looked across the slope to the place from where they were being thrown. He recognised Sean and Conor Phelan among those hurling missiles at the drivers and the police. So much for talking to these people, he thought. So much for a calm spirit. Then he heard McCafferty's voice, loud and hoarse against the general tumult:

'Dismount! Fix bayonets!'

Townsend turned to watch as the policemen obeyed, moving across the hill to place themselves between the tenants and the drivers. Then they flinched as they were met by another volley of stones.

'Prepare to fire!' ordered McCafferty. Townsend could not believe his ears. The man was exceeding his authority. He looked for Brady, who was sitting on his horse a short distance away. The man had turned green.

'Read them the Riot Act, Mr Brady!' shouted Townsend, though he had a sinking feeling that it was already far too late for that. In any case Brady, sick with fear, could clearly hardly get his mouth open.

'Take aim!' shouted McCafferty. The police raised

their carbines. A jagged stone caught one of them full in the face and he fell, rolling down the hill. The crowd cheered.

'Don't shoot!' yelled Townsend, but at the same moment McCafferty had bellowed 'Fire!'. Townsend had time to notice several things at once. The worst, perhaps, was the expression on McCafferty's face. The sound of the guns was not loud – a dull popping absorbed by the grassy hills. The agent looked towards the stone throwers. He could see Michael Dolan running towards Sean and Conor. How long had he been running? People were screaming and scattering, women falling over their long dresses. Michael was still running. It seemed a miracle that he did not lose his balance. The Phelans were watching him too. A red rose was blooming in the side of his head. A rose with black spores. Could such a thing be? His arms were spread wide. His mouth was open. Then the rose turned into a perfect fountain which spattered those standing closest as Michael fell. He seemed to embrace the earth, and then lay still.

There was a lull. The police were reloading. But the crowd had realised what had happened. It was collecting itself. Then there was a furious roar. People, led by Conor, began to run and stumble across the hill towards the police. Townsend was aware that they were impelled by pure rage. The police knew it too. Some of them had already reloaded. Townsend knew what would happen if he did not do something quickly. He tore at his reins and drove his horse between the two sides.

'Hold your fire!' he shouted at the police. Then, glaring at McCafferty, whose face had resumed its normal expression, he said: 'Withdraw your men. Now.'

At least he had broken the mood. Almost gratefully, the policemen broke ranks and ran for their horses, remounting before the order was given and riding away for dear life. But people were descending on the track from all sides. Townsend's expression was bitter as he watched one policeman tumbled from his horse and beaten, while another reined in and fired his carbine point-blank into a small knot of people who blocked his path. McCafferty sat rigid on his mount, unable to move. Brady, the bailiffs and the drivers were already vanishing in the direction of Brannocktown.

'Mister McCafferty! Withdraw, for God's sake!' said Townsend. The sub-inspector pulled himself together and spurred his horse. Townsend followed him and the others back in the direction of the barracks. His thoughts were black.

There was a strange stillness after their departure, soon broken by the scuffling and groaning of the wounded, and the demented lowing of a cow that had caught a stray bullet in her udder. A small group of children stood about the tortured animal, holding hands, respectful in front of such agony, not comprehending it. People were picking themselves up, helping each other. Sean and Conor knelt beside Michael. The grass all around his head was stained dark crimson. Sean took off his jacket and bundled it behind Michael's neck. Michael frowned. His eyes were open. His mouth twitched. He was trying to say something. Con cradled him in his arms, gently rocking him.

Away over the hill near the Dolans' farm, where Daniel and Mary were walking arm in arm by the lake, you could not hear the faintest whisper of the commotion, and Townsend's drive had ended in disaster long before it had reached this part of the estate. So the lovers were surprised when they looked up at a faint cry and saw a man running towards them along the shore.

'My God, he's got the wind in his tail,' said Mary, smiling.

But the man had started to wave his arms frantically and Daniel looked grave. The man was calling now.

'Is it us he's after?' said Mary. 'We can't hear you!'

But Daniel had heard: your brother has been shot, the man had shouted. Your brother has been shot. Mary caught the expression on his face and her smile died.

'What did he say?'

'Michael's been hurt,' replied Daniel after a pause. 'Mary, stay here with your mother and father. We'll bring him to you. Stay here with them.' He squeezed her hand and left her, running to meet the man. Mary watched them hurry back over the brow of the hill together.

As Daniel followed the man to the scene of the battle, Townsend pulled his horse to a standstill alongside McCafferty in the yard of the police barracks. All the mounted men were back now, together with a clutch of riderless horses. Several of the police were cut and bleeding, their black uniforms scuffed and their gold epaulettes dull with mud. Townsend did not wait until he had dismounted to tell McCafferty what he thought of him. He had meant to teach the tenants a severe but disciplined lesson – to bring them into line once and for all. Instead, he had made himself appear cruel and inept. These police were supposed to have had military training! He knew from experience how good Irish troops could be – hadn't he served alongside them under Elphinstone during that terrible time in Afghanistan? And could that only have been four years ago? The memory intensified his anger.

'You had no business opening fire,' he said to the Sub-Inspector, keeping his voice low. Despite his rage, he knew there would be no point in upbraiding the man openly in front of his men. 'Warning shots would have served.'

Equally angry, McCafferty gestured to his wounded men. 'As you can see, we fired in self-defence.'

'They'll live,' replied Townsend in a tone of great contempt. 'Michael Dolan won't.' Already he was wondering what he could do to redeem the situation.

They had managed to get Michael on to a low, one-wheeled turf-barrow by the time Daniel reached them. Daniel knelt by his friend and put a hand on his brow. Michael's eyes met his, but Daniel could not be sure that there was any recognition in them.

'Don't die,' he whispered to him. 'Don't leave me alone in this struggle.'

'We can't let his mother see him like this,' Sean was saying.

'We'll take him home,' said Con. 'It's much closer. Get him cleaned up, make him comfortable. Maybe there's a chance yet.'

They set off, manhandling the barrow gently over the rough ground to minimise the jolts and bumps. Michael kept watching the sky. But they had scarcely reached the track when his breathing stopped. Sean lowered the handles of the barrow. They stood around, looking down on their friend with horror.

'Oh, God,' said Daniel. 'I'll see them dead and buried. Every last bitch's son of them.'

Con covered Michael's face carefully with his jacket. They moved on.

All Maeve saw as they came up to the house was that her husband and her brother-in-law were covered in blood. Her eyes flared in panic. Then she saw the body on the barrow, recognised the clothes.

'It's Michael's blood,' said Sean. He and Conor lifted their friend carefully off the barrow and carried him into the house, laying him on the table. Con's jacket had fallen from his face.

'Oh, Mikeen, Mikeen,' grieved Maeve.

'I told you no good could come of this,' said James, emptily. He was lost. What would happen to them now, he thought.

Con looked down at Michael's ruined face. Then he darted out into the yard and crossed it hurriedly, ignoring the curious bystanders who had accompanied Michael's body to the house. He was shaking violently, and as soon as he was out of sight, he crouched down behind a field-wall and retched like a dog. Then he rose, and clutching his clothes tightly round him, stumbled away towards the sea.

Maeve had shushed the children back into the bedroom where she had shut them for safekeeping while the raid was on, and now, with a bowl of water and a cloth, she started the job of cleaning her brother's head. Her hands trembled as she picked the loose pieces of bone out of his blood-clogged hair, and the men left the room one by one as she worked, but she stuck to her task, and like all such things, it became easier as she went on. There was even a grim reward in seeing her brother's look return to something like what it had been in life. When she had finished her cleaning, she went to the alcove by the fireplace and took from it a length of linen with which she bound Michael's head. Then she took a shirt of Sean's and an old, clean waistcoat of Con's, and dressed him in them. They were big for him, but that hardly mattered now. The bloodstained clothes she bundled up and put to one side. There was a smell of Michael on them that made her weep as she looked at her finished handiwork.

'Oh, my darling, my darling,' she grieved.

Sean and Daniel returned to the room when she called them. Sean squeezed her shoulder and the two men picked Michael up to lay him once more on the turf-barrow, which James had cleaned and dried. As they did so, Conor reappeared, shivering and pale, dark rings round his eyes.

'We're taking him home now,' Sean said to him.

Con nodded, taking the handles of the barrow.

A group of people had gathered at the Dolan farm to give comfort to the parents, Patrick and Sarah, and to Mary, as they stood at the door of their farmhouse to receive the body of their son and brother.

'The Lord have mercy on the soul of the dead,' intoned Patrick as the barrow was brought up. He was a small, thin man who looked much older than his fifty years. Life had not brought him much luck, and he had not always sought his fortune as energetically as he might have; but this loss was a cruel blow. With one daughter already married and gone and the other soon to be, what help could he look for with his farm, small as it was? Things were bad with him – he knew his rent had been left hanging for far too long, and he knew the penalty that would soon be upon him, as sure as night followed day. Michael had, to some extent, protected him from that penalty, and he had not the same resources of strength and character that his son had possessed.

'The Lord have mercy on us all,' answered the voices of all those present.

Sarah bent over the barrow. 'My boy, my boy,' she keened. Gently they drew her back as Sean and Daniel lifted the body and carried it into the house.

Later, Sean found Patrick standing alone by the lake, staring out over the water, watching the sunset.

There was no colour in the land. Everything was as grey as the smoke that spiralled eternally from the stack. Patrick had his knife in his hand, but he had cut no rushes.

'Don't worry, Patrick,' said Sean. 'We'll give him a good wake.'

'I have no money, Sean.'

'I'll pay. He was my family too.'

There was work to do for the wake, but the people rallied round and it was quickly done. Maeve made a face at the cost, but kept her thoughts to herself. The coffin-maker at Brannocktown came and measured, and soon Michael was laid out in the Dolans' main room, asleep in his box, looking like a waxwork of himself. Forms had been borrowed from the people round and placed along the walls of the cleared room, and on a trestle supported by stones there were tobacco and clay pipes, and plenty of stone jugs of poteen. A kilderkin of stout stood just outside the door, as there was no space for it in the room. By the door, too, stood all the members of the two families – James, Con and Daniel, Sean, Maeve and their children, and Patrick, Sarah and Mary. All were dressed in their market-day clothes, the men in grey and black, the women in a variety of hues – red, purple, olive, yellow, peach and pink, which splashed colour onto the bare land, though round their shoulders their shawls were black. They were waiting for their visitors to arrive for the wake.

The first to arrive was an old couple from up the valley.

'I am sorry for your loss,' said the old man, greeting Patrick.

'We're thankful to you,' returned Patrick.

He conducted the old couple into the house where they knelt before the corpse in prayer, before rising and being offered a place to sit. It was all very ceremonious and formal. Soon, others began to arrive, and it was not long before the house had filled up. Mercifully, the rain held off, though the ground was still muddy. Seated on a broad flat stone, an old woman was singing a lament. The faces of most of the mourners outside the house were turned to her, listening, so that at first few noticed the arrival of the figure in black on his strong, white horse. But as more did so, the people turned to face him, and the old woman stopped singing.

Townsend dismounted and removed his hat. He was dressed soberly, and Daniel, studying him, quickly noted that he was unarmed and that there were no holsters attached to the saddle. There was not a policeman in sight. The mourners watched him approach in silence.

Townsend walked forward and came to a halt three yards away from them. Daniel could read nothing in his grey eyes. Townsend cleared his throat.

'The parish of Galready has been too long without a priest,' he said. 'I have written to the Bishop of Raphoe in the hope that he will be able to send someone.' He paused. 'I regret that this will be too late for Michael Dolan. I know that your prayers will help him on his way to God. May he rest in peace.'

'Amen,' muttered some of the mourners. Others

took up the word, crossing themselves. Townsend watched them carefully.

'As a mark of respect,' he continued, 'I have decided to defer collection of the rent until the autumn – until after the harvest has been gathered. I pray that it will be a good one.'

A ripple ran through the people.

Townsend replaced his hat. 'Please forgive the intrusion. I wanted to offer my condolences.' He returned to his horse, mounted, and rode off.

'He's a clever one,' Daniel told Con. His voice was cold.

Sean took up a jug of poteen and moved among the people, pouring a drink for all those who were gathered there.

By the evening, the kilderkin was half drunk and plenty of empty poteen jugs were stacked by the door. A fire had been lit outside and some of the young people were dancing near it to the tune of a piper playing *Out on the Ocean*. Con sat by the piper, playing a bodhran to accompany the tune. Maeve stood near him, her face lit by the fire, watching her sister and Daniel dancing. She saw the look in their faces as they danced together and it stirred memories. She felt the warmth of the fire on her body. She stayed the hand in which Con held the drumstick.

'Come,' she said. 'Dance with me.'

Later, they brought Michael out into the air as the piper played *Taimse Im' Chodlach*. The sky was clear and the stars out, like a perfect spring night should be. Daniel, Sean and Con raised Michael's light body in their strong arms above their heads. It was Daniel who spoke for them:

'Say farewell to the stars in the sky. Farewell to the mountains and the rivers.'

As he spoke, the mourners gathered round, raising their hands above their heads. Borne aloft, very gently, Michael was passed from one to the other. Daniel followed him as he moved over their heads in the night.

'Say farewell to the strand and the sea. Farewell to the trees and the flowers in the grass.'

Michael's body was received by the women now, Mary and Maeve among them. Touched and kissed.

'Sail across the water,' said Daniel. 'Pass beyond the edge of the world. Find the Cave of Cruachan. Enter into the Otherworld. Dwell there in happiness. Michael. Dwell there in happiness.'

The long summer continued. It was one of the wettest people could remember, but the crops grew and ripened in the sunshine when it came. Meanwhile, the people grew leaner, and some were seen on the shore, gathering seaweed to eat. The early hay was gathered and stacked in small cones. Maeve worked with the men gathering the dried turfs in kreels to stack under the eaves. Sean and Con sheared the oats. Daily, James blessed the potatoes in their lazy beds and they seemed to respond to the blessing, the stalks thick and strong, the leaves dense and a rich green, striving up from the lazy beds, decked with gaudy, butter-yellow blossom. It looked as if the horrors of the previous year would not, indeed, be visited on the people again.

If only it would not rain so.

On a day in late summer, the whole family stood or sat in the living room of the farmhouse, watching the rain hurl down against the glass of the small windows, hearing it thud into the turf of the roof. The sky was slate. When James opened the door to the yard he could not see the wall opposite, the sheeting water was so dense. It was hard to tell what time it was. It might have been evening or night.

A heavy mood oppressed them all. When the greyness outside intensified to darkness, they ate their supper in silence. Even the children caught the mood, and the dog stayed under James's chair, head on paws, looking out anxiously.

The rain did not stop all that night. Out in the fields, the stems of the potatoes waved like a miniature forest under the downpour. All looked well, but if a man had been out there, with light enough to see the leaves, he would have fled from that place. Or, already despairing, raised the alarm.

In the morning it was Maeve who was first up, raking out the fire and stoking it up to put on the cauldron of potatoes she'd prepared the night before to boil. The men were down to two pounds apiece for their breakfasts now, and this was a wealthy farm. The rain still fell in torrents and above its noise she did not hear the man approach the door across the yard, swathed in a black cloak with the broad-brimmed hat of a priest pulled tight down over his eyes. The man had come through the potato fields at first light and the urgency of his walk seemed to indicate more than just a desire to get into the dry. Reaching it, he hammered at the door of the farm, making Maeve start.

She crossed the room to open it. He came in, dripping on the earthen floor. As soon as he had removed his hat she saw who it was. A priest – perhaps the priest Townsend had promised. But not just any priest – Liam. Liam Phelan, the youngest of the brothers, who had taken the cloth.

'Welcome, Father,' she said.

'Maeve.'

Sean emerged from the inner room, pulling on his shirt. He smiled to see his brother and crossed the room to embrace him.

'Come in, come in. Get that cloak off and sit by the fire.'

But Liam's expression was grim. 'Wake the old man. We have work to do.'

Sean looked at him. 'What is it?'

'We have to lift the potatoes,' replied his brother.

'In this weather?'

'All the more need. The brown spot is on the leaves. Hurry, or you may lose them all.'

Quickly, the house was roused. Not daring to believe the news, the men took their spades from the shed and set out for the lazy beds. The rain was finer now – you could see across the valley to where other farmers were already at work. The plants, so tall and strong, seemed at first glance to be unchanged. But when you got up close, you could see that the leaves were beginning to shrivel and that the edges of them were black, while brown spots like liver-flecks covered their surfaces.

'Dear God, no,' said Conor, plunging his spade skilfully under the nearest plant. When he lifted it, the spade brought with it not plump, round tubers under the stem, but a filthy, stinking mass that dripped and oozed over the blade.

'It's the potato blight. It's all over the valley,' said Liam. 'I have come to you in an evil time.'

'Lord have mercy on us,' said James.

Liam took out a scarf and tied it over his face. Seizing his spade, he began to cut and dig along the nearest bed. The others followed suit. Not all the potatoes seemed ruined yet, though many already had the dull marks just below the skin that spelt their end. But the blight had spread with the terrible speed they'd heard tell of. Sean, working his lazy bed, took hold of a stem. It broke off in his hand like dead wood. He dropped to his knees by the plant, and, resisting the stench which made his stomach heave despite the handkerchief he'd tied over his nose, scrabbled away the muddy, slippery soil at the base of the plant with his hands to uproot the tubers beneath. As he grasped them, they collapsed in his hands into a putrid, stinking mess. But, among them, two were still firm enough. Wiping them on his shirt, he placed them to one side of the bed and proceeded to the next plant. On either side of him, his brothers worked along their beds in feverish silence. The rain intensified but they did not heed it. All that morning they worked like demons, while Maeve, James and the children struggled back and forth with kreels carrying the good and almost-good potatoes to the shelter of the byre. By noon they looked like demons themselves, covered from head to foot with mud and mire. Under the weight of the kreel on her back, Maeve fell headlong near Liam, cutting her hand on a sharp stone in the soil. He dropped his spade and reached over to steady her. She looked at him.

'God help us all, Father. God help us all.'

FOUR

They were exhausted, but the rain eased off enough at last for them to be able to pit the potatoes they'd saved by late afternoon. Taking it in turns to dig and rest, they excavated a long, shallow trench. Along the bottom of this, Maeve strewed a quantity of dried ferns which she brought from the byre. Then the men piled the potatoes on the fern-bed in pyramids, which Maeve covered with more dried ferns and grasses. The men took their spades again and covered the potato piles with earth, beating it down gently but firmly until the piles were evenly covered and sealed. They had sifted through the potatoes carefully before pitting them, and another pile of tubers that already carried the brown spot, or were suspected of carrying it, were set aside in a separate pile to feed to the pigs before the rot set in. A smaller pile was of blighted potatoes which still had clean portions big enough for human consumption. There would be a huge dinner that night, because every part that was edible on the diseased tubers would have to be eaten before the blight spread into it.

At last they rested on their spades in the rain, heads bent. They did not speak. Each had his own thoughts about what had come to them. They thought of the blight. No-one knew where it had come from or what caused it, but it had arrived in Europe during the last few years and in 1845 had visited Ireland to terrible effect. A bevy of English scientists had come over to study it and issued complicated instructions about what to do to salvage a crop when it struck – but as to a cause or a cure, few conclusions had been reached.

Maeve had gone into the house some time before them, joined by Mary, who had come over to lend a hand as soon as she could. They had been able to save scarcely two bushels of potatoes from Patrick Dolan's small field. Now Maeve reappeared in the doorway to call them in. Wearily, they roused themselves from their reveries and dragged themselves into the dry and the warmth. The women had prepared a large wooden tub, which stood in the centre of the room. Into it they were pouring hot water from jugs which they dipped into the large cauldron which hung over the fire. The room was steamy and comfortable. One by one, the men stripped, their bodies gleaming white in the light of the oil-lamp, arms and torsos of marble, in contrast to the darkly weatherbeaten colour of their faces and necks, hands, forearms and feet. They bathed in silence, letting the women pour water over them, washing the mud and the grime from them. They were all thinking about the blight still.

'Thank God we've lifted them,' said Maeve. 'Some

are sound. We've saved some, at least.' She was trying to cheer them up, to make them look on the bright side. But it was a hard task.

'It smells like it's come from the bowels of the earth,' said Mary.

'Perhaps it fell from the sky in the rain?'

Liam had towelled himself as dry as he could with a piece of linen. His clothes were damp and earthy, and clung to him. He spoke with conviction: 'Like all good things and all bad, it has come from God. We must pray to him for forgiveness.'

It was still pouring with rain the following day when the cart bearing Liam's belongings arrived at the edge of the town of Galready. It had made slow going on the road from Raphoe, mired by the rain. They had tethered Liam's horse to its backpost, and the animal picked its way along behind the lurching vehicle. By the driver, in front of the heaped tarpaulin which offered some protection from the rain to Liam's modest luggage, sat the priest with his brother Conor.

They were close to the modest stone house adjoining the tiny Catholic chapel when the left-hand rear wheel of the cart became stuck in a muddy hole where the road had sunk. Con leapt down immediately and put his hands to the spokes to free it. Liam followed suit, but people had noticed the mishap and came running from their houses to offer help. They welcomed the priest with their eyes, not allowing him to sully his clothes.

'Leave that now, Father,' they said. 'Get back up

on the cart.'

The cart was clear of the pothole now, but more and more people arrived to push and steady it, and to escort their new priest on the last few dozen yards of the journey to his house.

'God bless you,' said Liam. 'God bless you.'

The interior of the house was far from welcoming. It was bare and cold and damp, and no fire had been lit against his arrival – for he had come unannounced. But there were a few signs of the occupancy of Liam's predecessor, an old man who'd died many months before and been taken home to be buried at Bundoran. His cape hung behind the door, and on a shelf above the narrow bed was a handful of books, including a *Confessions* of St Augustine and Newman's *Lyra Apostolica*. The covers of nearly every volume bore traces of mildew. Liam wiped some off the *Confessions* with his thumb.

There was wood and kindling stacked in the hearth and Con squatted down to lay a fire.

'Did you ask to come back to Galready?' he asked Liam.

Liam interrupted his unpacking to turn to his brother. 'No.'

'Still, I'm glad you're here,' said Con warmly.

Liam smiled. 'God's blessing on you, Conor.'

'The same blessing on you, Father.'

Too many people turned up for Mass on Sunday for the little chapel to accommodate them all. But it was a blustery, fine day and the priest was able to hold the service in the open. The people stood, heads bowed, in the long grass among the headstones of the cemetery. After they had taken communion, they stood attentive to what their new priest had to say to them. Liam knew that his words would be weighed carefully. He had arrived among these people at a time of appalling stress. Perhaps God had willed it so, sending His servant to His people in their hour of need. Liam felt the spirit of God strong in him.

'I am proud to stand before you here today,' he said. 'Many of you I know and love, for this is where I was born and raised.' He searched their faces. 'We know what has befallen us. We must all look into our hearts and ask ourselves what we have done, so to displease the Lord that he has visited this punishment upon us.' As he continued to speak, his eye caught a figure in black on a white horse, almost silhouetted against the sky, as it rode along a far ridge among the blackened stalks of the potato fields that surrounded the town. As Liam continued his homily, the rider spurred his horse and vanished around the other side of the hill.

'Oh God, heavenly Father,' prayed Liam, at the conclusion of the service, 'Whose gift it is that the earth is fruitful, behold, we beseech Thee, the afflictions of Thy people. Grant that the scarcity and dearth, which we now suffer for our sins, may through Thy goodness be turned into plenty …'

He could not look at the faces of the people now, as he prayed. He could not even look at the faces of his family among the congregation. A thought was within him that he could not yet acknowledge, though he knew it was there, and that it had come like a storm cloud as he had watched the black rider among the blackened plants.

'Come, fetch your basket,' Maeve said to her daughter, later that day. 'It's time we dug up some of the good potatoes for the men's supper.' It would be necessary, she knew, to eat the food they had salvaged as soon as possible. They could not risk it spoiling, and she did not have as much confidence as she would have liked in the pit. If wet had got in, who knew what the result would be? Molly cheerfully bounced up to her with the shallow reed basket that Patrick Dolan had woven for her last winter. The little girl looked paler than Maeve would have liked, though that might have been from the lack of sunshine. And she smiled cheerfully enough. Maeve fussed for a moment with her daughter's plum-coloured apron, pulling it straight over the buff, homespun skirt beneath it.

Outside, it was still dry, though the fresh winds were already gathering clouds overhead. Away in the east field, Sean was with James and Conor, beginning to get in the barley which would have to be sold to pay the rent. The period of Townsend's deferment, occasioned by Michael's death – could Michael have been dead so many weeks already? – was nearing its end.

Suddenly, Maeve stopped. The breeze had brought an odour to her nostrils. It was very faint and her first instinct was to deny that it was there at all, to presume that she was imagining her worst fears realised. But another gust brought it to her more strongly.

Her scalp crawled. She put her hand to her hair.

Molly caught her distress and her smile vanished. But Maeve was already hurrying towards the potato pit. On her knees, she started to shovel the soil aside with her hands. Once the seal of earth was broken, the stench hit her with its full force, but it was from shock as much as from nausea that she recoiled, as if from a punch in the stomach. She caught Molly's distressed eye and covered her face with her hands, unable to stop the sobs of panic and dismay that came to her. She heard Molly running, her voice fearful, calling her father. She heard the men approach. Now she looked at them, pointing mutely at the potato pit. Conor had a spade in his hands, but he did not need to use it. They could all see what had happened. Their entire stock of potatoes had collapsed into a putrid mess of rottenness. Conor delved into it, but the few solid pieces of tuber he was able to draw out smelt so vile that his gorge rose at them. James watched with opaque eyes. Sean drew Molly into his arms, squeezed her, held her up, close to him.

On the day following his Sunday ride among the ruined fields, Townsend had bidden McBride into the inner office to dictate a letter to him. The agent had learnt much in the months he had been here, though beyond a few words the Irish tongue itself continued to elude him – Hindustani had been easier. Now he had not hesitated before making his decision to write to his employer. McBride was reading back to him what he had taken down so far:

'The potato fields of Ireland are utterly destroyed. Your Lordship will be aware that the potato is the staple diet of your tenants, who have thereby lost six months' supply of food overnight.' McBride cleared his throat. 'Following, as this does, hard upon last year's partial failure, many of your tenants will find it impossible to pay their rent. There is a danger that any attempt to collect the rent in full will result in a fiasco. I am sure the new Government under Lord John Russell is doing all that it can to expedite matters, but in the meantime I humbly suggest that your Lordship reduces the rents or agrees to forgo them altogether until this terrible situation has passed.' McBride stopped reading and looked up, dipping his quill, ready to continue.

'The lives of thousands,' Townsend dictated, 'may depend upon what is done now. *Bis dat qui cito dat.*' McBride hesitated, looking at the agent quizzically.

'He gives twice who gives promptly,' Townsend translated.

For days and days it rained. Everything was grey under the rain: the rocks, the land, the grass. Father Liam was spurring his sturdy little horse towards a group of wretched cabins that nestled on the upland of Cluain-Cuas, at the foot of the Carrickduff mountains. When he had reached them, he dismounted. There seemed to be no sign of life, but in response to his call a thin little grey figure appeared in the darkness of a doorway. Boy or girl, Liam could not tell. It was skin and bone, but for the swellings at its elbows and knees, and its taut, rounded belly. There was a curious smell, too: a dry, sweet smell that, while not being obviously unpleasant, made the hair on his neck rise. Liam approached the door. The child watched him without any expression at all.

'Is there sickness here?' Liam asked, directing his question half to the child, and half to the darkness beyond the doorway. From within there came a slow, scuffling noise, and soon a man as wasted as his child appeared, looking at the priest with weary eyes.

'No, Father. Only hunger.'

'Let me see.'

Liam made his way into the cabin. It was empty and even the fire had gone out. The air was close and tired. There was a small, pale shape on a litter of brown grass in one corner. Its arms and legs were drawn up to its body and it lay on its side. Its eyes were open and hollow. The dry smell came from it. It lay too still.

'Why have you not buried this child?' Liam asked the man.

The man made an empty gesture with one hand. 'I have not the strength,' he said. 'We have eaten what there was to eat on the moor.'

Liam took the dead child in his arms. As he did so the rags it was dressed in fell away and he saw that it had been a little girl. He took the corpse outside and laid it gently on the ground a short distance from the cabins. For the first time he became aware of the stillness in the settlement.

'The others have all gone,' said the man, watching the priest's face. Liam walked over to his horse and delved into the saddlebag, from which he produced the loaf and the flask of buttermilk he had packed for his lunch. Without speaking, he gave the food to the man who took it without a word and broke the bread carefully, giving the larger part to the living child.

'Eat slowly,' said the man; and truly it seemed that the child was too tired to do anything else. Liam had found a spade by the side of one of the other cabins, and with it he dug a shallow grave in which he laid the little corpse, before covering it with earth and stones. Then he stood by the grave and said a prayer for the soul of the departed, and the Lord's Prayer. But the thought in his mind was: why does God do this? Is it a test? Is it a challenge? How should a man respond to it?

'God is the source of all truth. His Word is truth,' he said to himself.

That evening, back at his house, he bathed his tired face in cold water, lit the lamp, and sat at his small desk, drawing a notebook towards him. He had eaten nothing since the morning, but he was not hungry now. He thought of the survivors up on the moor. How many like that father and child were there? How fast hunger came on the land. As for his own resources, he could scarcely help one, let alone thousands. But perhaps there was a way. He started to write:

This is the testimony of the Reverend Liam Phelan, PP, Galready, County Donegal, 17th August, 1846. I travelled today to Cluain-Cuas, the Meadow of the Caves,

one of the most remote parts of the parish.
I found a family reduced to a single meal
a day of cabbage, and the first instance of
death from want. The poor people of this
parish are already eking out an existence
on nettles and blackberries. In my journeying
today I saw women and children scouring
the seashore for seaweed and sand-eels,
like scavenging birds. A famine, with all
its baneful consequences, presses, if the
people be not immediately relieved.

When he had finished writing, he counted out the money he had and placed it all in his pocket. He undressed and lay down to sleep, but he was too impatient for dawn to close his eyes for a long time.

The next morning, early, he made his way across to Brannocktown, where he arrived at Coulter's Stores soon after it had opened. He knew Coulter, who'd been a bullying young man – one to put the fear of God into the children of the district when Liam was little. Lord Hawksborough had still been in residence for at least part of the year at Galready House in those days, and Coulter's father had built up his business supplying food and drink to the gentry. Coulter had inherited the business after the Catholic Emancipation Act of 1839, which marked the end of the Hawksboroughs' sojourns in Ireland. As a Catholic himself, Coulter had had an interest in Irish nationalism, because he wanted the trade that, in the days of direct English patronage, had gone to his Protestant rivals. Coulter's father had died a few years ago, leaving his son a business that had seen better days, but the son had developed a tidy sideline in loans at high interest. Reinvesting in his Stores, he was able to build up a clientele among the big farmers and the agents, as well as doing a bit of modest exporting. The beauty of the business was that everyone needed food and drink, and often what the locals got from Coulter for their produce, they spent on his stout and whiskey. Coulter was now a man of about forty-five, but he looked older. Though he still carried the traces of his youthful good looks, he was grey and balding and running to fat, and his skin under his stubbly beard was always shining and greasy. He had fat, wet lips, and cold, careful brown eyes. He knew what he was, a gombeen man, one who flourished on the misfortunes of others; but as long as he flourished he did not mind in what contempt he might be held. He did not even think about it.

Liam gave his order to Martin Ferry, who worked in the Stores. As Ferry packed a basket with the food, Liam watched Coulter, who lounged at the bar counter at the far end of the shop, pencil and pad in hand, checking his stock of bottles. Catching the priest's eye, Coulter shambled easily over to him.

'Throwing a party?' he asked, glancing at the food in the basket.

'It shames me to do business with you,' said Liam. Coulter looked at him expressionlessly. 'Thank you, Father.'

Liam glanced around the shop. A cornucopia. Heavy flitches of bacon hung from the beams. Sacks of grain, oats and barley were ranged by the counter. On shelves behind, all manner of food, vegetables and fruit – for those with the money to buy them.

'Remember what happened to the money-lenders in the temple,' said Liam. 'Our Lord made a scourge of ropes and drove them out.'

'I help more than you know,' said Coulter. 'I have no reason to be ashamed.'

Liam spent the day distributing the food he had bought. The people he took it to received it gratefully. But was he inspiring hope which he could not fulfil? His money was finite, and one priest alone could not stop the tidal wave of hunger that was crashing over the land. How could he help his fellow man without arousing expectations, without appearing to make promises which he could not keep? And how could he tell his flock to bear their lot patiently, as a test sent from God, or a punishment for some unidentified sin? They bowed their heads humbly when he preached, but their children were dying. There had to be another way to help them.

'Vanity,' he thought angrily and bleakly. 'All is vanity.' Yet he continued, as the days passed, to keep his journal. The first notebook was quickly filled and another started. An idea to make use of them was forming in his mind.

As the hunger mounted, so the Government in London introduced measures to ameliorate the predicament of the people. As in the previous year, schemes for relief works were got under way – those who were unable to gain a living from their farms would be put to work on schemes beneficial to the community as a whole, and would use the money paid them to buy corn to eat. Unlike the previous year, however, there would be little or no free or subsidised food available to the people, for the Government had a horror of interfering with free trade. Means would be made available for the people to earn money with which to buy food, and works of improvement would be the result of those means. It was a beautiful theory. And loans for the works would be provided. The result of that, however, was that at the presentation sessions where local committees sought suggestions for works, they were deluged.

In the Babel of one such session at Brannocktown Town Hall a week after Liam had shopped at Coulter's Stores, Townsend, sitting at a table with McBride, McCafferty, Mr Brady the justice, Parson Denny, Dr Davis and Father Liam, desperately tried to instil some order into the proceedings. In the body of the room sat the more-or-less prosperous ratepayers of Galready parish. Among them was Coulter. In another group Townsend identified the schoolteacher, Daniel Phelan. A beautiful girl with cream-coloured skin and golden hair sat next to him. Armed police were near the doors, and at the back stood a heavily-built man with grey, blank eyes, whom Townsend recognised as the one who had pleaded with him on his knees the day he was attacked by the mob. It had never been possible to prove that it had been Martin Ferry who dealt the first blow that day, but Townsend had the man marked down as a potential troublemaker and resolved to keep a close eye on him.

At the moment, however, he was grappling with other problems. He stood and banged on the table, spread with maps in front of him, to elicit silence, or at least enough of a lull to make himself heard. There was no making sense of these people. Attracted by the advantageous loans the Government in London was offering, every man jack of the ratepayers was proposing a scheme for the relief works – with little regard to the need for it to benefit not one, but all.

'We need to put forward one proposal,' Townsend said when he could, at last, command some attention. 'Not two hundred! One scheme large enough to provide employment for all the distressed in the district. There is no point in everyone here presenting schemes. The Board of Works will not build you a pigsty and you a barn, or make you a new field. The works, to be fair to all the local ratepayers, must be non-productive. That is, it must not confer benefit on any one individual.'

'Who will pay for your relief works?' asked Daniel. Townsend looked across at him, his eyes lingering on the girl next to him a moment longer than he knew they should have, for she became aware of his look, and he knew that she knew what had fleeted through his mind. Parson Denny was answering for him:

'His lordship will pay, and all other persons possessed of property.'

'The money advanced by the treasury is a loan,'

explained the fat Mr Brady patiently. 'A loan payable in its entirety after ten years at three-and-one-half per cent. The terms are generous.'

'They are. But if we have to pay in the end,' a farmer said, 'why shouldn't we reap the benefits? Why shouldn't I get a pigsty?'

'Because you are not starving, my son,' put in Father Liam. 'In my view, the loan should be used directly to buy food which we could resell at cost or even give away to the really needy.'

'That is not the Government's view,' said Coulter, warmly. 'You cannot interfere with free trade.'

Liam looked at him with contempt. 'Yes, "free" in the sense that you can charge what you like, Coulter!'

By now Dr Davis was on his feet, siding with Liam. 'The people need to be fed, not worked to death building a road that begins nowhere and ends in a bog.'

Townsend looked at him. The road Davis was referring to was, in fact, the scheme the agent favoured. It was true that another road was superfluous, but there was no other project that could not be identified as benefiting someone more than another. With the road scheme, Townsend could count on a degree of agreement and thus attract the loan needed to pay the poor workers to enable them to buy meal.

'I know full well where the road starts and finishes, doctor,' he said evenly. He had expected more support from Davis. 'It is in a good site because there is a quarry nearby. It is a good scheme because it will be approved. Those of you who wish to present alternative schemes to the Board of Works may of course do so. In the meantime, I am declaring this meeting closed.'

He gathered his papers together and turned, followed by the other members of the committee, to leave the assembly room by a door at the back. In the hubbub they left behind, Ferry made his way across to Daniel. He spoke quietly, not looking at the schoolteacher.

'When do we make our move?' he asked.

In the ante-chamber beyond the assembly room, Davis was speaking to Townsend. 'Who exactly will be eligible to work on this road?'

The agent replied stiffly. 'It is our task to draw up a list to submit to the Board of Works. I suggest we start by relieving Lord Hawksborough of the burden of the poorhouse.'

Davis was silent for a moment. Townsend's motive was obvious: Lord Hawksborough would look kindly on any employee who could save him money. 'Many of the men in the poorhouse aren't fit to work,' he said firmly.

'But many are,' said Parson Denny, who had overheard. 'Since begging has become so unprofitable, the place has filled with malingerers,' he added spitefully.

'How would you know, Mr Denny?' asked Davis, rounding on him, but keeping his voice polite.

'Clearly there's no sense in encouraging farmers or fishermen to give up their endeavour for road-building,' said Townsend.

'How then are they to be assisted?' said Liam. 'There are no fish except out in the deep waters where the curraghs cannot sail. The tenant farmers have lost their food supply and have no seed potatoes to grow more. It is too late in the year for anything else and after harvest, when they have sold their cash crops to pay rent, they will have nothing! His lordship must understand that.'

Davis made a very impatient gesture. 'Lord Hawksborough has not been in Galready for nigh on twenty years. He can have no idea of the distress that exists here.'

Townsend was pulling on his coat. Outside, the night rain beat at the windowpanes. Liam walked over to him:

'His lordship must be made to understand the situation. If his tenants have to sell the rest of their produce for rent they will starve. They must be allowed to eat their oats, their eggs, their butter. They must know that there is no threat of being turned out to die on the road. Persuade his lordship to forego the rents until this crisis is over. Give the people hope.'

'I have written to Lord Hawksborough, asking him to remit the rents. I am awaiting his instructions.' There was a blast of cold air as McCafferty appeared at the outside door with the agent's armed escort. 'In the meantime, I will submit the road-building scheme to the Board of Works.'

The others watched Townsend go. Putting on his own coat, Denny moved to the door. His hand on the knob, he addressed a parting shot to Davis, but it was clear that it was also aimed at the priest. 'Would there be a "crisis" at all if the land weren't so overpopulated?'

When he had gone, Liam said to Davis wryly, 'He thanked God for that "overpopulation" when each and every Catholic family paid a tenth of their income into your church year after year – though they neither shared your kind of Christianity nor required Mr Denny's services.'

Davis, putting on his hat, was silent. Liam watched him, relenting. 'Can his lordship really be so ignorant of what is happening here, on his own property? Do the English really not know?'

'Come back with me and have a drink, Father,' said Davis. 'We should talk of these things. I must say I had hopes of the new agent, but ...' He let the sentence hang. The two men left together.

The doctor's study was cluttered with books and papers. It was a warm, untidy room with thick walls that shut out the cold night, a night which already carried the threat of winter. Davis poured two large whiskeys and handed one to Liam, nodding to a leather armchair. Rummaging on the desk, he produced a copy of *The Times* and handed it to the priest. 'A little old,' he said. '3rd August. But there's a sentence or two in the leader that will interest you.'

Liam scanned the column and read: 'It is possible to have heard the tale of sorrow too often.' He cast the paper aside. 'I am aware that the English press has little sympathy for our plight,' he said.

'There's worse than that,' said Davis. 'They published

a letter on the first of this month from someone writing under the name "B". You ought to hear what he has to say.'

Rummaging again, the Doctor produced a more recent copy of the paper and read aloud: 'They inhabit a country a great part of which is at least equal in fertility to our own, with more that is capable of being made so. There is no reason, except their own wilful mismanagement, why they should not grow as fine crops of wheat as are raised in the Lothians, and, after feeding themselves, export the surplus to our shores. Yet, after years of present suffering and fearful expectation, they idly and stupidly persist in staking their very existence upon a crop the precarious nature of which is no more than a fair set-off against the small amount of labour required to produce it.'

The two men exchanged a glance. 'I may safely assert,' Davis continued to read, 'that the prejudices and ignorance of the Irish people are at least as inveterate and as fatal as their misgovernment and the ill example of their superiors have been culpable and injurious ...'

'Whom does he mean there?' asked Liam. 'The English?'

Davis smiled drily. 'The great object of his life,' he read, 'is to rent a miserable patch of land, to build himself a hovel, or burrow in the earth, to marry, and, if possible, to live as well as his pig. For a month or two our farmer is busied with planting potatoes; for another month or two he leaves home and comes to reap where he sowed not, in the smiling harvests of England; while for the remaining two-thirds of the year he does nothing but sleep, drink or beg. I verily believe that if the potato famine in Ireland were to continue five years longer, it would prove a greater blessing to the country than any that has ever been devised by Parliamentary commissions from the Union to the present time.'

Liam sat in silence for a moment. Then he drank a deep draught of whiskey to cover his anger. 'God help us,' he said, 'if they really think like that.'

'You want my opinion,' said the doctor. 'They neither know nor want to know what is going on here.' He refilled the priest's glass.

'I can't believe that,' said Liam.

The doctor shrugged. 'We both have jobs that show us the truth. We are both Irishmen. What can we do? O'Connell failed to find a political solution. I cannot accept that the answer lies in violence.'

'Do you keep a diary, doctor?' asked Liam.

Davis looked at him. 'Of sorts.'

Liam sat forward in his chair. 'Could we work together, do you think?'

'In what way?'

'I'm keeping a journal. We could draw on our accounts of what we see to write a report on conditions here in Galready. We could get it published in London. So that the people might know at last what is going on. I cannot believe that the ordinary people of England think like that man whose letter you have just read.'

'You mean,' said the doctor, smiling wryly, 'that we should tell the tale of sorrow once again?' But he raised his glass to the priest.

The following day, towards the end of the morning's lessons, Daniel received a visit from his brother Liam at the schoolhouse. He dismissed his class of fifteen ragged children a few minutes early, and they stowed their slates and chalks with a happy clatter. English language lessons were not their favourite, and did they but know it, they were not the favourite of their master, either. But learned they had to be, if these children were to have any hope of a future away from the land.

They chorused 'Good day, Father Phelan' and filed out into the quayside square. Daniel opened the door that led from the schoolroom into his own lodgings. The room he lived in was as simply furnished as the priest's. There was an upright chair next to a table piled with books and papers, an easy chair by the chimney-piece, and a settle bed against the far wall. Under the window were a basin and ewer, rather cracked, on a stand. As Liam outlined his plan to his brother, Daniel prepared tea. He listened attentively, but his face displayed little enthusiasm.

'If the Protestant doctor and the Catholic priest are writing this "report", what need do you have of the poor national schoolmaster?' he said at last.

'You are the one with the gift for language.'

Daniel smiled bitterly. 'A "gift for language." Is it a poem you're writing?' He handed his brother his tea.

'I'd like to work with you.'

Daniel looked at him. 'I don't think so, Liam.'

Liam sipped the tea before replying. 'Do you

remember when we were boys? In the summer, we drove the cattle to the mountains. To Cluain-Cuas. Pastured them there. Lived on milk and blood.'

'Yes.'

'I was there a few days ago. I buried a child who had died of starvation. Less than a day's ride from here. Do you not think the English should be told that?'

Daniel had seated himself at the table. Now he rose. 'Let me show you something.'

Liam followed the schoolmaster back into the classroom. Over the chimney breast there was a painted sign, worn and chipped, but still perfectly legible and written in English. Daniel looked at it and read it aloud:

'*I thank the goodness and the grace*
That on my birth have smiled,
And made me in these Christian days
A happy English child.'

'I stand beneath that every day teaching Irish children. I show them a map of the world that is covered with the red of the British Empire.' He pointed to the map on the wall nearby as he continued. 'I tell them British troops are stationed here in India, in Australia, in Hong Kong, and here in Ireland. And I remind them that every soldier has three square meals a day. That every day food is shipped to Bombay, Calcutta, everywhere. Food that comes from Ireland. And then I ask them why, do they think, despite all that, people are so hungry in Donegal? Why can't we eat the food that is under our noses? Or – if there is not enough food for us to eat – why is it beyond the resources of the richest nation on earth, whose ships sail every ocean, to get food from there to here? And they don't know the answers.' He stopped, looking at his brother with cold eyes.

'Your rhetoric will not put food into anyone's mouth, Daniel.'

'Perhaps not, but I still won't waste my time appealing to people who more and more behave as if they'd like to see us dead.'

Townsend sat at the table in his dining room. The room seemed cold and cheerless despite the fire that roared in the grate. The remains of his supper were pushed aside – he was waiting grimly for Mrs Brogan to bring the second bottle of wine he'd asked for and to clear away. The bare surface of the rest of the table reminded him of his loneliness. Near his hand lay the letter which had arrived that morning. He had read it a dozen times and could still not believe its contents.

At last he heard footsteps in the corridor outside and Mrs Brogan entered, another bottle uncorked on the tray. She placed it by him without a word, though she glanced at him sidelong as he poured himself a glass immediately and drained it, pouring another before watching her himself as she cleared the plates and cutlery on to her tray. He pulled himself upright in his chair and addressed her, tapping the letter.

'This will interest you, Mrs Brogan. Apparently, poverty is the natural condition of the Irish and no extraordinary measures for relief are necessary. Quite the reverse. Lord Hawksborough, "after the fullest and most mature consideration", has come to the conclusion that the rents, and all arrears, must be collected. His Lordship believes that "with better management and husbandry the tenants will be able to pay without hardship". All this, of course, can be seen from the window of his drawing room in Eaton Square.' He made a sweeping gesture with his hand, throwing the letter down in disgust and upsetting the bottle of wine, which spilt over the letter despite Mrs Brogan's attempt to rescue it. 'Oh, damn it, woman! Damn it!' he swore, letter in one hand and bottle in the other. Mrs Brogan took up her tray and retreated from the room without a word. Townsend attempted to shake the wine from the letter, placing it on a dry part of the table top and looking at it once again as he poured himself another glass, willing its instructions to be other than they were. He put the bottle down. It would be a hard enough day tomorrow without having to contend with a hangover as well.

Maeve straightened her back and eased it, placing her hands on her hips and turning her face to the sky, which was assuming its wintry aspect after the mild and rainy summer. She felt how bony her hips had already become. She put the mattock she had been holding down and rubbed her hard hands together. They were big, capable hands, but she thought ruefully that they would never be beautiful. She could feel her baby, Hannah, stirring in the shawl which swaddled her and tied her to Maeve's back. She turned her head and nuzzled the tiny, pinched face.

The little patch of ground above the house which she was cultivating gave her a good view of the farm. In the yard, Sean was flailing the oats. Toiling up the short incline towards her came Conor, with a kreel full of good earth. She looked with some pride at the heap of furze and stones she had cleared.

Con tipped the earth out of the kreel. He picked up the water flask and offered it to her before drinking himself. He drank long and deep. At least water was plentiful and filled the belly. Then he nodded at the new field they had made.

'We'll fold the pig in here. She'll soon have it dug over,' he said.

Sean had raised his head, watching them. Now he too walked over. 'I don't know why you're wasting your time with that,' he said. His tone was easy, but there was a hint of nervousness in it. Sean was not a man for new things.

'It's our rainy day patch,' said Maeve. 'In the spring there'll be cabbages, onions, turnips. Food for us.'

Sean continued to look unconvinced. 'People will laugh at us.'

'Let them. We won't be left with nothing to eat but the air.' Maeve looked at him more seriously. 'Don't stop me from doing this, Sean.'

'I won't,' he replied. 'But tomorrow, Con works with me.'

As he walked back to his task, the sun came out, brightening the morning and warming their faces.

'It's a good sign,' said Con, pouring a little water from the flask into the palm of his hand and rinsing his face before taking up a fork and beginning to spread the earth over the cleared land. The sun went back behind its cloud.

They worked for half-an-hour before the black figure on the white horse rode up and disturbed them. He reined in close to the edge of the field. He wore an overcoat against the weather but Con saw that he had a revolver in its belt and that there were long pistols in the saddle-holsters. Still, Townsend gave them a tight smile.

'Good morning. I would speak with your husband,' he said to Maeve.

She looked over to the yard, but Sean was not there. 'He must be in the house, sir.'

Townsend tipped his hat and rode down to the yard, where they saw him dismount and enter, taking the saddle-pistols with him. They looked at each other. They stacked their tools and followed.

It was as if Townsend and Sean had been waiting for them. They sat at the table. Con leant against the doorpost. Maeve went into her room and tidied herself briefly. The children were at school. James was down at Patrick Dolan's for a bit of a talk. When everyone was settled, Townsend began:

'I remitted the rents in June as a mark of sympathy and regret at the way Michael Dolan met his end,' he began. His voice was completely neutral. Despite the firearms, if anything, the agent's manner was friendly and relaxed. 'But now they must be paid in full,' he continued. 'I have selected two or three tenants who I know have the means to pay – yourselves included – and I am taking the unusual step of visiting them personally to ask them not to hold out against their landlord's people. To ask them, in fact, to set an example, and pay promptly on Gale Day.'

They had listened to him in silence, heads bowed, but Townsend was aware of the effect of his words. He had been aware of what their effect would be ever since he had received Lord Hawksborough's letter. But what could he do?

Conor spoke first. 'Mister Townsend, we have lost our entire crop of potatoes. We don't even have seed potatoes.'

'We will have to sell everything to pay our rent in full,' said Maeve. 'We will have nothing to sow in the spring.'

Townsend met her eye. 'Those with the means must pay.'

'And what will happen to those who haven't the means to pay?'

'They must pay what they can.'

'And what will become of them?' said Sean.

'Let them pay what they can,' repeated Townsend, less easily.

There was a pause before Con said: 'And what if we don't "set an example"?'

Townsend looked down at the table. 'Then I shall have no choice but to proceed against you by law.' He looked up. 'I will eject you from this farm altogether.' He rose and made his way to the door. Once there he turned, as if to add something, but said nothing, and a moment later they heard him riding away.

They finished work on the new field that day. Conor

hadn't so much heart for it, but Maeve made him go on, hiding her own despair. They ate cabbage at midday, and nettle soup at night. The children came home with some hard biscuit which Daniel had given them, they said. Sean sat at the table, in his father's chair, which James had never sat in again since the altercation on the last Gale Day, the old notebook in front of him. He looked up from his calculations to Maeve, who sat on a low stool by the fire, staring into it, nursing Hannah. It was early evening. James, hearing the news on his return, had retired to his room. Conor was still out, making the most of the fading autumn light. The children, Joseph and Molly, nestled at their mother's feet. They were listless. From time to time the baby whined.

'I think we can keep one of the cows,' said Sean.

'We should keep Derdriu.'

'Nes gives more milk.'

They were interrupted by James, who came in stony-faced, carrying his Sunday suit of grey frieze over his arm. He placed it by Maeve.

'Here. Make the boy some clothes.'

Maeve looked at him. 'But …'

'He needs warm clothes for the winter. I won't be going to market again.' James left as abruptly as he had arrived.

Sean and his wife looked at each other. 'Do as he says,' said Sean. 'It's all he's got left to give.' He closed the book and got to his feet wearily.

'Where are you going?'

'It's late and the cows are not yet milked.'

She watched him go. She knew what his father's gesture meant to him. No wonder he needed to be alone to think. Left alone, she picked up the jacket of the suit. She had already noticed the children eyeing it. She exchanged a glance with Joseph and smiled.

When Conor came in half-an-hour later – he'd been building a low wall around the new field as a surprise for Maeve but it was too dark to work any more – he saw that she had her workbasket and scissors out. The children had gone to bed. Hannah slept, very still, wrapped in the shawl, in a basket nearby.

'What are you doing?' he asked.

'Cutting down your father's suit,' she replied. 'He's given it to me to make clothes for the boy.'

Con couldn't resist a joke: 'His best suit? Ah, no – what'll we bury him in now?' But he saw the seriousness in her face and came to sit by her. She spoke without looking up from her work. He knew every nuance of her voice, though, and she could not disguise from him how close she was to tears.

'We spent so much money on Michael's wake. If we have to pay in full we won't even be able to buy seed for the new garden.' She looked at him then. 'It's bad enough now. What'll we do when there's nothing at all to eat?'

Conor returned her gaze and smiled with his eyes. He started to sing gently:

I had a first cousin called Arthur McBride;
He and I took a stroll down by the seaside
A-seeking good fortune and what might betide,

Being just as the day was a-dawning.
Then after resting we both took a tramp,
We met Sergeant Harper and Corporal Cramp.'

'Stop, now,' said Maeve.

'And besides a wee drummer who beat up for camp,
With his rowdy dow-dow in the morning.
He said, My young fellows, if you will enlist,
A guinea you quickly shall have from my fist…'

'Stop it,' she repeated.

'Besides a crown for to kick up the dust
And drink the King's health in the morning.'

Conor fell silent. The song didn't seem so jolly any more.

'Do you not think a uniform'd suit me?' he asked.

'No, I do not.'

'There's plenty of Irishmen who've made a living in the British Army. Look at all those gallant lads in India last spring, at Aliwal and Sobraon, helping General Gough put down the rebels there.'

'And where are half of them now?' asked Maeve. 'Dead. And for what?' She took Con's hand. 'We need you here.'

'But for how much longer?'

The whole valley, the whole estate knew of Lord Hawksborough's decision to order payment of the rents, and of Townsend's determination to impose that order. Fear of eviction was uppermost in everyone's mind, and while Townsend had done little in that line since he'd taken over from Jenkins, it did not mean that he wouldn't. The threat he'd held over the Phelans was held over every tenant in Galready, and only the landowning men breathed easily. People would do anything, sell everything, not to be turned off. So there was a fever of activity in the country against the next market day.

It dawned soon enough, and before first light Conor and Sean were loading the big horse with sacks of grain, while Maeve and the children coaxed all but a handful of chickens into baskets which Patrick Dolan had made. Maeve was anxious: she knew how prices would be depressed by the degree of supply, but on the other hand, the Phelans' produce could be held up next to anyone's and pronounced the better. They would just have to hope and pray, as they always had to. Why were hope and prayer all the poor were ever given? You couldn't eat either, or pay for anything with them.

She put her thoughts aside as James came to the door of the house and watched them. He was in his everyday clothes and had risen late, not turning a hand to help. Not catching anyone's eye, either, he strode across the yard and out of it, walking up the hill behind the farm and only pausing to look at Maeve's new field, waiting to be sown. Maeve saw him walk on and then find a flat stone where he sat. She ushered the children into the house and pulled Joseph into his new suit of clothes. A little big, but warm and tidy enough, and the boy's eyes shone with pride.

'There,' she said to him gently. 'Go and show your grandfather.'

James was looking down at the farm. He was crying, but when he saw the boy running up towards him he wiped his eyes on his sleeve. Joseph arrived, and he hugged him. Then he held him at arm's length and looked at him, nodding his approval and smiling.

'Take care of your father today,' said James.

By sunrise, the horse was laden with produce. All the sacks of grain, the two baskets of chickens, a store of eggs packed in straw, cheeses in linen wrappers and butter wrapped the same way were all placed on his broad back. Sean and Con had changed into their best clothes, their hair washed and neatly tied back. Their shoes and stockings they carried round their necks to save them from the mud. The pig and the cow, Derdriu, stood nervously tethered by the horse. The children stood near. To save her from envy, Maeve had made Molly a little red shawl, out of material left over from a scarlet cloak of her own, which she now wore over her best blue gown. Under the cloak, Hannah snuggled warmly in a shawl tied across Maeve's shoulders. Like the men, Maeve carried her shoes and stockings round her neck. She caught her husband's look of admiration with pleasure. It made them all feel good to dress well. But she saw how Sean's clothes hung too loose on him. Only Con still filled his coat completely.

People were already on the track when they set off. Others, those left behind, the old ones, or those with nothing to sell, watched them go with mixed feelings. From his hilltop seat, James watched too, though none of his family turned back to look at him or to wave. But he watched them out of sight on the way to Brannocktown. Then he looked down at the farm. The dog in the yard cocked his head at him.

Just above the town, where the track joined the cindered road, the family stopped by a small stream to wash their feet and put on their shoes and stockings. Sean and Maeve sat on the bank a little upstream of Con, who had Derdriu in the water and was washing the mud from her legs. 'Must have you looking presentable,' he told the cow sadly. He turned to look at his brother and sister-in-law with something like longing. Sean was holding Hannah, while Maeve washed her long, pale legs in the stream. Joseph and Molly stood on the road, holding the pig and the horse. Their faces were sad. Sean was saying something to Maeve, but Con could not hear what it was above the rush of the water.

'You know I've only ever wanted to make you happy?' said Sean.

'Yes,' replied Maeve, taking his hand and kissing it. Con saw the kiss and turned away, back to his task.

Early as their start had been, the market was already in progress when they arrived, and a meagre affair it was. Sean was glad for his father that he was not there to see it, for James remembered the good times. Ragged people sat by the walls, surrounded by a few wretched bits of produce for sale: perhaps a few tired heads of cabbage, a scrawny chicken, a pile of little brown apples, a dead rabbit – but that was a rarity. The game, such as it was round about, had all been taken and eaten by now. Most people's faces were empty of hope and, seeing that most people were here to sell and not to buy, those few with money in their purses passed the humble vendors by without so much as a glance. The family proceeded down the street in a little procession until they reached the quayside square, where there was a scene of some activity around Coulter's Stores. Some men had already bought drink from Coulter's Shebeen and one or two were even beginning to be drunk, doing a shuffling, almost angry dance to the reedy sound of a fiddle outside the Stores. It was not until he heard the music that Con realised how silent the town was. All these people and so little noise.

A nagging drizzle began as Sean unloaded the sacks from the horse's back and he and Con carried them into the Stores. Inside there was a hum of conversation as men queued to sell their produce to Coulter. At the back, those who had been paid were being served drinks – whiskey and stout – by a boy at the counter of the Shebeen. The money went from Coulter's hand to the farmer's and then into the boy's without seeing the inside of a pocket.

One man, angry at what he'd got, handed his sack to Martin Ferry but said to Coulter, who sat at a desk with money: 'And what will you sell it for now? Forty shillings a hundredweight?'

'You've got what everyone else is getting,' said Coulter without looking at him. 'Be satisfied.'

The air in the Stores was thick with the dust of oats. Con gave the sacks the brothers had brought to Bryan Meagher, who weighed them on a hook and spring suspended from a beam.

'Satisfied?' said the man to Coulter. 'Who here is satisfied?' But having delivered his parting shot he pushed through the throng to the Shebeen, where you could hear him ordering stout and a whiskey to keep it company. Sean and Conor took their money from Coulter without a word and left. Coulter watched them go.

Outside, the drizzle continued; but it was not bad enough to drive anyone away. People huddled under sacks. Chickens, looking bonier than ever now that their feathers were wet, scratched forlornly in the dirt. Maeve had caught sight of her father, sitting in a corner of the square on a box. Before him, spread out on sacking, were examples of his rushwork – mats, ropes, baskets and babies' rattles. His clothes were threadbare and torn at the elbows and along the seams. His hat, once jaunty, perched on his head like a broken chimney. The face beneath it was an old man's face. She walked over and bent to kiss him.

'I haven't sold a thing, Maeveen,' he told her sadly. 'Not a thing. Mary wanted to come with me, but I told her to stay with Mother. She's still grieving for Michael sorely.'

She shook him gently by the shoulder and smiled. 'Your work is the best in the county. You'll sell it, Father. Have patience.'

On the other side of the square, near the agent's office, Conor was discussing the price of his pig with a man.

'What are you asking?' said the man, a Protestant farmer whose land abutted the estate. Conor knew him by sight from other market days.

'Twenty-eight shillings,' said Conor.

'Get away. The going rate is twenty-five, and I can see her ribs.' Conor glanced across to Coulter's Stores, where Coulter stood with Sean, taking a hard look at Derdriu, who stood between them, switching her tail. She sensed the impending change of ownership and she was not happy.

Coulter knelt by her and felt her teats. He was not a fool and knew the signs for mastitis. Then he opened the animal's mouth and peered at her teeth. He straightened up.

'What are you asking?'

'Six pounds,' said Sean. No point in starting higher and he still had the better cow back at the farm.

Coulter had another look at the udder. 'She's got a blind quarter.'

'I know.'

'I'll give you four pounds for her.'

'I see you're as generous with your offers for livestock as you are with your offers for grain,' said Sean, caressing Derdriu's neck. She turned her face to him and nudged him. 'She's worth six pounds of anyone's money.'

'Not mine,' said Coulter, turning on his heel and disappearing into his shop.

Another pig-fancier was approaching Con meanwhile. He prodded the animal. Con told him the price.

'Hold out your hand,' said the man. Con did so and the man placed a penny in it, striking Con's fist. 'Will you take fifteen shillings?'

'I will not.'

The man stood back, giving the pig an appraising look. 'Hmn. Ask seventeen shillings, see if I'll give it to you.'

'Twenty-eight shillings.'

'Take the seventeen shillings, son,' said a bystander. 'You won't get better today.'

Con was getting angry. He rounded on the man. 'And who asked your advice?' Wisely, the man backed off.

'Seventeen-and-sixpence,' said the pig-fancier. 'I'll go no higher.'

'Your offer insults me,' retorted Conor.

The man shrugged and started to move off.

'Wait,' said Con. He was still holding the penny. The man turned. 'One pound.'

'Eighteen-and-sixpence,' said the pig-fancier, holding out his hand. Angry and disappointed, Con handed him the penny and they shook hands on the bargain.

The day wore on and at last people began to pack up what they had not sold and drift out of the town and back up the valley. The number of drinkers, for they could hardly be called revellers, at Coulter's Shebeen had increased, however, with those out of cash begging drinks from those who were still flush. There were outbursts of temper and scuffles. The anger was fierce but it had no direction and soon fizzled out. The drizzle had long since ceased and there was even a bit of late autumn sunshine which turned the grey of the town into a curious, watery yellow.

The Phelans sat together by the quayside and counted the money they had made. Maeve had sold all the butter and eggs, and the chickens had gone too, at fivepence each, only slightly less than the going rate. But no-one had offered for the cow – each prospective purchaser had spotted that she was dry in one teat – and they needed the money she would fetch.

'I'll have to ask him for what he'll give,' said Sean despondently, looking towards Coulter's Stores. The others were silent, watching him as he crossed the square, leading Derdriu.

'You haven't sold her then,' said Coulter, standing in his door.

'I'll take the four pounds,' said Sean.

Coulter was chewing a straw. Now he took it out of his mouth and looked at it. 'It's not four any more. It's three.'

Sean had no choice. He accepted the money and gave Derdriu's leading rope to Martin Ferry, who came up and took her away. Sean did not stay to watch her go, but walked slowly back across the square, looking at the three heavy coins in his hand.

'Is that your horse over there?' a man asked him. He looked up to see the Protestant farmer who'd refused Conor's asking price for the pig. The horse was tied to a bollard by the quay. Joseph and Molly stood by him. Conor and Maeve were walking slowly towards Coulter's Stores along the far side of the square. There was still some cheese to sell.

'Yes.'

'Are you selling him?'

Sean considered. 'What would you give me?'

'Let's have a look at him.'

Together they walked over to the horse, a solid chestnut, who watched them placidly. The children drew to one side. Sean avoided catching Joseph's eye. The boy loved the horse. Sean took the bridle and led the animal a little way along the quayside, getting him to trot and turn. The farmer ran his hands along the animal's legs, opened its mouth, rubbed its nose and smiled.

'I'll give you a fair price,' said the farmer. 'Eight pounds. No bargaining. You can take it or leave it.'

Sean argued briefly with himself. But it was a good price. He put out his hand. Watching them, Joseph now turned away.

Near the Stores, Con had left Maeve to speak to an acquaintance among the drinkers. She leant against the wall and closed her eyes. A couple of yards away, Coulter was examining chickens, dragging each bird from the basket placed in front of him and roughly feeling its pelvic bones, peering into its vent, before shoving it back and withdrawing another. When he had finished his business, he sidled over to where Maeve was standing, her eyes still closed, though he knew she was aware of him. He placed a hand on the wall near her.

'You know I dreamed about you last night, Maeveen,' he said, his face close to hers. 'You were standing at the foot of my bed. Naked as the day you were born. You held out your arms to me ...'

He did not finish. Strong hands seized him from

behind and hurled him to one side. He skidded across the stony ground, scattering baskets and chickens until he came to rest against a pile of sacks. But Con, his eyes dark with fury, was on him again, pulling him up like a sack himself by the lapels. Behind him, Maeve was shouting:

'Con, for God's sake!'

'Take your hands off me, you bastard!' spat Coulter. Con roared and butted Coulter hard with his head. Then he flung him away into a pile of mud and dung. He was getting ready for more, but as Coulter cowered away he saw Ferry and Meagher come up and grab Con's arms, pinioning him. Con struggled free and managed to land one punch full in Meagher's ample stomach before Sean ran up and placed himself between them.

'Stop it now, for Christ's sake,' he yelled. 'That's enough!'

Coulter had dragged himself to his feet. His nose was bleeding badly. For a moment the two groups of men confronted one another. Then Coulter turned and made for his shop, followed by his henchmen. Maeve turned on her brother-in-law, her eyes blazing.

'Now look what you've done!'

Sean looked from one to the other. 'What happened?'

Maeve was crying now. 'Look what you've done!' she repeated. 'He's the only one with any money. Do you think he'll ever buy anything else from us again? And he hasn't paid us for everything he's bought today yet. You fool!'

Sean looked at his brother more closely. 'Why did you hit him?'

But Con ignored him and walked after Coulter, vanishing into the shop. He found the storekeeper at the back, drinking a whiskey and holding a pad of wet cloth to his grimy face. Meagher and Ferry, flanking him, balled their fists. Con ignored them.

'Coulter,' he said.

Coulter looked at him.

'Our produce is the best in the valley. You'd be a fool not to buy it. Don't punish my family. If you want to punish someone, punish me. Don't punish them.'

Coulter's hand went to his pocket. He drew out some coins and gave them to Meagher. 'Give the Phelans that,' he said. 'It's what I owe them.' To Con, he said: 'Don't go back to the farm. You come to the Shebeen this evening. Then we'll see.' He turned his back and drained his glass.

On the road home, the family paused to rest. Maeve made herself comfortable on a stone by the track and uncovered her breast to feed Hannah. Sean watched her tenderly for a moment. Then he knelt by her. She looked at him expectantly. From his pocket he drew out a small paper packet.

'I got these for you.'

She opened the packet. It contained six little buttons, cut from blue glass.

'You bought them?' she asked, and there was an edge to her voice.

Sean spread his hands. 'Yes.'

Her eyes were angry. 'When we don't have enough

money for food? Oh, Sean, Sean!'

She threw the buttons into the mud, glaring at him. Sean stood up, turned away, walked on.

FIVE

Con helped Patrick pack up his unsold rushwork
after the rest of the family had left. Then, having
failed to find his brother the schoolmaster at home,
he mooched about the quay until darkness fell.
More and more frequently he threw glances in the
direction of Coulter's Stores. The Shebeen part of
the shop had taken over from the grocery by this
time, and though a few drunks were lounging about
outside, most of the people were within. Con could
hear raucous shouts and snatches of tuneless song as
he approached the door at last. Whatever it was he
had coming, he had better get it over and done with.

Plenty of men who had done some good for
themselves at the market were now turning their
profit into oblivion, and Coulter presided over the
proceedings from a high stool behind the bar, like a
demon might over damned souls. He noticed Con
the minute the young man entered and, quitting his
perch, waved to him. As he drew close, Con saw by
the light of the iron lamps that hung from the beams
that the left half of Coulter's face was spread with an
ugly bruise.

At the counter, Coulter poured a generous glass for Con. 'You're lucky I didn't lose any teeth,' he said. 'You might have been in trouble then!' He paused while Con drank, then added: 'So, Con Phelan, you like to fight?'

Con was immediately on the alert, tensing his back. Was he going to be jumped? He didn't dare look round. Slowly, he finished his whiskey. Coulter immediately refilled him. 'Can you fight with a stick?' he asked.

'What is this, Coulter?'

Coulter smiled, all innocence, repeating. 'Can you fight with a stick?'

'I don't have a stick.'

'Well, that's easily remedied.' Coulter looked around, with a shout. 'Does any one of you have a stick my young friend here can borrow?'

His voice had risen above the general babel and now the men in the room fell silent. They realised the request meant that there was going to be a fight. Some seemed uneasy. Others looked forward to the diversion. Con knew what he was in for, too. His mouth was dry despite the whiskey. Against his better judgement, he swigged the rest of the liquid in his glass.

A man nearby gave him a long, stout stick. Con weighed it in his hands. It was good and straight. He stood up, looked about him. A space cleared round him. At his ear, Coulter said, 'If you want to fight someone, fight Ferry.'

As if on cue, big Martin Ferry came through the

door behind the bar counter. He had already taken off his jacket and he carried a heavy staff as tall as himself. His cold eyes looked at Con and a little, frosty smile was on his lips.

'Let's see what you can do,' said Ferry.

The crowd was looking eager now. There was a greedy look, too, on Coulter's face. 'Into the yard with you,' he said, almost heartily. 'I'm taking bets now!'

He led the way outside to the broad walled yard at the back. There was a cart along one side, and stables and a pile of lumber. But in the middle was an open space and the men from the Shebeen formed an audience, thrusting Ferry and Con into its centre. Ferry laid his stick on the ground, not taking his eyes from Con's face. Con did likewise, laying his own stick parallel to that of his opponent. The gates of the yard were closed while the men clamoured around Coulter, squandering the last of their money on bets. Nearly all the money was going on Ferry. Coulter, cashbox at his side, smiled a secret smile. He was offering long odds on Con. A few men accepted them. One such was Bryan Meagher, who exchanged a look with his boss. Anyone watching closely might have wondered how Meagher had come by so much money to place. But now everyone fell quiet. Con felt that he'd entered a dream. It seemed that he and Ferry were alone on the planet.

'Right, then,' said Coulter. 'On a count of three!'

His voice came to Con from far away. He dipped his right shoulder, mirroring Ferry's similar move-ment, to grasp his stick. He heard the sharp crack as the sticks crossed in the air between them. Then the fight began. They circled each other, fencing and feinting, neither getting a blow in yet, as if they were fearful of starting the attack in earnest. Each man was probing for the gaps in the other's defence, sounding out the other's reactions. Their movements were dance-like, almost delicate.

But Ferry had more experience of fighting this way. Suddenly, like lightning, he moved in to hit. Crack and crack! And Con's head sang with the pain from the first blow, and the knuckles of his left hand went numb from the second. He went down on one knee but kept his eyes up and adjusted his grip. His hand was bleeding. He didn't want the stick to slip. Ferry was on him again now, bringing his stick sharply across to smash into Con's mouth and then, in a following blow, up towards his crutch. Just in time, Con straightened and stepped aside, but Ferry had not lost the initiative and brought his stick swinging round towards the side of Con's neck. In that moment the younger man realised that he was in a fight for his life. He parried the blow and managed to follow it with one to Ferry's shoulder, but though he heard his opponent gasp in shock he knew that he had connected with muscle, not nerve or bone, and that he had not drawn blood.

Ferry was dancing round him now, and he had to keep swivelling to keep his face to the man. How fast Ferry could move that big body of his. And all the time the cold grey eyes were on him, in which nothing could be read – neither pity nor cruelty, nor even much interest. Only calculation. There could be no appeal to the brain behind those eyes.

Ferry's stick whirled round to land heavily against Con's kidneys, but he had managed to jump enough to the side to lessen the force of the blow, and this time Ferry staggered forward, off balance. Con let him pass and stooped, swinging his stick as hard as he could against the other man's shins. This time there was a loud crack and Ferry howled in agony, but he did not go down. Still, he was breathing hard and a dull look had come into his eyes. Con felt better. He followed the shin blow through with another, fast to the elbow, and another to the temple. Blood gushed from the wound Con had opened in his head, and Con saw that the man's legs were bleeding too. Ferry jabbed towards Con's kidneys again with the point of his stick. This time the blow made Con gasp and for a second blacked out his vision. But he had time to recover and saw that Ferry was out of control, staggering around the ring with blood in his eyes. He aimed for the precise point on the elbow he had hit before and struck it again. Ferry shrieked, dropping his stick and putting his hand to the place. His wounded arm hung limp. He went down on one knee. The fight was over.

'Declared in favour of Con Phelan,' he heard Coulter say, and there was almost a laugh in the man's voice. Con looked to see the few men who had backed him come up to take their money. Even after he had paid up, Coulter could not close the cashbox, so full it was. Meagher had not collected his winnings. Con turned to Ferry. He wanted to shake his hand, now that it was all over. But the man growled in pain and turned away. Someone came up on his other side, took his elbow and steered him away. It was Coulter. Coulter counted ten shillings into Con's hand.

'You're good,' he said. 'Very good. I knew you would be.' He patted Con on the shoulder. 'Have a drink or two. On the house. You deserve it.'

Con accepted his offer. He was surrounded by people congratulating him. No-one bore him a grudge for winning. People bought him drinks. He was the hero of the hour. After a while, Coulter came over to him again. He handed him a package, which Con stowed under his coat.

'From now on, you fight for me,' said Coulter.

About the time Con was squaring up to Martin Ferry, there was a knock at the door of the Phelan farmhouse. The children were in bed. James barely reacted, continuing to sit and stare into the fire. Sean looked up from the table where he sat, counting and recounting the money they had made at the market, and making calculations in the eternal notebook. Now he swept the money into a leather pouch he had by him and placed it out of sight. It was Maeve who crossed to the door and opened it. Her father stood on the threshold. He looked at her with rabbit's eyes. She stood aside to let him in. Her lips were already tight. She knew what he'd be after.

'God save all here,' said Patrick Dolan.

'And you too,' replied Sean. 'Come in, Patrick. Come in, and sit by the fire.'

Patrick placed himself opposite James. They were

of an age, more or less, though if truth were told Patrick was the younger by a year or two. He looked older and frailer and was, in fact, the smaller man. But as for James, with all his bulk, the fight seemed to have gone out of him.

Patrick reached out a hand to his old friend. His voice when he spoke was piteous. 'Are you ailing, Seamus?'

Maeve folded her arms and crossed the room impatiently. She hated her father when he adopted that wheedling tone.

James came out of his reverie. He looked at Patrick. 'What?' he said.

'I thought, with you missing market and all – '

James turned back to the fire. It seemed to comfort him. 'No, I'm not ailing,' he said, but his voice was still resigned.

After a pause, Patrick said, more piteously than before, 'I sold nothing, Seamus. Nothing at all. I don't know what I'm going to do.'

Now Maeve was angry. 'If it's money you're after, you must speak to Sean,' she flared at her father.

Patrick continued to look at James, but his friend sat without speaking. He turned to face Sean.

'How much are you short?' asked his son-in-law.

'Ten pounds,' replied the old man, his eyes filling with tears. But his self-pity only angered his daughter the more.

Sean considered the matter. 'The most I could let you have is three.'

This was too much for Maeve. 'You can't let him have three pounds!' she shouted. 'We haven't enough for ourselves!'

'So my own daughter would turn me away empty handed, would she?' said Patrick, getting a little fire into his own voice.

'We have hungry mouths to feed here too.'

But Patrick was on his knees to Sean now. 'I beg you,' he said.

'Why must you do this?' Maeve asked him through her teeth. 'In my own home?' She turned away from them in a fit of rage and humiliation. But Sean put out his hands to Patrick and raised him up, speaking gently to him as he drew out the pouch.

'I cannot give you more than this. Here. Take the three pounds.'

But Maeve spun round on them like a harpy, knocking a stool flying as she came towards them. 'Don't you dare, Sean! Don't you dare to give him anything!'

Patrick backed off, looking at her with shock in his face. To Sean it seemed as if he were seeing his wife for the first time. But Maeve's fury was spent. 'Why must he shame me?' she asked.

'Have you no charity in you?' said Sean.

'Why must he shame me?' she repeated. She went through to the bedroom and closed the door behind her.

Sean righted the overturned stool. Patrick watched him in silence. James sat like a rock, staring into the fire. Without speaking, Sean went over to the alcove where the jug of poteen was kept and poured a measure each for the three of them. The stock was running low and needed rationing but this, he felt, was a time that called for a drink. The three men raised their glasses and drank in silence. Then Sean counted out the three pounds for Patrick and the little old man, bobbing his head in gratitude, disappeared into the windy night. When he had gone, Sean sat to his calculations again. He felt more tired than he had expected to, after the rigours of the day. He hated the disharmony Maeve had created. He wished it were possible for him to create a world where they would not be the prisoners of their tenancy. If he owned his own land, what might he not achieve? He thought of the improvements he would like to make here, but could not, for fear of having the rent raised as a result of them. He closed his eyes. There seemed to be no escape.

He must have dozed, for when he opened his eyes again James had gone and the fire had burned low. He got up stiffly, arching his back, and then bent to stoke the turfs and to lay two more on to keep the fire in until morning. He took off his shirt and splashed water from the basin in the corner on to his face and arms. Then, with a trace of reluctance, he made for his room.

There was a shaft of moonlight that came through the small window and settled on the children's sleeping faces. They were quite dead to the world after their day's adventure and when he kissed their foreheads they did not stir. The baby was in her cot in the darkness away over on Maeve's side of the bed. Maeve did not move as he got into bed, though once he had settled she turned to him in the darkness and kissed him. He returned the kiss and noticed that her cheeks were wet. She kissed him again and again without speaking; anxious, tender kisses that were meant to make amends. Sean felt a great wave of relief wash over him. He took her in his arms and she snuggled to him. They kissed each other harder now, and their hands, with gentle urgency, sought out their bodies' secret places.

Entering the house a short while later, Con was cautious not to make much noise, but it was dark and he was tired and drunk. His head hammered from the blow Ferry had dealt him, and he was hot in his thick suit. He pulled at the collar of his shirt and eased off his jacket. His muscles were already stiffening up after the fight. He would have liked to wash in the tub, but that would have to wait until morning. He put the money Coulter had given him, and the package, carefully on the table. Taking a taper to the fire, he lit a stump of candle and sat by it, willing his head to clear.

As he sat, he became aware of the noises from Sean and Maeve's room. He looked towards their door. He heard a low laugh from Maeve that he had rarely heard before, and that he found exciting. He knew what he was listening to. He had tried to disguise or translate his feelings for his sister-in-law as much as he could – the gifts of eggs, the helping with the new vegetable garden, defending her against Coulter's advances, which had got him into this state – but he could not bear to hear her making love. He stood up quickly, intending to go to his room, but his head swam and, reaching out to steady himself, he knocked over a tin jug which fell with a clatter onto the hard earth floor. He sat down again heavily, fighting the nausea, listening to hear if he'd disturbed anyone.

In their room, Maeve broke off, raising her head. 'Do you think he's hurt himself?'

'He sounds drunk,' said Sean without sympathy. But Maeve was getting up. Ignoring his objections, she drew her smock back over her head and got out of bed.

She found Con sitting on the form by the table, his head in his hands. He raised it at the sound of her approach and she saw that his forehead was cut and bruised. Concerned, she knelt to touch it. Their faces were close. She smelt the whiskey on his breath.

'It's nothing,' said Con. But she was hurrying back to her room.

'His face is cut and bruised,' she told Sean. 'I think he's been fighting.'

Sean sighed heavily, turning his back on her in the bed. She found the piece of cloth she was searching for, glanced at the children to make sure they had not been disturbed, and returned to her brother-in-law. She wet the cloth in the basin and then stooped to him again, cleaning his face, cupping his chin in her other hand, stroking his forehead when it was clean. Con closed his eyes. He looked like a child then.

'Wasting our money on drink,' said Maeve.

Con opened his eyes again. He took the package he had got from Coulter and held it out to Maeve. 'For you.'

She unwrapped the paper, looking from it to him, asking herself what he'd been up to, knowing he'd tell her in good time if he felt like it. Within the paper were three sacking bags closed with string. She opened one, and tipped some of the contents into the palm of her hand.

'Onion seeds,' said Conor. 'There's turnip and cabbage too. Enough for our… Enough for your plot.'

'Where did you get them from?'

'Coulter.'

'Why would he give you seed?'

'In payment.'

'For what?' Maeve looked troubled.

Con averted his eyes. 'I did some work for him. Behind the bar.'

Maeve decided to ask no more questions. Very carefully she tipped the seeds back into the bag.

'There's this too,' said Con, showing her the money. As he did so, she noticed his battered left hand. Whatever he'd been doing, he'd earned what Coulter had given him. But, knowing Coulter, he would have taken revenge and made a profit at the same time.

'Your poor hand,' she said, cradling it. She took the cloth to bathe it, her head bent over it.

Con looked down at her hair shining in the candle-light. He was trembling. 'I love you, Maeve,' he said.

She looked up at him.

'I love you,' he repeated, his eyes full of hunger.

She returned his look. Then she got up. She stroked his cheek kindly. 'I know,' she said. 'Thank you for the seeds.'

Taking them with her, she returned to the bedroom. Con watched the door close. He looked at the ten shillings, still lying by his hand.

In her room, Maeve regarded Sean's sleeping back. Then she examined the bags of seeds, before stowing them carefully in her workbasket. She climbed into bed and lay on her back, her eyes open in the darkness, shining, excited.

Gale Day arrived. All too soon, but such days are never welcome. At first light there was an armed police guard right outside the agent's office in Brannocktown, and when an iron-faced Townsend rode up a short time later, it was with another, mounted escort. At the desk in the outer office, Bailiff Harkin was seated. In the book already open in front of him he would mark off the names of the tenants as they arrived to pay. They would then be ushered into Townsend's inner sanctum, where the agent and his chief clerk would receive payment of rent.

Townsend was anxious. He had not slept well until the small hours, but by that time he was fully resolved on his course of action. He needed this job. He needed to do it well. There was no escape from it for him. Therefore his solution was to fulfil the function he served without further question. He had not created this situation, and he could not be the author of its resolution. If he failed to carry out Lord Hawksborough's orders, he would not relieve the misery of the people here, and he would increase his own. He had even reasoned with himself that by making an example of a few, he might yet be able to buy time for the rest; but in his rational mind he knew what a sop to Cerberus such reasoning was. He would be a soldier, then. He would carry out his orders. The law was on his side. Perhaps there was a rightness in all of this somewhere after all. He had read the articles in *The Times*. He had had evidence of drunkenness and fecklessness before his own eyes. And, last but not least, who was he to doubt the judgement of the Government in London? He was not one of these people. He did not wish to remain here longer than he had to. If an unpleasant job had to be done, then so be it.

He looked at the clock on the wall. It was time. He turned to his chief clerk.

'Open up, McBride,' he said.

Dawn that same day found Sean walking his fields, deep in thought. James watched his son from the narrow window of his room, then, pulling on his coat, went out into the raw weather to join him. Seeing him approach, Sean waited. It was a long time since father and son had spoken to any point. But once James had come up, he seemed unable to find words, and the two men stood in silence, looking at the land.

'I was born here, Sean,' James said at last. 'I will die here and I will rot here.'

'Yes,' said Sean. His father's speech had come as no surprise and he knew what was behind it. He was the head of the family now and the decision was his. The rent would have to be paid, come what may. Better to die on the land than lose it. That's what his father was telling him. He turned away and walked back to the house.

He stripped to the waist and shaved himself carefully in front of the bit of looking-glass. Near him, baby Hannah slept. She slept a lot these days. Looking closely at himself, something he rarely did, Sean noticed lines on his forehead he had not seen before, and there was grey in his hair. He paid these things little heed, but they reminded him of time passing. In the glass, he could see Maeve's indistinct reflection as she came across the room to him.

'They say relief works are about to start,' he said, unburdening some of his anxiety. 'They say that Indian corn is on its way. They say that the Government in London might be providing seed potatoes for planting, even this late in the year.'

She did not speak, but slipped her arms around him to silence and reassure him. She squeezed him, stroking his pale body. He turned to face her and they smiled at each other.

'We'll get through it somehow,' he said.

'Of course we will,' she replied. 'Now, let's see what a handsome figure you'll cut in your best shirt.'

Con was waiting for him at the table when he emerged in his dark suit. Con, too, was dressed in his Sunday best, and the demeanour of the two men reflected the solemnity of their clothes and the seriousness of the occasion. The canvas bag containing the rent money, painstakingly calculated to the last penny, lay buckled up on the table. Sean took its handle, and he and his brother said goodbye to Maeve and the children who stood at the door to watch them go. James was still out in the fields, but he waved to them as they passed.

The rain had eased off after daybreak; the ground was mushy underfoot but they were thankful it was not mired. They made short work of the walk to Brannocktown, and even felt a glimmer of pride as they strode down the main street. Sean kept an eye out for Daniel, but the schoolhouse was shut up as it was Gale Day and his brother was nowhere to be seen. In the main street, worn-out, hungry people watched them from street corners. There was a faint smell in the air – a sweet, dry smell that he had not noticed before. The water in the harbour was sluggish and dirty. Perhaps it came from there? And yet it was not a sea odour.

Outside the agent's office stood a group of men, Patrick Dolan amongst them. The debate was of money – how much to pay, if at all, and what the consequences might be. Several of the men, Dolan included, already had eviction orders hanging over them. The mood was sombre. Conversation fell off as the Phelan brothers approached. Seeing Patrick, Sean said something to Con, who waited by the agent's door. Sean walked over to Patrick and took his hand, as if shaking it. No-one saw the money he pressed into the old man's palm.

'I managed to find a little more,' said Sean. 'Pay him what you can. It's all you can do.'

Patrick looked at him with emotion. 'God bless you,' he said. That pernicious jade, hope, awoke in his eyes again. Sean turned and rejoined his brother. Together they entered the office.

Inside, they saw Harkin taking a couple of coins, slipped him by another tenant, a big, ruddy man called Connachton, who was leaving after having paid.

'Good of you to remember my work,' smiled Harkin. Sean watched the sweetener change hands with contempt. Harkin looked across at him as Connachton left, brushing past Con with a muttered greeting. Harkin's face had resumed its usual fixed expression.

'Sean Phelan,' he said, marking the name off in his book. He continued to look at Sean.

'There's nothing you can do for me,' said Sean.

Harkin gave the faintest shrug. 'Go in,' he said. Conor took a seat on one of the ladderbacks, settling to wait for his brother.

In the office where Townsend and McBride sat, the atmosphere was close. A fire had been lit but it had blown back. The window, its lower half still boarded, had been opened a crack, to no effect. Sean went across to where McBride sat and placed his bag on the desk. McBride emptied its contents and counted them, putting the money into a large strongbox by his side. As the transaction took place, Townsend studied Phelan. The young man stood there with a kind of quiet dignity that made the agent feel obscurely uncomfortable. McBride turned the ledger towards Sean, pointed to a space, dipped his pen and held it out.

'Make your mark there,' said McBride.

Sean took the pen, leant over the book and, as both

the other men could see, signed his name in full. He had a firm, rounded hand. Then he took his empty bag and straightened his back. Without a word, without looking Townsend or McBride in the eye, he turned and left. Townsend watched him go. He was angry. Who were these people to make him feel at fault?

Once outside, the brothers did not pause, but started immediately to walk away. Patrick's voice called after them, asking the question the town wanted to know:

'Have the Phelans paid?'

'They have,' Conor called back.

'In full?'

'In full.'

Patrick watched them go, making their way through the crowd of tenants that had gathered outside by now, then adjusted his stock and made his own way into the office. He was nervous. He wished he still had a strong son to support him.

Forty-eight hours after the agent's office had closed on Gale Day, Captain Townsend called a meeting. Present were his clerk, McBride, the magistrate, Mr Brady, the two bailiffs, Harkin and Curran, and Sub-Inspector McCafferty. They sat around the table under the oil-lamp in the inner office like a council of war – which, in a manner of speaking, they were. Lying on the table between them was a piece of paper, covered with names written in Townsend's narrow, even hand.

'I've made a study of the returns entered in the rental book since Gale Day,' Townsend was saying. 'This is the list of defaulting tenants, and those who have not paid a sufficient contribution to their arrears – who have either been served with notices to quit in the past, or have had unenacted notices drawn up against them.' He leant forward and picked up the list, handing it to Brady. 'I should like you to draw up ejectment papers forthwith.'

'I may not be able to offer you adequate protection if you move against so many,' objected McCafferty. Like the others, he was surprised at how Townsend had hardened his heart. But he did not know the details of the letter the agent had received from his employer.

Townsend looked at him. 'Then we shall have to apply to Dublin Castle for some reinforcements. Fortunately, there isn't any lack of troops or police in this country to enforce the upholding of the law.' He looked at the men seated at the table. 'It is time to wipe the slate clean, gentlemen. I have had enough of compromise.'

No-one there said a word to him in defence of the people, and pretty soon the meeting broke up, each man taking himself off to his own snug little home, though Brady and McBride at least took one or two looks over their shoulders as they went.

The morning chosen for the raid was dark and freezing – it looked as if the unusually wet and mild summer would be followed by an unusually cold winter. At the police barracks, the locals had doubled in strength through reinforcements mustered and seconded by the Lieutenant-Governor's office in Dublin. Each policeman carried a sword and a carbine. Townsend led on his white horse with McCafferty at his side. The rear was brought up by Magistrate Brady and Bailiff Curran, whose job it would be to look after Mr Brady's welfare in the event of the people attacking them. Accompanying the police force came Harkin and a band of destructives recruited from the unemployed townspeople – barefoot men carrying crowbars and cudgels with which the bailiffs had supplied them. It was unpopular work they'd be set to do, but in Harkin's experience it was never too tough a job to find people prepared to attack their fellow-sufferers, provided they were hungry enough, and the price was right.

Townsend drew up to review his force, and from his saddlebag took with a gloved hand the list of tenants slated for ejectment. They had been arranged in order, and he read the first name. Recognising it, and well aware of the implications of moving against such a family, he bit his lip. But his resolve did not falter – indeed, now it could not. In any case, he had reasoned that disaffection had better be taken out at the root. He shouted his orders and the troop galloped out of town.

Patrick and Sarah Dolan were awakened from sleep by the noise of the horses. Patrick knew what it was immediately, but for a moment he lay there, protected, as it seemed, by the rough blanket which covered them. He put an arm round his wife, who looked at him with fearful eyes. 'Oh, God in heaven, no,' he said. He did not want to get up, to leave the safety of his bed, to face this most terrible of days. But rise he must. He could hear the horses move as their riders encircled the farmhouse.

By the time the Dolan family appeared at their door, their home was surrounded and the police had unslung their carbines. In front of the door a small group of men in black sat on their mounts. Bailiff Harkin, on foot, took a paper from Brady and handed it to Patrick. Brady spoke:

'I serve this ejectment order on you, Patrick Dolan, in the name of the Sheriff of the County. It places this farm in the hands of Lord Hawksborough's agent.'

'Spare us, sir, for God's sake,' cried Sarah. Mary put her hands on her mother's shoulders. The faces of the men on horseback were impassive. Mary looked at Townsend. She thought of Mrs Brogan, who worked for him and with whom she'd been talking of him only two days before. Mrs Brogan had said she found him a reasonable employer and not too demanding.

'Remove your belongings from this house forthwith!' said Harkin, taking a step forward. Patrick flinched, as if the man were about to hit him.

'If you do not go into the poorhouse,' Townsend told them, 'you must quit this estate, and no person may give you shelter, on pain of eviction themselves.' He had recognised the girl as the one who'd been with Daniel Phelan at the presentment session. So she was Michael Dolan's sister. Well, he could not change anything now.

'Remove your belongings from this house,' repeated Harkin, beckoning to his men.

Patrick, Sarah and their daughter stood in the doorway, unable to move for fear and grief. Pushing past them, Harkin and Curran entered the building, while the destructives, taking their cue from them, took torches to the roof of the outhouse. The family were pulled away from the door to allow those inside to throw their belongings out on to the wet earth. Harkin re-emerged. 'Quit the estate by tomorrow morning,' he told Patrick. The old man did not answer. He watched as the destructives attacked the mud walls of his home with staves, undermining them so that at last the roof fell in. Their home was smashed. His wife wept in his arms. He watched as a destructive savagely kicked one of his two poor remaining chickens out of the way, stamping on it and killing it instantly. He watched them trample over the remains of his fields and he watched as the outhouse roof collapsed, wrecking the rushwork he had made for sale that was stored within.

The men on horseback were already riding off. Mary continued to stare at Townsend. Not once had he met her eye. A door closed in Mary's heart then. She knew that she would do whatever she had to do to avoid a similar fate and, in the end, to take vengeance on those who had brought this on her family – if only by surviving their cruelty.

After the work of that day, Townsend took himself

home and, sending Mrs Brogan away, sat down and drank. He felt better when he was drunk. He had, he told himself, done all that a reasonable man could do to avoid this destruction. He was not responsible alone for what had occurred. He thought of the letter he had received from his employer. How could anyone be so cold-hearted? But then again, Lord Hawksborough was entitled to make a profit from his own land!

By the end of the third bottle Townsend was telling himself that, after all, these people should be made to pick themselves up and show a bit of integrity themselves. Did they expect to be carried along by the generosity of others all their lives? And yet he could not rid himself of the memory of the look on Sean Phelan's face as he'd paid his rent, nor of the memory of the look the Dolan girl had given him that morning. That morning! It seemed an age away already. Townsend looked at the picture of his wife. Had she ever really existed? Had anything, outside this nightmare? He took himself to his cold bed, but he could not sleep.

In the morning, however, he had pulled himself together and dressed with more than his usual formality. He ignored the breakfast Mrs Brogan had prepared for him, of half-cooked bacon swimming in grease, and, his revolver in his belt, as it always was nowadays, rode to work. He was aware of the people staring but he looked neither to right nor left.

Hardly had he sat down in his office than he was disturbed by the outer door banging and a commotion in McBride's room. He went to his own door and opened it to see McBride attempting to restrain the Catholic priest.

'You cannot turn people off their land! Not at a time like this! You cannot!' Liam Phelan shouted at him.

'Father, please,' said McBride.

'Let him go, McBride,' ordered Townsend. He beckoned the priest to join him, holding the door for him.

'Have a seat, Father,' said the agent, once he had closed the door of the inner office behind him.

Liam remained standing; Townsend did so too. From a drawer in his desk he took out Lord Hawksborough's letter and handed it to him. 'I can carry out his instructions or I can resign,' he said. 'I do not choose to resign.'

Liam read the letter swiftly. Then he looked up. 'Nowhere here does he order you to turn people off their land.'

'No. But that is the landlord's right when tenants do not pay.'

Liam made a gesture of despair. 'Why in the name of God should the poor man not have the same property rights as the rich?' His voice was so passionate that, spoken in such tones, it hardly sounded like a rhetorical question at all. Townsend knew the bitter answer, and he suspected that Liam did too, but he replied with another question:

'If I do not eject the defaulter, what am I to say to the man who has paid in full? To the man who asks how it is that his neighbour can flaunt the law with impunity?'

Liam answered him at once: 'Say "Give to him who begs from you. Do not refuse him who would borrow from you."'

'That doctrine I will leave to you, Father,' said Townsend grimly. He made a move towards the door.

'You must not do this,' said Liam.

'It is done.'

'It is theft! "Thou shalt not steal", Mister Townsend. "Thou shalt not steal"!'

The Phelans and the Dolans had gathered by the ruins of Patrick's farm. It was a misty day and the cloud swirled about their legs, making them look like ghosts. The colours of the day were dark-green and grey, and the lake beyond the tumbled dwelling was peat brown and still. The Dolans' belongings were tied into bundles, those of them that could be carried. The rest remained where the bailiffs had scattered them, though Sarah Dolan had set the chest of drawers her mother had given her when she had married back on its feet. Now, Sarah sat on the stone where the old singer had sat at Michael's wake, and keened. There was no other sound than the sound of her lamenting. The children stood about miserably, comprehending only the unhappiness, not its cause. Baby Hannah slept in the crook of her father's arm. Nothing moved, except when, on the track above the house, another evicted family walked slowly past, leaving the estate with backs bent under their loads.

'Come away now,' said Maeve to her father. 'Come home with us.'

'They wouldn't allow it,' replied Patrick, his voice hollow with despair. 'We'd be turned out again. It's best we go.'

'Go where?' said Mary. 'Where is there to go?'

Sean put an arm round his father-in-law. 'You can't go anywhere in this weather. It's coming on for winter. Come home with us now.'

But Patrick shook his head.

'If you won't stay with us, then at least go into the poorhouse,' said Maeve. 'Where there's a roof over your head and some food.'

'They'd separate us in the poorhouse,' said Patrick. 'And you'd be at risk if we came to you. We've always been together. We're better on the road.'

Maeve was losing patience in her grief. 'God in heaven, Daddy, you're not …'

'We've been on the road before.'

'Forty years ago.'

'There might be work somewhere. Relief work. It's best we go.'

Maeve was silent, though inside she was screaming. Suddenly, as they watched, Patrick turned to his home and walked back to it. Simply, unselfconsciously, he kissed the walls goodbye. Then he turned to face them again. James could not meet his eye. Mary lowered her head, her eyes masked, and walked slowly down to the lakeside. After a moment, Daniel followed her.

When he caught up with her, he wrapped his coat round her shoulders. It was only late morning, but the light was already dying.

'What am I to do?' she asked.

He was silent.

'Daniel?'

After a long moment he spoke: 'Mary. I do not know.'

Mary broke from him and walked away, but he followed. 'Mary,' he said. 'Please.'

'Do you not want to help me?' she said.

'Of course I do.'

'Then help me.'

There was another silence. 'What am I to do?' she said.

Daniel could not find words. His thoughts were floundering. He would have liked to be able to cut his way through to some kind of freedom, but the events of the past few days had overthrown him entirely. Now, he knew, he would have to concentrate less on affairs of the heart, and more on matters of the head. The only way the English yoke could be thrown off was through rebellion. And to work for rebellion he would have to stand alone. He loved Mary, his heart ached as he watched her. The smell of her hair, the feel of her soft skin, these things made his head swim. But the time to be together with her was not now. How could they be happy in such a cruel world?

'We're supposed to be betrothed,' she said.

He hung his head. 'I know.'

'So will we marry?'

He looked at her. 'I love you.'

'Will we marry?' Why wouldn't he answer her question?

'Mary,' he said, 'where would we live?'

He saw his betrayal register in her eyes before she spoke, though her words still clung to hope. 'You live at the schoolhouse.'

'For how much longer? Half the children have stopped coming. How long before the school is closed?' He wished he could tell her what his true work was. But would she approve of it? Would she admire him? Would she want him to do it? And how could he involve her in it?

She had turned from him and was walking away, back to the ruin where the others stood. Sarah had stopped keening; there was no sound at all now except the wind in the reeds and the cry of one seagull in the distance.

'Mary! Please give me time. I'll think of something.'

But she did not turn back.

'Please ...'

She walked on. She knew that her only saviour now was herself. But she would survive. Come what may, she would survive.

When she reached the others, her parents had taken up their sticks. She helped Maeve with the bundles of their belongings. She and her sister would carry them for their parents a part of the way, up to the main road south. She did not know how her parents would manage them alone.

She took up her own bag as well.

'You can leave that with us,' said Sean. He and Con had exchanged glances, but decided not to offer to help. The women should spend their last time with their parents alone.

'No,' said Mary. 'I want it with me.' She was aware of Daniel standing a little way off. She did not look at him. Patrick took up a last small bundle and gave it to Sean.

'These are some of Michael's things,' he said. 'They might be of use to you.'

'Thank you,' said Sean.

'You'll tend his grave, won't you?'

'You can be sure of it.'

'I hope we meet again – in better times.'

'If God wills it.'

Patrick cast an eye over at James, who now sat hunched on a rock, his back to them. He and Sarah looked at each other. They were ready to go.

'God guide and protect you,' said Sean.

He and Conor stood together, watching them go. At a turn in the track above the farm, the little party disappeared. They did not turn back to look or to wave.

A mile down the track, Patrick, Sarah and their daughters met a man coming the other way. They could see from his face that he knew what had happened to them. He called out a blessing. They walked on. The track was wet and stony, but it soon levelled out to follow the headland. They walked in silence, the bundles swinging against their legs and hips, clumsy and hard to carry. An hour later they arrived at the main road. The sky had cleared a little and you could see how the road stretched far and away to the south, where it vanished in the mists of the distant blue mountains. Patrick stopped.

'Let me take that,' he said, reaching for Maeve's bundle.

'We'll come a little further with you.' Maeve wanted to delay the moment of parting as long as possible.

'No, Maeve,' replied her father. 'We must carry our own things now.'

His daughter gave in. They placed the bundles on the wet ground and embraced each other, there at the top of the lonely moor. All were weeping. Then Patrick and Sarah hoisted the baggage to their shoulders and walked south. They did not look back, but the women watched them out of sight. They knew that when they vanished, it would be for the last time in this life. At last, hand in hand, Maeve and Mary turned, and set off back to Galready. A fine rain had begun to fall, and it washed the tears from their faces.

It was late afternoon by the time they reached the path that led down to the Phelans' farm. Maeve set off down it and had gone a little way before she realised that her sister was not following. She returned to where Mary stood.

'What is it?' she asked.

'I'm going into Brannocktown,' replied Mary. There was a firmness in her voice that made Maeve wonder.

'To Daniel?' she asked.

After a pause, Mary replied: 'Understand me, Maeveen.'

'What do you mean?'

'Whatever you do, try to understand me.' Mary embraced her sister and was gone, swinging her bag as she walked.

It was dusk when she reached the town. In the angles of buildings, poor people were bedding down in the street for the night. No-one paid much attention to Mary as she took refuge behind a cart. There, sheltered from the rain, she undid her bundle, taking from it a blouse and a light grey flannel dress, together with a belt. Changing into these things and stowing her everyday clothes away, she pulled the belt tightly round her waist so that her figure would show to its best effect. Then she combed her hair carefully. From where she stood, she could see the light in the land agent's office. She also saw Daniel, going up the steps to Coulter's Shebeen. She noticed that he looked round carefully before going in. But it was not Daniel she was concerned with now. Daniel would not help her. She *must* help herself.

'There's someone here to see you, sir,' said McBride as Townsend looked up from his work. Behind his clerk, the agent could see who was standing in the outer office. 'Show her in,' he said. His heart had started to pound hard. The first question he asked himself as Mary came into the room was what she could possibly want with him. He had just evicted her parents. At a raid organised by him, her brother had been killed. But she did not look at him with loathing or contempt. Her look was simple and straightforward. He offered her a seat, which she declined. He found that he did not resume his own chair.

'What can I do for you?' he asked, a little stiffly.

'Mrs Brogan told me you were looking for another servant. To help her out.'

Townsend placed the tips of his fingers on his desk. The idea of Mary in his house was one, he realised, that he had not dared contemplate, but one he knew was attractive. And yet his rational mind advised caution.

'I need a job. I have nowhere to go,' she said. But her voice was steady and free of self-pity. Could she really be this matter-of-fact? He felt like explaining himself to her. Could it be that she knew he had just been doing his job? That there had been nothing personal in his actions? And yet how could she view him other than as a brute?

'Do you think you'd make a good servant?' he asked. He could not help looking at her figure. How long was it now since he had been with a woman? Since he had been with one he found attractive?

'I can cook and clean and sew,' said Mary. 'I can read and write. I can speak your language.'

She could, too, Townsend admitted, and well. He looked at her again. Perhaps his credit in the community would go up if he gave her a job. Perhaps such an action would show the people that he could show mercy and understanding. That he would give someone a chance if she were prepared to help herself a little. There could be no impropriety, after all. Mrs Brogan would be there, and there was another maid's room for the girl to sleep in. Even so.

'You'd work for me, though?' he had to ask. 'A man you have every reason to hate?'

'Yes, sir.' She looked him straight in the eye.

'I have to ask you why.'

'Because I have to survive,' she said.

'I thought there was something between you and the schoolteacher? I'd heard talk that you were affianced.'

'Every Irish town is full of rumours, sir. Besides, even if it were true, I'd still have to work.'

'But would he approve?'

'My employment is not a matter to concern him,' she replied.

Townsend knew he was acting entirely against his better judgement, against all that was sensible. 'Well, let's see how you do,' he said. 'Can you make your way to the house by yourself? I'll ride on ahead and tell Mrs Brogan to make ready for you.'

Mary was scared, but still she smiled to herself.

The room behind Coulter's Shebeen had walls so thick that you could hardly hear the row from the bar. Not that many were in drinking tonight. The raid had cast a pall over the town, and there were few men inclined to demonstrate that they'd a penny to spare on drink. But it would blow over, Coulter knew. People were fickle. Things always got forgotten. In the yellow light of an oil lamp, he sat with Martin Ferry as the third man in the room read to them from a sheet of paper. What he was reading amounted to the minutes of the meeting they'd just had. Coulter listened with half an ear. He was tired, and there were accounts to be totted up before he slept tonight.

'Captain William Townsend, Land Agent for the Manor of Galready,' read the man. 'You have been tried and found guilty of crimes against the people of Ireland, and duly sentenced to death. You showed no mercy when you ejected eleven families and destroyed their lives. Expect no mercy now. Signed: The United Sons of Freedom. November 10th, 1846.' The man looked up, his eyes shining.

'That's fine, Daniel,' said Coulter. 'And I know just the men to be his executioners.'

SIX

Mary was thinking. She had been in the agent's house a day. Mrs Brogan had shown her to a room the like of which she had never seen in her life, so luxurious it seemed. She had taken the job with gritted teeth, prepared to hate herself for doing so, seeing it as a means to an end only – but within this short time she felt the intensity of her feelings reduce. She was not siding with Townsend, far from it – but she did not find him the ogre she had expected. He was kindly to her, almost as if he meant to make amends for what he had done to her family. He was teaching her English manners. She already knew how to decant wine, from what side to serve, which glass was reserved for each drink. By the second evening she was already beginning to feel at home, though she would not allow herself to be comfortable, aware of the attitude her behaviour would arouse in some of her countrymen, and not entirely happy herself with the route she had chosen for survival.

The letter arrived, as if in confirmation of her doubts, on that second evening of her stay. It was in a sealed envelope, and it had been pushed under the front door. Whoever had delivered it must have avoided the police guard at the gate, as well as the one who patrolled the perimeter of the grounds, and climbed the railings to cross the garden. Somebody brave and determined, it seemed. She handed the letter to the agent immediately, having been on her way to the dining room to clear dinner when she noticed it.

'This came for you, sir.'

Townsend's name was printed on the envelope in block letters, but the hand, though clearly disguised, seemed educated. Townsend frowned as he took a butter knife and sliced the letter open. He unfolded it and read its contents impassively. 'You have been tried and found guilty of crimes against the people of Ireland, and duly sentenced to death.' Townsend studied both paper and envelope, but could find no clue about where it had come from.

'Leave that,' he said to Mary, who had begun to clear the plates and glasses. He showed her the letter. 'You are working for the agent now, Mary. That puts your life at risk.' He spoke gently, watching her face, which remained without expression. 'You have the protection of this household, but you must be aware of the threat to your person as well, should you choose to stay.'

She gave the letter back to him. Clearly she did not know who it was from, either. 'Thank you, sir,' she said. But it was impossible to read anything into her voice.

Townsend sat back. 'You may clear the table now,' he said.

Alone in her room, later, Mary wept – for her parents, for Daniel, for herself.

Another copy of the death threat had been left on the altar of the Catholic chapel, weighted down with a stone. Liam found the copy the following morning – Sunday. He was holding it in his hand as he preached to his congregation, searching their faces with his eyes as he spoke:

'This is wrong! The "United Sons of Freedom", the "Ribbonmen", are a curse to themselves and their neighbours, for they will bring down the wrath of the British Government. The same Government we have to turn to in our hour of need.'

As he spoke, he saw Mary arrive. Maeve looked round and Mary caught her eye, but she was at the back of the congregation. Several other people had noticed Mary, too, and drew away from her. Liam saw this happen. It was a bitterly cold day and the frost had not yet left the grass among the headstones, which were rimmed with frost themselves.

'For it is written,' continued Liam: '"Be not overcome by evil, but overcome evil with good: avenge not yourselves, but rather give place unto wrath."'

He saw his brother Daniel start to walk away. Mary looked at him but he would not look at her. One or two of the other men were making to follow him.

'Stay where you are!' commanded Liam. They did

so, shamefacedly. Daniel let Liam see how angry he was. Mary's eyes were on Maeve now, appealing. Maeve did not look at her sister again, but watched the priest.

"'Vengeance is *mine*; I will repay, saith the Lord,'" continued Liam.

"'Therefore, if thine enemy hunger, feed him; if he thirst, give him drink.'" He fixed Daniel's eyes with his.

When the service was over, Mary walked back to the agent's house alone. She had hoped to speak with her sister and waited after Mass to see her, but Maeve was with Sean and Conor. She exchanged another glance with her sister but that was all. Mary sensed Maeve's sympathy, but wondered if the others really didn't understand what had motivated her. Daniel clearly didn't. The degree of hatred that she had seen in him made her realise how much she still loved him. Why had he let her down? Why had he not helped her himself?

Mary did not know all that was in Maeve's mind. Throughout the service, Maeve had been praying for her baby, Hannah. Hannah was crying for milk all the time now. Maeve was not getting enough food herself to provide her with it, and it would soon be December. Three babies had already died in the valley. The people who could had paid their rents, but in doing so they had deprived themselves of the food they needed to live. Coulter's seeds would not provide food until the spring, though Maeve went to look at her vegetable garden every day, as if the hope of food could feed her. No supplies had been forthcoming from the Government in London, or, if they had, they were not getting distributed; though exports of grain sold to pay rents continued. The winter was upon them and, with it, Hunger – and Maeve knew that whatever their past prosperity had been, it would go hard with the Phelans now. Con and Sean knew it, too; neither man smiled much any more. As for James, he kept to his room and his bed for much of the time. Joseph and Molly were silent and listless, and they seldom played. Only the dog still seemed to be able to fill his belly somehow, though what he did for food, Maeve could not think: there was nothing for them to give him at the farm.

As Mary walked along the road, she became aware of people following her. She glanced round, and saw a small group of men and women, Martin Ferry among them. They looked at her jeeringly. Worried, she quickened her pace, but they kept the same distance behind her. Ahead, she could see the gates of the agent's house. Townsend had bought her a pair of shoes and her feet felt cramped and uncomfortable in them. Their soles made what seemed to her to be a deafening noise on the hard-frozen road. The policeman on duty at the gate was blowing on his hands. He was not looking in her direction. The people behind her were silent, but she could feel their menace.

Then something hard and sharp hit the back of her head, making her gasp and stumble – a stone. More stones scattered around her, skeetering on the road.

'Traitorous bitch!' yelled someone. Another stone

hit her on the neck, and another in the waist. She started to run. The policeman was looking in her direction now, unslinging his gun. The crowd had seen him do this and no longer pursued her, though their abuse continued. One more stone hit her in the back. They'd wrapped it in dung and she felt the muck spatter on her dress as the impact sent her flying. The policeman fired. Somehow she got herself through the gate into the safety of the garden. The shouts of hatred were still in her ears. It was too late to go back now.

Once inside the house she threw herself into Mrs Brogan's arms, sobbing bitterly. Townsend emerged from his parlour to see the women sitting on the hall seat. Mrs Brogan was stroking Mary's spun-gold hair.

'I saw what happened,' said the agent. 'From now on you will only leave this house with an armed escort. Is that clear?'

Mary nodded. Townsend returned to his study, poured himself a brandy and attempted to return to his book. But his thoughts continued to distract him: why had Mary attracted such great disgrace? Mrs Brogan was tolerated, and there were plenty of other Irish in Brannocktown who worked with their English masters, but were left in peace.

'God forgive me – what have I done by coming here?' said Mary to Mrs Brogan.

'Hush now, child; hush.'

Liam found his brother in the schoolmaster's room, sitting at his table. In a fury he hauled Daniel up by the collar, so that their faces were close.

'You do not do that! You do not walk out during a sermon.' Daniel tried to free himself, but Liam kept a tight hold. 'Thanks to you, Mary was attacked in the street – by her own people.'

'Thanks to me?' Daniel's voice was without expression.

'Don't you care for her at all?'

Daniel shook himself free. 'She is nothing to me now.' He faced his brother, almost lecturing him. 'Love is a trap. I see that now. It holds you back. I have something more thrilling than love to seek now.'

'And what might that be?'

'Freedom.'

'Freedom?' Liam made the connection. 'Are you telling me that you have something to do with this death threat – with these so-called "United Sons of Freedom"?' He waited for an answer, but Daniel was silent. Moderating his tone, Liam continued: 'That is not the way, Daniel. Skulking under the cover of darkness, with blackened faces, dressing as women to ambush the English? Writing death-threats on scraps of paper? It all seems to have more to do with the schoolroom than with true revolution.'

'And what is the way, then?' retorted Daniel, stung. 'Your way? Begging letters? "I have the honour to remain, sir, your most obedient servant"?' He sneered.

'Such phrases do not diminish me, Daniel – not if they help to feed the hungry.'

'The relief committees haven't been very successful

in feeding the hungry,' replied Daniel scathingly. 'They can't levy enough money to buy grain for the poor. The price has risen beyond everyone's pockets, and still the Government in London refuses to distribute food. The protection of free trade is all they're interested in. It was better under Peel. But this man at the Treasury, Trevelyan, is a monster. You don't reason with monsters, Father; you cut them down.'

The next day early, heavily swathed against the biting wind, Townsend was accompanying Mr Brewster of the Board of Works to the site of the new road. The project had been approved, and Townsend was hoping to get things under way before the ground became too hard to work. What, he wondered irritably, had become of the famous mild Irish winters he had heard tell of? This was certainly not going to be one of them.

There were men working already, skilled men, driving stakes into the ground to mark out the course of the road. The work was well advanced, and Townsend could see the stakes stretching ahead of him away into the clouds which had come down to settle their bellies on the tops of the hills.

'We'll dig a ditch on either side,' Brewster was explaining. 'Throw the earth into the middle. Cover that with broken stones which we'll bring up from the quarry. Then we'll put a thin layer of clay over that, and over that, a layer of gravel from the pit.'

There was a big wagon parked nearby and Townsend looked under the tarpaulin that covered it.

It was loaded with tools.

'We were lucky to get them,' said Brewster. In many of the unions the people have to provide their own. I've seen some digging roads with their hands.'

Townsend was silent. The first contingent of workers, from the poorhouse, was due to arrive and start work that very morning. He wondered what Brewster's reaction to them would be. He did not have long to wait.

'Good God,' said Brewster, looking at something beyond the agent's shoulder.

Turning his head, Townsend saw what at first sight appeared to be an apparition. Out of the freezing mist a motley, ragged, barefoot company of people was emerging. They looked bewildered and they moved like sleepwalkers. Their naked limbs were grey and blue with cold. Not only men, but women and children as well – even three-year-olds tottered along by their mothers. They seemed to come out of the mist endlessly, and stopped in a loose semicircle around the agent and the official, looking at them with vacant eyes, in silent expectation.

'That, Mr Brewster, is your workforce,' said Townsend, grimly.

'Do they know they'll be on task-work?' asked the official. 'That they'll be paid according to results? Half of these people will never earn enough to buy food at the price grain is reaching.'

'I can only help ameliorate the fate of these people with the means I have been given,' said Townsend. 'You know that.'

Liam Phelan and Dr Davis stood in Davis's study over a table on which four bound bundles of paper lay. Both men were in a state of some excitement. In his hand, Liam held a letter they had just finished writing to accompany the document they had written: *A Report on Famine Conditions in the Parish of Galready, Donegal, in the Year 1846*. Liam read it back aloud to the doctor:

'Even as we write, autumn has turned to winter, and the nettles and blackberries, the nuts and roots on which your neighbours, the Irish poor, have been eking out an existence, are to be found no more. Two thousand people in this parish alone are living, or rather dying, on a diet of turnip-tops, sand-eels and seaweed. We therefore respectfully and earnestly beg you to publish our report in your widely-circulated journal, so that the people may know what is happening within forty-eight hours' journey of the capital of the world; so that the Saviour's words may be ultimately fulfilled: "Let your light so shine before men that they may see your good works and glorify your Father who is in heaven." We are, Sir, your obedient servants: Doctor Michael Davis, Physician; Father Liam Phelan, Parish Priest.'

Davis nodded his approval. 'That letter can go with the copies we'll send to *The Times* and *The Dublin Medical Journal*.' He picked up a third copy and laid it on one side. 'This copy we'll send to Lord Hawksborough, telling him what we've done. And this last copy is ours.' He looked at Liam. 'We've done what we can, Father. Let us hope the seeds we are about to sow bear fruit.'

The days passed. In a makeshift tent at the head of the new road, Brewster sat at a table. He was cold despite his scarf and gloves, and he could hardly hold the pencil he used to write on the papers in front of him. Work was continuing on the road, and more and more people sought to register to labour on it. The hunger was taking hold of the land, and the only way anyone could eat now was by earning money toiling for the Relief Works – money with which they could then buy grain from Coulter.

He raised his head to the queue that stretched away from the table in one direction, just as the roadworks stretched in the other. At the head of the queue stood an old couple – both man and woman were over fifty. Privately, Brewster thought they would not last a week on the road, such was the state of their emaciation already.

'What are your poorhouse numbers?' he asked them wearily.

'One-one-six-seven and one-one-six-eight,' said the old man.

'You know you forfeit your place in the poorhouse if you work on the road?'

'Yes, your honour.'

'Very well. Here are your work-tickets.' Brewster issued them with the coveted permits. But their places in the poorhouse would be soon filled. There were those less fortunate even than these people. 'Report to the quarry,' he told them. Neither of these two would be any good at trench-cutting. They'd have to go on the stone-fetching detail.

He looked up at the next applicant – a tall

youngish-looking man whose clothes hung loose on him now, but who might still have some strength in him.

'Poorhouse number?' he asked.

'I've not been in the poorhouse.'

'But you're of this parish?'

'Yes.'

'What is your name, then?'

'Sean Phelan.'

The name rang a bell with Brewster, who consulted another list. 'You're a farmer,' he said. 'You hold land.'

'Yes. But there is nothing to farm.'

'That isn't my concern. You're a farmer. That means you don't qualify for relief works. You are not to be employed.'

'But I have no employment! I have nothing to farm.'

'You must work on your farm. There are always jobs to do on a farm. Be grateful that you still have it.'

'You must know how things are here. We lost all our potato crop. We have nothing to eat.'

'I'm sorry. You are not eligible. Step aside, please.' Sean did not move. 'Step aside,' repeated Brewster.

'I must work,' said Sean.

Brewster nodded to a policeman who stood nearby. The policeman was solidly built. He came forward and took hold of Sean's arm in a firm grip. Sean shrugged him off and made his way back down the hill. People in the queue stared at him. They were nervous. Would they be turned away too? From behind him came the sounds of the men digging the trenches. Up the hill came women and children with barrows and kreels, bringing stones from the quarry to be broken up and spread on the road. Splinters of stone flew everywhere from under the hammers of the stonebreakers. Children too small to work sat in huddled groups where they had been left by their mothers, their backs to the wind. A freezing rain began to fall.

Sean trudged on homewards. As he reached the end of the queue, he saw Townsend riding up on his white horse, dressed in his habitual dark clothes, going to see how work was progressing. Sean watched him ride by. Townsend did not look at him – perhaps he did not recognise him.

Con was with Nes, the cow they had managed to keep since there was grass enough for her. But she was ailing and her milk was falling off. No-one would buy her. In any case, Coulter could name his price and get it, things were so bad.

'What's her yield like?' asked Sean.

'Not what it was. There's still some.' Maeve was trying Hannah on the milk. 'Where have you been?' asked Conor.

'Up to the public works. They turned me away.' Sean ran his hand along Nes's flank. 'If we slaughter her, the baby will have no milk. Besides, we couldn't afford to salt the meat.'

Conor dipped his finger into the pail of milk he'd got from the cow and made the sign of the cross on her lean hip.

'Jesus,' said Sean, watching him. 'Perhaps Michael was the lucky one. Not having to face all this.'

'We'll think of something,' said Con.

'I suppose I could ask Coulter for credit, but asking anything of that man sticks in my craw.'

'He'd charge you interest enough to put you in his debt for life,' said Conor, handing his brother the pail. 'Here, take that in to Maeve.'

Sean took the bucket and made his way to the house. It looked dirty and grey now the year was old. Con watched him go, his hand on the cow's back, stroking her. She looked at him with sad eyes. Con shook himself and tethered her by a fresh patch of grass, not without wishing he had the same kind of stomach as she had to eat it, for if they could eat grass and get some nutrition out of it, they'd be all right. But, as it was, other ways of getting by had to be found.

Leaving her, he set off for the town.

He arrived there at dusk, passing the agent's house and thinking how warm it looked, with lights at every window, but he did not dare to linger, for the policeman at the gate was already looking at him with suspicion.

He made his way straight to Coulter's Stores. A few men were in the Shebeen, mostly Protestants who worked in the town, and men from among the handful of landowning farmers who'd shown a profit on their grain sales. He recognised Brewster from the Relief Works, drinking with two of his assistants. How they assessed the task-work was beyond Conor. He knew one of the assistants at least to be quite illiterate.

Coulter sat in his habitual place by the bar counter;

but his expression was disconsolate.

'What are you after?' he asked Con. 'I'm giving no tick here.'

'You said you wanted me to fight for you.'

Coulter spread his hands. 'There's no-one to fight! And no-one to bet on a fight. Bad times are bad for business, too, you know. What they don't realise in London is that you don't solve a problem by ignoring it. They're forcing us to go on as if in times like these you can just do business normally, and the result is that everything's getting worse!'

'There must be people with money somewhere. Get me a fight. I won't let you down.'

Coulter considered. 'There is one possibility,' he said. He looked at Conor. The man had lost weight, there was no denying that, but he was still big and strong and the light in his eyes had not gone out. And now Coulter had thought of a group of men who had food in their bellies and money in their pouches. 'Come back tomorrow,' he said. 'I'll see what can be arranged.'

Late the following afternoon Con was riding behind Bryan Meagher on a broad-backed shire, followed by Ferry on a cob. They were on a track above the shore near a little bay just beyond Brannocktown.

'Where are we going? Who is this man I'm to fight?' asked Con for the fifth time. He'd arrived at the Stores to find that Coulter had gone on ahead, leaving his men to wait.

'He just told us where to come,' said Meagher. 'But

I think you'll find it's now that you'll have a chance to strike a blow for Ireland, if you're so minded. Look down there.'

Conor peered over his shoulder and saw a knot of men on the beach. He could see Coulter among them, so there could be no doubt. There was no mistaking the men either, in their red coats and white crossbelts. English soldiers from the lines outside Galready town.

'Fight a soldier?' he said.

'You said you wanted a fight,' said Ferry. 'Odds are a bit tough for you, but then, they were when you beat me.'

'We might have guessed,' said Meagher. 'That Coulter's a sly one. We might have known he'd sniff out the only people in Donegal with money.'

'Surprised it took him so long,' said Ferry. 'Must've been your asking for a fight that set him thinking. You should do well out of it.'

Con was silent.

'Turn back if you want to,' said Ferry, but his voice was mocking.

'I don't want to,' said Con.

They took the track that led down to the beach. Heads were turning towards them. They were close enough now for Con to see that Coulter was already taking bets. There were a dozen or so fusiliers and a sergeant major. Con eyed them all, wondered which one of them it was he would have to fight. They, too, eyed him with interest. They were all big men. The English spent no money in feeding the Irish, but they stinted nothing when it came to paying for the army to come over and stamp out any trouble that hunger might cause the people to make.

The sergeant major, a black-eyed bull of a Manchester man with no neck and a cleft chin, Peter Ewence by name, came over to them as they dismounted. He carried a stoneware half-gallon whiskey jar by its loop and twirled it as he came.

'Which one of you is the stick fighter?' he said.

'He is,' replied Meagher.

The sergeant major handed Conor the jar. 'Here. Fortify yourself.'

Con drank from the jar and handed it back. He'd felt from its weight that it was less than a quarter full, and he hoped his opponent had had more than his share of what had gone. He watched the sergeant major waddle back to his men – curious to see that the infantryman had the gait of a rider. Then he took off his coat and, without thinking, began to limber up, easing his shoulders in circles and dancing on the sand to get the blood going in his legs. But his look was still apprehensive.

The soldiers moved back and formed a loose circle, while Ferry went over to the sergeant major and the two men compared the sticks that were to be used. Satisfied, each returned to his fighter. Now, for the first time, Con was able to identify his opponent and his worst fears were confirmed. By the look of him he was Irish, a Kerryman from his accent, Con later established. He was a big brute, but what gave Con a glimmer of hope was the battered condition of his face. It made him seem tough, but Con knew that the fighter to fear is the one who's kept his looks.

Meagher and Ferry backed Con up as he took his place in the centre of the ring formed by the men. Dimly in his mind was the thought that here were two Irishmen fighting each other for the pleasure of the English and the profit of a gombeen man, but he had no time for reflection. He needed whatever cash he could gain from victory, and he felt a sort of pride in the fact that Coulter had laid money on him heavily.

Coulter drew a line in the sand and withdrew. 'Gentlemen,' he said. 'I have only one thing to say to you: we are looking for a fight of unsurpassed ferocity.' The soldiers laughed and cheered. Half of them were drunk. Scarcely a one, except the sergeant major and Con's opponent, was out of his teens. 'On the count of three you will commence battle.'

'They say he's good,' Meagher whispered to him. 'But watch him. He'll fight dirty.'

'One, two …'

The Kerryman had laid his stick on the sand but not let go of it yet. Con made to lay his stick parallel and, as he stooped to do so, the Kerryman brought his own up and smashed Con's nose with it.

'Three,' said Coulter, laughing.

Con reeled back, but kept a hold of his own stick, adjusting his grip and swinging it through the air, aiming at the other man's shoulder. But the blow sliced wide. Con lost his balance and was face down on the sand. Above him, the soldier lifted his stick high, aiming to bring it down on Con's head.

Just in time, Con rolled aside, pushing his stick upwards as soon as he could and hitting the Kerryman hard in the crutch with its point – a lucky blow. The soldier gagged in pain but his eyes were mad with anger. This was no fight, Con thought. This was a no-holds-barred brawl. Ferry had been a gentleman compared to this rowdy.

By the time he'd got to his feet, the other man had recovered, and for the next five long minutes they hit each other wherever and however they could. Con's nose was numb and his mouth was full of salt blood which he had to keep spitting out in order to breathe, for there was no breathing through his nose. By the end of that time Con, who had eaten nothing but a bowl of nettle-soup and two turnip tops in the past twenty-four hours, was weakening. His head was light, but he clung to the thought that the soldier's greater confidence might provide an Achilles heel to cut at. Then the Kerryman aimed another blow at Con's head, which glanced off the cranium but caught on his ear, tearing it. Despite the pain, Con gripped one end of his stick and, in a move which brought a gasp from the spectators, brought it upwards violently, to smash hard into the soldier's forelip, splitting the upper jaw and coming to a halt against the palate.

The Kerryman's face caved in. When he grunted in pain a mess of blood, teeth and mucus fell out of his mouth, drooling on to his shirt. He dropped his stick and rocked backwards on his heels. Then he fell forward on all fours, vomiting what was left in his mouth on to the sand.

'Finish him off!' yelled someone. Con, looking at what he had done, felt numb with misery. He threw his stick away, and staggered out of the ring. He could hear the oaths of the soldiers who'd lost money on their comrade. They came from far away. Someone – it might have been Meagher – gave him his coat. He managed to get away from the crowd and slumped down on a dune at the edge of the beach. The blood and the surf roared in his ears. He just had enough strength to put his coat around his shoulders. He did not seem able to get enough air into his lungs, which panicked him. He looked down at his bloody front as if dreaming. His vision was blurred. No-one came to help him. He could hear Coulter and the other two triumphantly discussing their winnings as the soldiers angrily made their way off.

He heard Coulter and the others approaching. He saw them. Coulter was grinning, carrying a heavy bag.

'Give me my money,' said Conor. He could not raise his voice above a whisper.

'What?' said Coulter.

'I want my money.'

Coulter snorted, and counted out two coins.

'It's not enough,' said Con.

'Times are hard,' said Coulter, looking affronted. 'You should thank me for my generosity. Take it or leave it.'

Con didn't have the strength to argue. Coulter tossed the money at him. He heard them mount up.

'God help you if he dies,' said Coulter from his

horse. 'I told them you were mad. Nothing to do with me.'

'God help you if he lives,' said Ferry. 'He'll want revenge for the face you've left him with.'

'I've never seen the fucking English so angry,' said Meagher.

They rode away.

It was nightfall before Con felt strong enough to stand. When he did, he vomited immediately. Still he managed to stagger to the shoreline. Scooping up water in his cupped hands, he bathed his nose and ear. The salt stung, but the water made him feel better. He vomited again, but after that his head cleared a little, and he began the walk home. By the time he had reached the headland, the tussock-grass was blowing in the wind and the remorseless rain had begun again. His head felt light with hunger and he could scarcely see where he was going. More than once he stumbled and fell. At last he felt he could go on no longer. He crawled into the lee of a clutch of rocks and huddled there, drawing his knees up to his chest and tucking his hands into his coat. Turning his face to the cold stone, he lost consciousness.

They found him the next morning. It was still raining. Townsend and Mr Brewster of the Board of Works were riding from town to the site of the road when a mass of rags under rocks near the track caught Townsend's attention and turned out to be Con. Immediately, the agent dismounted and went to help. He took Con into his arms and turned him on his back, pulling his flask from his coat pocket and letting the sick man take brandy. Con's skin was the colour of white marble, his body as wet and cold as the earth.

Brewster was still on his horse, nervous and obviously impatient.

'Help me,' said Townsend. He took off his greatcoat and wrapped Conor in it.

Together they managed to hoist Conor on to Townsend's stallion. Townsend mounted behind, putting his arms round his charge and kicking the horse into a gentle trot. They rode on from there.

They arrived at the Phelans' farm twenty minutes later. Sean and James were in the yard, inspecting Nes, the cow. They took extra care of their last animal, since they'd had to sell James's old cob at last. But their actions this morning were automatic. When they saw the riders, they came running. Once Townsend and Brewster had drawn up in the yard, the men took Con down from the horse. He was chilled to the bone and shivering violently. His eyes were open but focused on nothing. The top of his left ear hung down and his nose was pushed over at an angle to the left. The rain stood on his face in beads. They carried him indoors, Townsend helping. Brewster stayed mounted with the horses.

They fetched his palliasse and bedded him down by the fire.

'What's happened?' asked Maeve, coming out from the inner room with Hannah in her arms. Townsend was shocked to see how gaunt she'd become. The hollow-eyed children clung to her skirt.

'I don't know. We found him up on the moor.' Townsend looked around. 'Build up that fire. Give him something hot to drink. Keep him as warm as you can.' God, but he wanted to leave this country. The old man bent over his son, helping Maeve undress him. Joseph and Molly ran to fetch linen to dry him, and dry clothes. Sean went with Townsend to the door.

'Now we are even,' Townsend said to him.

Sean watched him go, feeling sorry for the kind of man so limited as to see acts of human mercy in terms of a profit-and-loss account. When he turned back to look at his brother, he felt panic. He sent Joseph to fetch Liam and Daniel. Then they dried and changed Con, and put him to bed under a heavy blanket. He had not ceased to shiver. They sat around him and watched over him anxiously.

It was not long before Liam and Daniel arrived. 'I wanted to bring Dr Davis,' said Liam, 'but he's away over at Ballyshannon.'

'Let us pray,' said James.

The family gathered round. They all laid their hands on Con. Liam said:

'Lord, give life and health to our brother on whom we lay our hands in Your name. Lord have mercy.'

'Lord have mercy.'

That night Sean sat with Con. The two brothers were alone now. Con was getting better. There was some colour in his face and his eyes, when they opened, registered awareness.

'What happened to you, Con?'

Conor looked at his brother. You could see the realisation come into his face that he knew where he was, that he was alive.

'What happened?' repeated Sean, gently.

Con struggled to reach into his pocket.

'What is it?' asked Sean. 'Gently, now.'

He tried to help; but Con had found what he was looking for. He withdrew his hand, pushing his clenched fist into Sean's palm. He released the contents. Sean couldn't believe what he saw there. Two half-sovereigns. Sean looked at his brother's battered face and dared not ask himself what Con had done to get this money – enough to tide them over a little longer. He patted Con's shoulder as his brother once more lapsed into unconsciousness. Then he took the money through to the inner room, where Maeve lay in bed. She was not asleep. He gave her the money and she looked at it in wonder.

'In his pocket,' said Sean.

She rose and went into the main room to see her brother-in-law. His eyes were closed. She knelt by him, caressed his forehead. 'Thank you, Conor,' she said, kissing his brow. From the doorway, Sean watched her.

It was late when the knock came at the door of Coulter's Stores. Inside, Coulter and Ferry looked up from their late dinner of mutton stew, washed down with whiskey. Ferry stood and went to the door.

'Who is it?'

'Daniel Phelan.'

Ferry looked across at Coulter, who nodded his permission to let the man in. Ferry slipped the bolt back and, as he did so, Daniel pushed it open violently, knocking Ferry off balance for a second. Ferry made for the knife in his belt, but Daniel already had a pistol on him – the pistol taken from the murdered Henry Jenkins. With it, the schoolteacher covered Coulter and his man.

'Don't go near my brother again.' Daniel's tone was calm, dispassionate.

'What?' snapped Coulter.

'Do not go near my brother again.'

'Which brother? You have so many.'

'The one you've sunk your stinking teeth into. The one you left for dead on the hillside.'

'I don't know what you're talking about.' Coulter turned back to his meal.

'My brother Conor was found by the agent. The agent brought him home this morning.'

'Put the gun down, Daniel.'

'He was half dead from exposure.' Daniel's voice was trembling now. 'You harm any member of my family and I'll kill you.'

'What do you know about killing, schoolmaster?' sneered Ferry.

'You have a short memory, shop assistant,' snapped Daniel, pushing the muzzle of the gun into Ferry's fat neck. 'Who helped you drown Jenkins?'

Coulter spread his hands. 'You forget your oath, Danny,' he said. '"I will do no injury to any other member of the Honourable Society." Remember. You swore brotherly love to us.'

Daniel shifted his aim to Coulter.

'Look,' said Coulter, hastily. 'We paid Conor what we owed him. It was a stick-fight for a wager. He wanted it. Would we have left him out there to die, and the money still on him? Use sense, man.'

Daniel swung the pistol to just past Coulter's sweaty head and fired one of its two barrels into the bottles behind the bar counter.

'Jesus Christ!' yelped Coulter.

Daniel pointed the gun at Ferry, whose hand was on his knife.

'Please, Daniel,' Coulter whined. 'I didn't know about your brother. The last I saw of him he was fine. He begged me for the fight. He fought well. Very well.'

'He fought well?'

'Like Finn MacCumhaill himself.'

'But you made all the money.'

Coulter reached cautiously for a pouch at his side. 'Sure, I have that money here for you. Twenty pounds.' He counted it out on to the table. 'Twenty pounds to pay for Brian and Martin Sweeney to come here from Letterkenny and kill Captain William Townsend.' There was a pause as Daniel looked at the money. Coulter wiped a greasy lip. 'Your brother Conor made us that money.'

Daniel looked at him. 'You are a liar and a cheat and a usurer,' he said. 'You talk about brotherly love between Irishmen while you rob the people blind. You talk about the redress of grievances when it is you at whom the people are aggrieved.' He paused. 'And yet you'd pay that sort of sum to have Townsend killed?'

Coulter smiled. 'Yes. Because Townsend's death will be another nail in their coffin. Because the English aristocracy will be buried under the sheer bloody mess of it all, and I will be here to dance on their graves. More to the point, I will be here to buy up their land.'

'And what kind of landlord will you be?'

'An Irish one.'

Daniel looked at Coulter's cooling plate of mutton in disgust. 'English, Irish, still a landlord.'

Coulter laughed. He shoved the money across the table at Daniel. After a moment's hesitation, Daniel scooped it up. He looked at Coulter again, about to speak, but Coulter held up his hand. 'Spare me your political excuses. Everything and everyone, you included, has its price. But you'd better keep mum about all this – even to your family.'

'The end justifies the means,' said Daniel.

'That's my boy,' said Coulter.

The next day, Con was well enough to sit up. In the light they could all see the full extent of the hammering he'd had. His nose was broken, but Maeve knew enough to set it so that it would not look too bad when it healed. The torn ear was not as grim as it had looked. Once the skin had healed, it would hardly show at all. The important thing was to keep the wounds clean. Gangrene in the head would kill the man in a day. No-one asked directly how Conor had come by his injuries. He would tell them if he chose. Still, a question nagged at Sean, and he asked it as he helped his brother dress:

'Where did it come from?'

Conor did not reply.

'Where did the money come from?' insisted Sean.

'I worked for it,' came the surly reply.

'Doing what?'

'Does it matter?'

Sean helped his brother stand up, and fastened his trousers. 'Yes, if you've been doing someone else's dirty work.'

'What do you mean?' Con bridled.

Sean avoided his eyes. 'Tumbling houses somewhere.'

Con was furious. 'What do you take me for?'

'I don't know. I don't know how anyone would get two half-sovereigns without killing someone for them.'

Conor looked at his brother. 'I haven't killed anyone, Sean.' He was silent for a moment, then said: 'Spend the money. There's no blood on it but my own. Buy food while there's food to buy.'

And so it was that later that day the money found its way back to Coulter's pocket as Maeve and Sean went shopping for the family. Maeve chose several pounds of maize, some salt fish, a dozen eggs as a luxury, and two pounds of smoked bacon.

'Can you afford all this?' smiled Coulter, cutting the meat from a flitch.

Maeve showed him the money.

'Where on earth did you get those?' asked Coulter,

all astonishment.

'Wouldn't you like to know?' Maeve was gay. She smiled radiantly. Coulter winked at Sean. Sean looked away.

Dinner that evening at the Phelan farm was a fine affair. Maeve fussed over the pot, cutting a carefully-judged wedge from the bacon and adding it to the soup she had on the boil. The rest of the joint she wrapped and stored away carefully.

By the time the family was bidden to table, she was ready to serve them a corn porage with bacon and whiskey. Sean wanted his father to take back his old chair, but James took his place on the form, and it was for Sean to say grace:

'Bless us, Oh Lord, and these Thy gifts, which of Thy bounty we are about to receive; through Christ our Lord, Amen.'

They settled down to eat. Molly and Joseph ate greedily. Molly gagged on her meat.

'Eat slowly,' said Sean. 'You're not used to it, that's all.'

Hannah was taking a little warm broth from a spoon which Maeve held for her. Looking over the child's head, she caught Con's eye. Con embraced her with his gaze.

At the agent's house, Mary Dolan was pouring hot water into a zinc bath that sat by the fire in the bedroom. She looked at the level, tested the temperature. Both seemed well enough. There was no-one else in the room and, after a glance at the door, she crossed over to the chimney-piece to look at the daguerreotype of Townsend, in its red morocco-and-velvet case. The agent looked out at her with a gaze that was almost sad, though the man was still slim and handsome in his dark Hussar's uniform, the dolman hanging at its neat angle from his left shoulder. She picked it up to look at it more carefully. Unseen by her, Townsend entered the room. He watched her for a moment. Then she became aware of him and put the picture down in confusion. But Townsend was flattered and delighted. Despite the bottle and glass he was carrying, he managed a presentable salute.

'Captain William Townsend, Queen's Own Eleventh, at your service.' He drained his glass and refilled it. He crossed the room towards Mary. 'I'm afraid I don't cut quite such a dash in my dressing gown.' He looked at the picture and a cloud crossed his brow. 'You know, this was taken in London, at Richard Beard's studio, on 1st May, a few years back, and it cost me two guineas. It was taken on the day I retired, or rather, resigned in disgust.' He drank deeply from his fresh glassful. 'Lord Cardigan hates "Indian" officers, you see. And I was in India for seventeen years. Seventeen years at the rank of captain. Seventeen years spent watching the sons of the aristocracy buy their promotions over me. I had no money. How could I get on?' He looked into himself. 'Seventeen years of purgatory for my wife.' He put his bottle down and picked up the picture. 'We put on a splendid show in London, though. That I'll allow.'

He was silent. Mary waited. She knew she was

blushing. But he seemed to be paying no more attention to her, lost in thought.

'Will there be anything else, sir?'

He started, and turned to look at her, with an intensity that made her tremble. 'No,' he said at last.

She almost ran from the room, closing the door behind her. Cursing his drunkenness, Townsend undid his gown and stepped into his bath.

The next day, in the back room at Coulter's Shebeen, they were planning his death. 'He always carries two holster-pistols,' Daniel was saying. 'And he has a repeating pistol which he wears in his belt. He often wears a blue topcoat like an officer's and he rides a white stallion. You won't mistake him.'

'What about the money?' said Brian Sweeney. His brother Martin sat silently by, a blunderbuss across his knees.

'Ten pounds now,' said Daniel. 'Another ten when it's done.' He handed over a bag of cash and leant to point at the map spread on the table between them. 'The road works are here, which means that he has to come through this pass on his way back to Brannocktown.'

'It's a perfect place for an ambush,' said Martin Sweeney, taking a drink from his glass of whiskey.

'Yes,' agreed Daniel. 'If we position ourselves here, here and here, we should catch him in our crossfire.'

Brian looked across at his brother, then at Daniel. 'You're coming with us?'

'Yes,' said Daniel.

SEVEN

From their vantage point on the upland they had a clear view of the road works spread out beneath them, of the narrow valley and the track leading through it which connected the works with Brannocktown, and of the encampment that had grown up by the site – a shanty-town of shacks and drinking dives which housed the workers and would-be workers who had come from far and wide as news of the relief scheme had spread. Work on the road was progressing and, had it been necessary, it would have been a pleasing sight. Like a brown and black ribbon, it lay on the land surrounded by its ant-like builders and servants. Daniel surveyed the scene through a pocket-glass. Brian Sweeney crouched by him, the blunderbuss at his side. His brother Martin checked his double-barrelled percussion-cap pistol.

'Are you nervous?' Brian asked him irritably. 'That's the umpteenth time you've done that.'

Martin looked up. 'The man was a captain in the British army. I just don't want there to be any mistakes.'

'Isn't that the white horse?' said Brian.

'Yes,' said Daniel, watching Townsend mount up below them. 'God forgive us, he's coming.' He clambered to his feet and set off, crouching low, to take up his position. The Sweeney brothers quickly followed suit. About halfway up the track there was a bend as it passed through the defile. Brian settled himself on the upper curve of the turn. Daniel and Martin took up places on the high banks just above the pass, which was, in truth, small enough for them to conceal themselves without worrying about Townsend being out of range of their pistols.

Daniel glanced at his fellow assassins. He knew little about them but they seemed to know their business. And soon they'd be on their way back to Letterkenny, and probably they'd never be traced. He knew he was taking a great risk himself, for if Townsend saw him and they failed to kill the agent, his life would be at hazard; but he felt he had to prove himself to the cause. He tried to remain calm and hoped he gave that impression to the others. His heart was pounding from fear and exertion.

Too soon, Townsend appeared on his big horse at the beginning of the bend. The land agent was proceeding at a trot, but his face was alert. The saddle holsters were unstrapped, and the repeating pistol was close to his hand in his belt. It was clear from watching him that he was aware that the place was a good one for an ambush; but it was the quickest route to the town, and perhaps that outweighed other considerations. How long had

Townsend been here now? Seven months? Perhaps he was getting slack after all. Daniel knew that the planned attack would have been impossible if the agent had not once again dispensed with his police escort.

Just as Townsend reached the middle of the curve, Brian Sweeney stepped forward and fired off his blunderbuss at the horse's chest. There was a great flash and explosion, and the horse reared and screamed; but he was a big animal and the clumsy weapon's load of tin tacks had done him no serious damage. Brian had done his part of the job. While Townsend was bringing his steed under control, he was at his most vulnerable. Daniel levelled his pistol and, in his nervousness, fired both barrels at once. The gun whipped round in his hand as a result and both shots went wide. Martin, on the opposite side, took more careful aim, missing with his first barrel, but getting the second ball plumb into the middle of Townsend's left thigh, where it lodged. They could see the agent wince, but he kept his seat and, drawing one of the long pistols, spurred after Brian, who was running up the path. Seeing Townsend coming after him, Brian threw the blunderbuss aside in order to get away the quicker, but anyone watching Townsend would have seen that his blood was up. He was closing on Brian.

Daniel had been watching as if transfixed. 'Reload, man!' he heard Martin yelling to him from the other bank, and saw his fellow assassin running and stumbling along to keep up with pursuer and pursued. Townsend glanced over his shoulder. Then he spurred his horse harder and in another second had ridden Brian down. The unarmed man lay sprawling on the path in front of the agent. Townsend wheeled his horse round, aimed his long pistol at Brian's head in an unhurried manner, and fired.

Daniel heard Martin yell with rage and saw him fire again, but the shots went wide. Townsend had holstered the pistol and brought up his revolver. He got off two shots with frightening speed at Martin, who turned and fled. Daniel heard more horses and looked down the track to see a group of six policemen riding up to join the agent. He turned and ran himself, his mind numb with panic, stumbling and scrambling over the rough ground.

Townsend looked down at Brian's body. It had been a clean kill. 'There were three of them,' he said as the police rode up. 'The other two fired from there, and there,' he pointed above the track with the barrel of his gun. 'Get after them.' Then he dismounted and, steadying himself with the reins and his good leg, ran a gloved hand anxiously and tenderly over his horse's chest. There were superficial cuts, but nothing had lodged in the flesh. 'You were luckier than me,' said Townsend, patting the animal, which, calming down, snorted and shook its head. He had to remount from the right, but managed to haul himself back awkwardly into the saddle by himself as a policeman held the bridle.

The police divided into two groups and rode up

the steep, grassy banks. More police were coming up now, over the crest of the hill. Daniel ran down the other side at breakneck speed, giving himself up to the momentum, praying that his feet would not find a rabbit-hole to tumble him. At last he threw himself behind a heap of rocks and lay there, forcing himself to breathe quietly. Not long afterwards, he heard his pursuers thunder by. When he was sure the coast was clear, he made his way back to the tumbled house where he and the Sweeneys had left their horses. It was a well-concealed spot and there was no-one about. The animals were quite unconcerned. He released the Sweeneys' mounts, hoping they were not so far from home as to be unable to find their way back in the end, and rode his own as slowly as he could bring himself to, by a circuitous route back to Brannocktown. As he rode, he wondered what on earth excuse he would give for being up there on the moor if anyone stopped and questioned him; but no-one did.

Martin Sweeney was not so fortunate. The police flushed him from cover after a pursuit of only five minutes. He had not had time to reload again and the fight seemed to have gone out of him. He gave himself up immediately. The police bound him and dragged him down the hill to where others had slung Brian's body across the saddle of a horse. They then set off for Brannocktown. The agent, despite his wound, had ridden on ahead.

Coulter, Ferry and Meagher were unloading mealsacks from a wagon outside the Stores when they saw Daniel ride by on his way to the schoolhouse. He exchanged a glance with them and it was enough for them to know that something was wrong. Coulter watched the schoolmaster go, and after waiting for him to disappear through his door, left the others and followed him. It was still early. The few children who remained for Daniel to teach had not yet arrived.

Daniel was leaning against the desk by the blackboard when Coulter entered. 'Brian Sweeney is dead,' he said. 'They must have found Martin, I think.'

'And Townsend?'

'He was hit, but …'

'Is he dead?'

Daniel sighed. 'No, he's not dead. Do you think Martin will talk?'

'How in hell should I know? Did you pay them?'

'Half.'

'Give me the rest back,' said Coulter. Daniel, after a moment's pause, did so. 'Now,' said Coulter, tying the pouch to his belt, 'collect your things together. From now on, you are on the run.'

In a bare room at the police barracks, Townsend, seated on a straight-backed chair, gripped the sides of the seat and gasped as Dr Davis twisted the blunt-ended knife he'd inserted into the agent's thigh and scooped out the ball with it.

'Not too bad,' said Davis, putting a linen pad on the

wound and getting Townsend to hold it there. 'It didn't go in far. Still, you might think of wearing silk hose if you're going to go in for this kind of thing a lot.'

Townsend, recognising the military allusion, smiled grimly. He was pale, but already he was feeling the relief that followed the removal of the shot. Davis cleaned the cavity with alcohol and was binding the leg up when there was a commotion outside, and Martin Sweeney was bundled into the room and thrown into a corner by two policemen. McCafferty was close on their heels.

'Has he given you his name?' Townsend asked.

'No,' replied McCafferty.

Townsend sighed. 'The names of his accomplices?'

'Hardly.'

On the floor, Martin groaned. One of his guards kicked him hard in the stomach.

'Must this man be treated like an animal?' said Davis furiously.

'Show the doctor out,' Townsend directed the other policeman. Davis was ushered from the room. Martin looked up, scared.

'Where is the body?' Townsend asked McCafferty.

'Laid out in the armoury.'

'Get them to bring it in here.'

The guards left, soon to return, struggling clumsily with Brian's corpse, which they dumped on the floor between Townsend and Martin.

'Strip it,' said Townsend. They'd tried to shoot him like a dog, so he'd treat them like dogs. The guards carried out his order, roughly, tearing at buttons, cutting away cloth. They piled the clothes on a trestle table against one wall. There was a crucifix around Brian's neck, which they pulled off and dumped there too. Brian's head was twisted round, and though the skull was intact, the skin around the eyesocket where Townsend had aimed his bullet was turning dark blue.

'Any distinguishing features?'

McCafferty touched the body with his boot. 'None here. Turn it over,' he instructed.

'Search the clothing,' said Townsend. The ten pounds scattered out of a small pouch. 'Ten pounds,' commented the agent, drily. 'Is that what my life is worth?'

'What was his life worth? He was unarmed. He'd surrendered. You murdered him.' Martin was in tears.

'Did you know this man?'

'I only met him today.'

'Who paid you?'

Martin did not reply. Townsend made to get up, but winced in pain. 'Get me a bottle of brandy,' he said to one of the guards.

Martin was staring at the body. Suddenly he could bear it no longer: 'For Christ's sake, cover him up!' Townsend looked at him coldly. 'Is he a beast, to lie naked on the floor?'

The guard returned with the brandy. Townsend uncorked it, and took a swig from the bottle. 'Strip search him,' he told the guards.

They did so, and found a piece of newspaper lining one of the man's worn-out shoes. 'It's the Letterkenny newspaper,' said a guard, holding it up.

'Do you have any Letterkenny men on your force?' Townsend asked McCafferty.

'Yes, sir. But they're Catholics.'

'Never mind. Find one.'

McCafferty left. Martin stood naked before Townsend. They had tied his hands behind his back again, and manacled his feet. 'You will give me the names,' the agent told him. 'The name of every Ribbonman you know. Or I will hang you and leave you hanging until you rot.'

Martin looked down to the floor. They waited in silence until McCafferty returned with a constable.

'Coyle, sir,' said the man. 'You wanted me?'

'I understand you're a Letterkenny man, constable,' said Townsend.

'Yes, sir.'

'Do you recognise this man? Or his dead friend?'

Coyle looked at Martin, then at the body. Then back at Martin. He was clearly hesitating. Martin raised his head and addressed the policeman in his own tongue:

'Be loyal to your native place, your country. Turn your back on the English tyrant.'

Townsend had a pretty shrewd idea of what was being said, but he chose not to press for a translation. Instead he repeated, more forcefully: 'Do you know them?'

'Answer now, or I'll have you birched,' added McCafferty.

Coyle hesitated a moment longer, but he knew McCafferty meant it, and he was frightened. 'Brian Sweeney is the dead one,' he said. 'And this is his brother Martin. They are Letterkenny men.'

'You villain,' Martin told him in Irish. 'You traitor.'

'Brothers, you say,' said Townsend.

'Yes, sir.' Coyle was discomfited.

'Thank you, Coyle.' Townsend waved his hand in dismissal. Coyle looked again at Martin, who would not meet his eye. Unhappily, he turned and left the room.

'So, Sweeney,' said Townsend, turning to address his prisoner. 'Who was your contact here in Galready?'

Martin was silent.

'All right,' said Townsend, angrily, and nodded to McCafferty.

The interrogation lasted a long time. They tied Martin to a chair and two policemen with belts wrapped around their fists to protect their knuckles hit him every time he refused to answer. McCafferty did the questioning. Townsend remained in his seat, drinking brandy to assuage the pain in his leg. By nightfall, Martin could hardly open his mouth any more and both his eyes were all but shut by the swelling around them. He'd lost several teeth, which glistened on his naked chest and on the floor near him. His brother's body still lay on the floor in front of him.

'Who gave you that money? Who was the third man?' asked McCafferty again.

'I never knew his name,' Martin replied.

'What did he look like?'

'I never saw him. My brother ...'

A policeman hit him. Townsend pulled himself to

his feet. 'All right,' he said in a tone of finality. 'I've had enough of this. This is a waste of time.'

'I don't know any names,' said Martin in sudden fear.

'Take him away and hang him,' said Townsend. McCafferty nodded to the guards, who untied Martin and manhandled him out of the room. He could hardly stand. He cast a last look back at his brother.

There was a gallows in the barracks yard. Lighting the way with lanterns, the police dragged him out into the bitter night and across to it. The ground was already hard with frost and there was a hint of sleet in the air.

'You will not do this,' cried Martin. 'You will not!' His voice was a wail. 'I haven't been tried.'

'Was I tried?' Townsend, standing at the foot of the gallows, asked him. 'Was I tried, before sentence was passed on me?' He turned to the police. 'String him up.'

They placed the noose around his neck and pulled it tight. One of them stood on either side of him. A third stepped back to grasp the lever. No-one put a sack over Martin's head. He looked round at the man with the lever. The man was watching for McCafferty's nod.

'Lord Jesus Christ, only begotten Son of the Father; Lord God, Lamb of God, who takest away the sins of the world, have mercy on me,' Martin babbled.

They sprang the trap and it clanged open. Martin fell the length of the drop, voiding his bowels, but then felt himself hit the ground, still alive. The rope had not been fastened off.

'Pick him up,' said Townsend. 'Clean him up.'

Somebody threw a bucket of water over the wretched, trembling man. Martin was crying openly now. Townsend came close. 'Now,' he said. 'Who was it?'

Martin hung his head. 'It was the national schoolmaster here.'

'What?'

'The national schoolmaster in Brannocktown. He was the one who gave us the money. Ten pounds down and another ten to be paid when the job was finished. He was with us on the hillside.'

Townsend turned back to McCafferty. 'Find Daniel Phelan,' he said.

A troop of men was despatched across the quayside square as quickly as possible and the door of the schoolhouse broken down. It did not take the officers long to discover that there was no sign of the teacher. He'd left in a hurry, that was clear – though hardly surprising. The search spread. Other police were sent to rouse their off-duty colleagues. Soon lamps were being lit all over the town and people in their night attire came into the road despite the cold to see what was going on. The homeless, huddled in the angles of the buildings, were rousted out and forced to spend the rest of the night standing in the barracks square, under the guard of armed police.

Liam was at his small desk writing letters when

he was startled by a sudden hammering on the door. He opened it and a group of officers forced their way into the cottage, knocking over a table and immediately probing into every nook and cranny.

'What is the meaning of this?' asked Liam, enraged.

'We have instructions to search for Daniel Phelan,' said the corporal in charge of the group, a southerner by his accent.

'I am here alone. What has my brother done?'

'Nothing here,' reported a constable, coming up. They had swept all Liam's papers to the floor.

'There's been an attempt on the land agent's life,' the corporal told the priest.

'But what has that to do with Daniel?'

'My instructions are to search for him. That's all I know. I am sorry, Father.'

Liam seized his hat and cloak, and followed the policemen out into the night. Leaving the town behind him, he climbed the hill above it and made his way across the moor to the family farm. As it came in sight, he noticed that there were lights in all the windows. In the yard, he could see his other two brothers, his father, Maeve and the children huddled together under the guns of two constables, while from the house came the noise of smashing and clattering as others searched it. Liam waited until the police had finished and ridden off before he made his way down to join them. He found them clearing up the mess the constables had left behind them. Even their frugal supper had been thrown on to the floor. His approach took them by surprise. Sean, already furious, had taken hold of a pitchfork and turned on him before he realised who it was. The children squealed in panic.

'They've visited me, too,' said Liam. 'Are you all unharmed?'

'Yes,' replied Sean. 'Look at what they've done.' He paused to survey the damage. The little bit of looking-glass was smashed to smithereens. James sat by the fire, holding two shards in his big red hands. 'Is it true? That Daniel is a Ribbonman?'

'They told me nothing. He has fled. That is all I know. But you had no idea what he was up to?'

'None.' Sean was confused, overwhelmed by the thought. 'Why didn't he speak to us?'

Liam almost laughed. 'What? To tell us he was plotting murder?'

'He should have spoken to us,' Sean persisted stubbornly. 'We're his brothers.'

Con had remained silent. Now he spoke: 'And we must do what we can to help him.'

'I will pray for him,' said Liam. 'More than that I cannot do.'

Mrs Brogan had left a lamp burning on the hall table, but otherwise the house was silent and dark when he entered it. Townsend had instructed his servants never to wait up for him if he were kept away later than ten. He staggered against the doorpost. He had drunk all the bottle of brandy and started another before leaving the police barracks. He paused for a moment where he was, to get his breath back, and listened to the noise of the trap that had brought him home as it drove away. He thought about going round to the stables to see his horse, but he felt too tired. The alcohol, and the events of the day, were suddenly overpowering. The wound in his leg ached dully.

Dr Davis had left him a stick and, with its help, he limped into the dark drawing-room, making his way to the tantalus on the sideboard, which he unlocked with a key on his watch-chain, and withdrawing the brandy decanter. He poured himself a generous half-tumbler and drank it off. Then he hooked his fingers round the neck of the decanter and made for the stairs.

Mrs Brogan had left at lunchtime to visit her husband in the caretaker's cottage in the grounds of the now empty and closed-up Galready House. She had only returned after Mary had retired. Mary had not left the house all day and, as it was on the edge of the town, she was unaware of the police activity there.

In her room, she sat at her table, writing the diary which she had begun soon after she had started work here. Having no-one to talk to, she found it a help and a relief to commit her thoughts to paper in this way. She stopped when she heard Townsend's footfall on the stairs. When the steps reached the landing on the floor below, but, instead of going along the corridor, continued to mount the stairs which led to the upper rooms, she closed her book and put it away in a drawer. She had on her long linen nightdress.

What might he want? He could have rung for her if he had needed anything.

The doorknob turned and Townsend entered the room. He collapsed on a chair by the door before raising his eyes to look at her. She noticed the bandaged left thigh and the cut trouser-leg immediately.

'Has your honour had an accident?'

'Yes,' said Townsend. He raised the decanter to his mouth and took a drink of brandy. But when he looked at her again, his eyes were clear and his voice was quiet. 'Help me off with these boots, would you? I can't manage them on my own.'

She knelt by him and grasped the left boot around his calf. Looking up at him, she pulled gently. Townsend winced.

'I'm sorry if that hurt you, sir.' She let go of the boot. She was worried that he was in her room. But his behaviour was calm enough, and though she could smell the brandy on his breath she realised that he'd been drinking to quell the pain. She wondered what the nature of his wound could be, but dared not ask.

He looked down at her. 'Do you care if I hurt or not, Mary?'

Her eyes were wide. 'Yes, sir.'

'Why?'

'I care for all my fellow creatures, sir.'

His face was close to hers as he leant forward. 'Is that what I am? Your fellow creature?'

She did not know how to answer, and began to feel frightened. He sensed her fear and she knew it. 'A creature,' he continued. 'Howling in the darkness.

Hungry and lost and cold.' He looked around the room and saw a water glass on the bedside table. 'Fetch me that glass,' he said. She did so. He poured some brandy into it. 'Have you tasted brandy, Mary?'

'No,' she faltered. 'It has a powerful smell.'

'Here.' She was still holding the glass. His fingers closed round hers, forcing the glass up to her lips. 'Go on. Drink.'

She took a sip and recoiled. 'I don't like it!'

He let go of her hand, but moved his upwards, to stroke her hair. She dared not move. His lips were close to her ear. 'What did he tell you to do, Mary? Unlock the door one night? So that he could stalk me in the darkness? Murder me in my bed?' he paused. 'No. It can't have been that. Or they wouldn't have tried to kill me on the moor. But you delivered his letter to me, didn't you?'

His voice had hardened. She didn't know what he was talking about.

'Is that why you came here? To spy?'

'Please sir, I don't understand.' She was close to tears. The gentle stroking was somehow almost worse than being hit.

'When you offered your services you said you spoke English.'

'I do.' She turned to face him. He removed his hand from her hair. She felt relief, but also, unaccountably, disappointment.

'All right,' he said, his tone openly harsh now. 'In plain English: Daniel Phelan tried to kill me today.'

She crossed herself.

'Where is he? Where has he gone? Where is he hiding?'

Distraught, confused, she stood. He stood too, and she saw the pain on his face; but he did not weaken. 'Where is he, Mary?'

In panic, she tried to get past him to the door, but he seized her wrist hard and spun her round to face him. In doing so, he kicked the decanter over and the room filled with the smell of brandy. Mary cried out and struggled. He held her tighter, hurting her. She struck out at him, and in their struggle she fell to the floor. He stood over her, then pulled her up, holding her close to him. Both of them were breathing hard.

'Where is he?'

'I don't know!'

As they stood there, she saw the expression in his face change. He continued to hold her against him. Her nightdress was pressed to her bod, and through it, against her stomach, she felt his manhood rise. He pushed her roughly against the wall, feeling her hair on his cheek. She twisted her head from side to side, struggling to avoid him.

'Don't you understand? I almost died today.' He was moving his body against hers. His eyes had become those of a stranger. 'I almost died.'

'Please don't …' she pleaded. 'Please don't do this to me.'

But he was not listening. He was too strong for her. She looked down and saw that through the bandage his wound had started to bleed. He held her to him and dragged her across the room to the bed, where they fell. He pinned her down by her arms, kneeling above her now. He watched as the tears welled into her eyes.

'Where is Daniel Phelan?'

'I don't know. Please, sir; I don't know.' She began to cry like a child – her face looked like a·child's. Her long neck arched and stretched as she still tried to get away from him, her body twisting under him on the bed.

'That's right, cry. You cry for him. That's right.'

He continued to watch her, all manner of thoughts in his mind. Then, abruptly, he pushed himself away and stood back from the bed. For a moment she could not believe it. She gasped, interrupting her tears. Then, suddenly, desperately, she scrambled free, ran across the room, opened the door and fled through it. He listened to her running down the stairs, heard the front door open and slam. At the final sound he seemed to come to himself. Picking up the decanter he made his way downstairs, calling for Mrs Brogan to get up.

The police guards at the gate had caught Mary, and brought her, struggling, back to the house. The outside air was cold. Townsend met them at the front door. 'Bring her inside,' he said. 'Gently with her – she's had a scare.'

The two constables exchanged a quick look but did as they were bidden. Mary had quietened already, and allowed herself to be placed on the high-backed settee in the hall. Mrs Brogan, holding a lamp, was coming down the stairs. She sat next to Mary and put an arm round her.

'Thank you, Mrs Brogan,' said Townsend. He nodded to the guards, who withdrew. He was still holding the decanter. He took it into the drawing room and replaced it in the tantalus. He did not come out until he heard the two women go upstairs. Then he made his way through the silent house to his own room.

The following morning he woke with bright, pale December sunshine full on his face. His head was clearer than he deserved. He rose and washed, putting on a dressing gown and going downstairs to be served breakfast by a cheerful Mrs Brogan, who told him some of her husband's news and who, having heard the news of his own adventure by then, was full of solicitous concern. Mary, then, could have said nothing against him to her. He wondered what explanation she had given. His bacon was crisp, his eggs perfect, his coffee piping hot. To his surprise he ate with appetite.

'Where is Mary?'

'In the kitchen, sir. Did you want to see her?'

Townsend hesitated. 'No – I'll see how she is later. She needs a little rest, Mrs Brogan.'

'Yes, sir. Oh – Dr Davis's man called. The doctor will be coming to re-bandage your wound at nine o'clock.'

After the doctor had left, Townsend dressed in a dark blue suit and ascended the stairs to Mary's room. He knocked gently on the door.

'Who is it?' said Mary.

He opened the door. She was sitting by the window. She turned to face him but did not get up. Townsend let this pass. What had happened the night before had, as far as he was concerned, blurred the relationship between master and servant. Perhaps it was the same for her? She was a strong girl – tough and independent. He did not bother to deny to himself his attraction to her.

He stood by the door a little awkwardly. The room had been aired and cleaned. Only the ghost of an odour of brandy lingered. 'Mary, I want to apologise. I realise that you had nothing whatever to do with the attack. What I did was unforgivable, and I am sorry for it.'

She said nothing, but turned to look out of the window again. He watched the sunlight dance on her golden hair. He left the room quietly, closing the door behind him. She listened as he went downstairs. Soon afterwards she saw him limping down the path to the front gate, which the guards were opening for him. His groom stood waiting there with his horse. There was something in his manner – a kind of lonely pride which drove him on – that thrilled her. She thought of the night before. And she thought of Daniel. She did not know what she should wish for.

Townsend's first action on arriving at work was to make an appointment to see Magistrate Brady; and now the two men sat opposite each other as the agent outlined his plan.

'I intend to induce the Phelans to quit the estate for

good,' he was saying. 'They can take their stock and crop, all that they have. We may, perhaps, find a way of making the prospect of departure attractive to them. But go they must – they must pass quietly out of the barony.'

'But there's no suggestion of any wrongdoing,' objected Brady. 'They've paid their rent in full.'

'Jenkins was murdered,' cut in Townsend. 'That is clear. And there have now been two attempts on my life. No-one has been apprehended or punished in this locality. The fact that Martin Sweeney will hang does not deliver a strong enough message to the people of Galready.' He paused. 'The tenantry here, if we are not careful, will come to believe that they may flaunt the law with impunity. I believe that they must be made to acknowledge the power of the law. If we cannot find Daniel Phelan, then we will make an example of his brothers.' He stood up. 'If you do not help me, Brady, I will see to it that you are removed and replaced by someone who will.'

He turned to look out of the window of his office, which had at last been reglazed, at the bleak square. He watched two or three bony, ragged creatures cross it, purposelessly. The whole estate bowed under the hunger, and the north-east winds cut like a knife. This was fertile soil for discontent, if for nothing else, and the Phelans and the Dolans were at the core of it, he was sure. Someone was helping Daniel – who, if not his own family?

On the farm a day later, Sean was leading Nes from

the yard to the track that ran past it. As he did so, he saw that Maeve and the children were already out on their hands and knees in the stubble, searching without much hope for any gleaning they might have overlooked. There was nothing left to eat, although Conor had managed to bring home a seagull with a broken wing which they had cooked and eaten two days before, the effect of the black and oily flesh had been to turn their stomachs. There was no wildlife left, no birds flew overhead. The fields were stripped bare and the hedgerows too – and now only the bright, poisonous winter berries coloured the cold land.

Some way down the lane was the low cottage where the bloodletter lived. The bloodletter was expecting Sean and already had the tools of his trade laid out on a large, flat stone in front of his house; a long, sharp knife and a copper bowl. Sean tied Nes to a post.

'I can't take more than a pint, or you might lose her milk.'

Sean nodded. he stroked Nes's flanks with great tenderness and the bloodletter honed his knife. Then, making sure the animal's head was turned from him, he made a quick cut in a vein in her neck, stanching the flow of blood with his fingers while he manipulated the bowl into place. He let the blood pour out up to a mark, then replaced his fingers over the cut. With his free hand he produced a thin wooden pin and closed the cut with it, tying it in place with hairs from the cow's tail. From the bowl he poured his commission – a tenth of the blood – into a can, which he showed Sean. The rest he poured into the jar Sean had brought with him.

'God bless you, Joe,' said Sean.

'God help us all,' said the man.

When Sean got back to the house with the blood it was early in the afternoon, and the day was beginning to lose what little warmth the morning sun had given it. His children sat listlessly in a corner by the fire. The baby slept in her crib. Her sleep was very deep. At the table, Maeve sat, holding a piece of paper.

Sean put the blood on the table. Maeve looked at it with tired eyes. 'Read this,' she said. 'Bailiff Harkin brought it while you were down at Joe's.'

Sean took the paper from her and scanned it. Then he looked around, running a hand through his hair. 'Where's Father?' he said.

'He went off out.'

Just then there was a noise outside. Sean saw James arriving in the yard with the dog. He was carrying a load of bogwood. 'I won't leave this place,' he said to his son.

'I don't know how he can do this,' said Sean, indicating the paper which he still held in his hand. 'Telling us to quit.'

'I won't leave this place,' repeated James. His tone was purposeful. 'Con's gone to collect stones. We'll barricade ourselves in with the wood. Seal up the windows and the doors. I told Con only to bring good sharp stones. We can hold them off for a while.'

'And then?' said Maeve, coming up. 'What good will it do? They'll still get in.'

The men got to work, ignoring her. She dogged her husband. 'I'm not barricading myself and the children in.'

Sean fetched a hammer and nails. He started to select broad boards for the windows.

'Sean! Listen to me! Think of your family.'

'Leave me be, Maeve.'

'I will,' she replied angrily. 'I will leave you be. I'll take the children and go from here.'

'Where? Where will you go?'

'Somewhere. Anywhere from this.'

'There is nowhere to go,' Sean said. He went into the house.

They did not know when Townsend and his men would come, so they worked hard. When, towards dusk, they saw a man in black on a horse riding from town towards them, they panicked – but it was Liam. By the time the priest arrived, the house was boarded up, all but the front door. Everyone, including Maeve, wore a resigned, even a sullen expression.

'This is not the way,' said Liam, taking a seat with Sean at the table. Even in this extremity, it troubled them both that there was no hospitality to give or receive.

'And what is?' retorted Sean.

'Oppose them with force and you're sure to lose,' said Liam, hiding the confusion and despair in his own mind. 'Sean, please. You've paid in full. You cannot be turned out. I'll speak to Brady. We'll appeal to the Lord Lieutenant if need be.'

'I appreciate your concern, Father Liam; but I think this matter is best left to me. We have to make a stand some time. We cannot be pushed around forever.'

His brother's tone took Liam by surprise. 'Sean, listen to me. At least let me take Maeve and the children in to my house.'

Sean looked at his wife. 'That is up to her,' he said.

Maeve returned his look and said, 'My place is here, Father. With my husband.'

Sean rose and picked up a plank, together with his hammer. Liam, understanding his meaning, got to his feet as well.

'God bless you all,' he said. As he walked to his horse, he heard the sound of hammering begin. Sean was boarding up the door, incarcerating the family in the house. Liam tried to pray as he rode, but no words would come. Darkness was in his mind.

When the work was done, the family sat round the table in silence. Maeve mixed milk in with the blood, giving cups of the drink to each of them.

'They'd better come soon, or we'll all die of starvation,' said Con. Despite herself, Maeve smiled.

The attack came shortly after dawn. The family had sensed it, and since well before first light Maeve had had the big pot on the fire to boil, and every container capable of holding water was gathered, near-boiling water and stones being the family's weapons of defence. Maeve had put the baby in the cradle and the cradle in the outshot – the alcove by the fire. Joseph and Molly were crouched under the table which had been moved against the far wall. They could see the light of day through the cracks in the boards but they could not see out, and it remained dim in the room. Then, far away at first, their straining ears picked up the sound of horses, the dreadful jangling of bridles. They heard the snorting and stamping of the horses as they drew up in the yard, the crunch of feet as men dismounted, and, at last, Magistrate Brady's reedy voice as he read the eviction order to them:

'This farm has been placed in the hands of Lord Hawksborough's land agent, Captain William Townsend. In full accordance with the law concerning the protection of Lord Hawksborough's interest, we are empowered to remove you by force.'

Under the table with the children, the dog whimpered.

Suddenly, there was a terrible banging on the door and the house shook.

'Start filling the cans,' said Sean.

Outside, Bailiff Harkin and three of his destructives were trying to prise the door off its hinges with crowbars. There were six mounted police around them in a loose semicircle, but people were running towards the farm from all over the valley and down from the uplands, as word had spread. As they came they armed themselves with stones. Liam, too, was riding back to the farm, gathering locals to him as he went. Townsend and McCafferty had brought a strong force of police and destructives with them, but they were soon outnumbered.

When Liam arrived the police, already nervous at the size of the crowd, let him through. Harkin and his men had given up trying to force the door, and had withdrawn to discuss an alternative strategy with Bailiff Curran and Townsend. They did not wish to set fire to the roof with the people still inside, except as a last resort. The indecision created a lull and Liam took full advantage of it. There was a regular crowd of people now, and they had surrounded the house. Liam stood by the door. It was a dry, cold day, the sort of still, winter day that in ordinary circumstances would make you think about how close Christmas was. Liam stood hatless, the wind tousling his long hair. He seemed to be defying the forces of the temporal law by his mere presence.

'If you attempt to stop us executing our lawful duty I will arrest you, Father,' Sub-Inspector McCafferty warned him. His voice lacked conviction.

Liam ignored him. The police had withdrawn to just outside the yard. Townsend looked about him. 'Read the Riot Act, Mr Brady,' he commanded the magistrate.

'We aren't rioting, Mr Townsend,' said Liam quickly. 'We have gathered here to pray.'

He made the sign of the cross. From his soutane he produced his prayer book. There was a ripple in the ranks of the police. McCafferty had been obliged to recruit all the men at his disposal for this job, and several of them were Catholics. They eyed one another nervously.

'*In nomine Patris, et Filii, et Spiritus Sancti, Amen,*' prayed Liam. The people all bowed their heads and repeated '*Amen,*' as, hesitantly at first, did many of the constables.

Townsend could see the initiative slipping away from him. 'Martial Law prohibits gatherings of this size for any purpose. These people will be evicted and there is nothing you can do.' He turned in his saddle to the fat magistrate, 'Mr Brady, read the Riot Act.'

But Liam had already resumed his service: '*Judica me, deus, et discerne causam meam de gente non sancta: ab homine iniquo, et doloso erue me ...*'

'Get on with it, Mr Brady,' said Townsend.

Brady began to read, in a timorous voice, as Liam continued to celebrate the Mass: 'Our sovereign lady the Queen chargeth and commandeth immediately all persons assembled to disperse themselves and peacefully depart to their habitations or to their lawful business, upon the pains contained in the Act, made in the twenty-seventh year of the reign of His Majesty King George the Third to prevent tumultuous risings and assemblies. God Save the Queen!' He rolled up his paper with some relief. But the people had not listened, and though the Protestant policemen gave a hurrah at 'God save the Queen', their Catholic colleagues had joined in the service.

'Silence in the ranks!' shouted McCafferty.

'*Emitte lucem tuam, et veritatem tuam: ipsa me deduxerunt, et adduxerunt in montem sanctum tuum et in tabernacula tua.'*

'If you have not dispersed in one hour, we will open fire,' shouted Townsend. His horse stirred uneasily beneath him.

'Confiteor tibi in cithara, deus, deus meus: quare tristis es anima mea, et quare conturbat me?'

Inside the farmhouse, in the dim room, the Phelans stood in silence, listening to the Mass. On and on the prayers continued, and time passed. Everyone knew that the Mass would draw to an end soon, and that, when it did …

Outside, the tension mounted. The police and the destructives did not move. Townsend, McCafferty and Brady sat their horses like statues, though from time to time the agent consulted his watch.

'Soul of Christ, sanctify me. Body of Christ, save me. Water from the side of Christ, wash me. Passion of Christ, strengthen me.'

'One hour has passed, McCafferty,' said Townsend, loudly enough for all to hear.

'Oh good Jesus, hear me. Suffer me never to be separated from thee. From the malicious enemy defend me.'

'McCafferty!'

The Sub-Inspector braced himself. His men looked to him expectantly, but there was disunity among them, and their leader knew it.

'Prime and load,' he said.

The people surrounding the house watched the police unsling their carbines and it was too much for them. From the ragged edge of the crowd, some of them began to flee. Liam and those closest to him stood firm.

'Bid me come to thee, that with thy saints I may praise thee for all eternity.'

'Take aim!' shouted McCafferty. But then one of the constables broke ranks and threw down his rifle.

'Coyle! Get back in line!'

Townsend recognised the policeman who had identified his would-be assassins.

'I will not fire on my own unarmed countrymen,' shouted Coyle. There were tears in his eyes. 'I will not fire!'

The other constables wavered. The crowd raised a cheer. Coyle undid his uniform belt and rid himself of his cartridge box, his hat, his crossbelts. 'I am no longer a member of the force.' Another cheer.

'Arrest that man!' yelped McCafferty. After a moment's hesitation, two Protestant constables pinioned Coyle's arms. Liam called over to Townsend as Coyle was dragged away:

'That man is right! His actions are a lesson to us all. Let there be no bloodshed.'

'It's in your hands, Father,' retorted the agent. 'Persuade your brothers to give up the farm.'

'You must first promise me there will be no arrests.'

'That I cannot do, but I promise that no-one will be harmed if they give up possession of the house.'

Liam considered for a moment. The balance was swinging back in favour of Townsend. None of the other Catholic policemen had followed Coyle's example – indeed, they seemed to have stepped more firmly back into line as a result of it. He turned to the door and spoke through the cracks between the boards: 'Sean, Sean. You cannot win. They will fire on us if they have to – I know it.'

There was no response.

'At least let Maeve and the children out.'

Still silence. At last Liam turned away. His whole body spoke failure. Townsend bit his lip. He turned to his bailiffs:

'Do your duty.'

Harkin and Curran grasped their sticks and nodded to their gang of rowdies. Knocking Liam aside, they stormed the house, smashing at the nailed-up boards with iron bars. They were met with volley after volley of stones from the crowd, but the police started shooting then, and two men fell during the first hail of bullets. More people fled.

Harkin's men had managed to wrench the front door off its hinges at last, and now they set about the business of ripping away the bogwood boards that were nailed up behind it; but as soon as the first ones came away and Harkin's red face was exposed, Sean threw a can of boiling water at it. With a scream, Harkin fell back, but the other destructives under Curran's direction were tearing down the barricades over the windows. Inside, the family fended off the attack as best they could with pitchforks, stones and jets of boiling water. Joseph joined in the stone-throwing but Molly cowered under the table, screaming for her mother, while the baby wailed in its crib. Suddenly, with a great rending crash, part of the wall, roped and pulled from outside by the destructives, fell outwards by the door, and the roof sagged dangerously; but still Townsend's men could not gain entry because of the ferocity with which Conor defended the gap. But Conor and Sean could not be everywhere at once and, under Curran, another team of roughs was now working away at the rear wall. Most of the local people had fled or retreated, injured, by now, and the Phelans were fighting alone. Still their supply of stones was good, and many of the destructives fell back with cut eyes and cheeks.

'You need shields, McCafferty,' said Townsend, watching the vicious melee. 'Order your men to charge that breach in the wall with shields.'

'We have no shields!'

'For God's sake, get them to use anything, man! Anything that will serve the purpose!'

Maeve was huddling with Molly and Hannah in the outshot as the table was dragged across to plug the opening in the wall at the front, but suddenly police protecting themselves with the planks of bogwood the destructives had pulled down charged into the house from a new breach at the back. The roof was in danger of imminent collapse – only the area beneath the chimney breast was completely safe. James withdrew unnoticed into the inner room. Con and Sean stood either side of Maeve and the children. They had both armed themselves with sticks but it was an impossible task they had set themselves and the fight was lost. Both brothers managed to fell several policemen, but at last Con succumbed to a blow across the bridge of his nose, and Sean was dragged away from Maeve and the children, who were pulled and dragged screaming from the house and flung out into the yard, the baby knocked from Maeve's arms.

'Are you proud of yourself?' Liam shouted at Townsend, who was watching the débâcle without expression. The priest turned to face the policemen. 'You will not manhandle them! You will not!' Pushing his way into the fray, he rescued Hannah and restored her to Maeve.

The house was being torched. The thatch was damp and would not catch fire. Suddenly, Sean looked about him wildly: 'Where's Daddy?'

Liam rushed towards the house. A policeman at the opening in the wall tried to stop him, but Liam hit him full in the face with his fist and he went down. Inside, the priest could see where three rowdies were breaking down the door to the inner room with a makeshift battering-ram. About the main room the family's possessions were scattered and trampled – Hannah's crib was on fire, James's chair smashed. Liam watched as the door fell inwards under the blows. Then the destructives fell back, momentarily silenced, and Liam saw his father hanging from the crossbeam above the bed.

'Cut him down. For the love of God, cut him down!' He wanted to go to his father but they held him back and led him out of the house. He saw Sean and Con being manacled and led away under a heavy police guard. Maeve stood holding Hannah in a corner of the yard, Joseph and Molly clutching her skirts. The children's eyes were wide and hollow, understanding but not accepting what they saw. Maeve's face showed that she was beyond tears. Liam had never felt such anger or such despair. Four men carried James's body out and laid it in the yard. As if it had been waiting for this moment, the house groaned and shifted, and the remaining walls, unable to take the strain by themselves, fell in, bringing the roof down upon them. Through the breach in the wall, Liam saw two men left inside fall under the heavy beams that had supported the roof, and his heart exulted.

EIGHT

Everybody had gone but Liam, Maeve and the children when it began to rain, putting out the sluggish fire which the destructives had made of the house. Liam had botched together a shelter for the children out of sticks and a tarpaulin, but he stood by his father's body uncaring of the weather himself, while Maeve picked and scratched about the yard like a hen, trying to collect together a few of the family's belongings that had been thrown out there, and that were not completely ruined.

Liam raised his face to the heavens. 'Dear God let it rain!' he said loudly. 'Let it rain for forty days and forty nights, and flood this place – let this place be washed from the face of the earth.'

Maeve turned to look at him. Under the wet tarpaulin, the children crouched miserably, their faces grey and pinched with hunger and cold. After a moment, Liam stooped and lifted his father under the arms. He dragged him from the yard and, pausing to rest every few yards, to the slope of the hill just behind and above the remains of his home. He laid him in a hollow there, and started to cast about, looking for large stones. Maeve watched him for a time and then went to help him.

In the narrow cell at the police barracks, where he'd been placed alone, Sean tried to picture his wife and children. He looked down at his filthy clothes, torn and bloodied in the fight. Cold and damp were in his bones and, try as he might, he could think of nothing else. He could not even worry about what fate might befall his family now. The one image that did come, unbidden and persistent, into his mind was that of his father as they brought him out and laid him in the yard. Well, he had escaped to where no-one could persecute him any more.

He heard the key rasp in the lock and the bolt drawn. A middle-aged policeman appeared with a tin tray. On it was a cob of brown bread and a wooden bowl of soup. The man placed the tray on the edge of the fold-down bed. His look was apologetic.

'Eat, if you can.'

He hesitated, as if about to say something more, but left without doing so. Sean watched him go, listened to the door being locked again. He looked at the food. He had been hungry for so long. He wished he could give the food to his children. Tears came to his eyes.

At the farm a cairn had risen over James's body. Liam and Maeve fitted the last rocks into place. The children had come out, Molly carefully holding Hannah, whom she passed to her mother. They stood in a little line as Liam prayed:

'Lord, have mercy on the soul of this poor man. His sin was to seek refuge from the miseries of this world, but he died in the Lord, and it is written that everyone who believes in the Son has everlasting life. May you live in peace this day, James Phelan; may your home be with God in Zion, with Mary, the mother of God, with Joseph and all the angels and saints. Amen.'

They stood in silence for a minute, then Liam looked at Maeve and the children. Without a word they gathered their bundles. He lifted Joseph and Molly on to his horse's back and led it down to the track, taking the direction of Galready town. Maeve lingered a moment, looking for the last time at what had been her home. What would become of them all now? Then she drew her shawl closer round her head and turned to follow the others.

Townsend returned to his house alone. He had achieved his aim, but far less tidily than he had hoped – though if he were honest with himself, he would have to admit that he had not expected the Phelans to go without a fight. His justification for evicting them was scarcely within the bounds of the law, but now he felt sure that he had broken the spirit of resistance on the estate, and that, if he could ride out this winter, he might expect a better year in 1847 – which he fervently hoped would be his last in this post.

He went to the drawing room and poured himself a brandy, and then another. He walked into the hall and looked both in the direction of the kitchen and up the stairs.

'Mary!' he called.

But the house was silent. Well, it was her sister he had turned out of her home this time, and her nieces and nephew. He took out his watch. She would come back. He would not be angry with her. He wanted her to understand him. He settled down to wait.

'I'm going to see them,' Liam told Maeve as soon as he had got them into his house and settled. The fire was built up and the children, dry blankets round their naked bodies and warm drinks inside them, were losing something of the look of desolation they had had.

'Will they let you, do you think?' asked Maeve. She was still tense. She knew this could only be a very temporary refuge. She was terrified for her children. She knew that without food or even the protection of a roof, they would die.

'I don't know,' Liam admitted. He was weary now, and had to drive himself on. 'I can try. I must try.' He looked at her. 'Bolt the door behind me when I've gone, and answer it to nobody. Don't even show yourself at the window.' To the children he said, 'Be good now, and don't make a noise.' They nodded solemnly.

The rain had abated somewhat, but not ceased, by the time Liam rode up to the gates of the police barracks. He rang the bell at the gate but no-one answered it for a long time. At last a constable appeared and looked at him through the grille.

'I'm sorry, Father, but I cannot let you in,' he said.

'I am their priest,' Liam told him, outraged.

The policeman shook his head, embarrassed. 'I am sorry, Father,' he repeated. 'Those are my orders.'

'I will wait here until I am admitted.'

The policeman said, 'You may have a long wait, then,' and walked back to the guardhouse. Liam watched him go, helplessly. He rang the bell violently, again and again, but the door of the guardhouse remained closed, and everything was still in the dripping rain. Not a creature moved in the town, not even a dog. Liam sat himself down on a mounting block by the gate and waited, as he had said he would.

An hour later he was still there, soaked to the bone, his arms folded under his cloak. He was stiff, and when he stood up to stretch his arms and legs, he found the sodden material of his clothes so cold and uncomfortable that he faltered in his resolve. Nothing would happen here today. Perhaps he had better go to the agent's house.

While he debated this with himself, he heard the sound of a pony and trap, and shortly saw one drive up, the noise of its tack deadened by the rain. On the box seat under the hood sat Dr Davis, whose face when he saw the priest registered surprise at first, and then immediate understanding.

'Come away from here, Liam,' he said. 'This can do no good.'

'I must see them,' said Liam, doggedly.

'They won't let you. I've heard what happened. I've

just come from patching up Harkin's face.'

'Is he badly burnt?'

'He'll live. He was lucky not to lose his eyes, though. Come on.' He leant forward and held out a hand to his friend. Gratefully, Liam took it and climbed up next to the doctor. Davis whipped up his little horse and it set off in the direction of his house.

Once there, the doctor took Liam to his study and settled him in a big carpet chair by the fire, while he sent the maid to make tea. Liam felt the warmth of the fire thankfully on his face and limbs, and drank the big tumbler of whiskey the doctor gave him in grateful sips. He was overwhelmingly tired, but he could not settle, and once he had had his drink he stood up.

'Where are you going?' Davis asked him.

'Back to the barracks. Or to see Townsend. I don't know.'

'Go anywhere on a day like this in the state you're in and you'll be meeting your Maker sooner than you should,' said Davis. 'Now, sit down and while we're waiting for tea you can just take this powder.' As he spoke, he tipped the contents of a folded paper he'd taken from his medical bag into a glass of water. The water turned milky white and the doctor shook the glass to mix its contents before handing it to the priest. 'Drink it down in one. It will help you to sleep.'

'I don't want to sleep.'

'Just do it.'

Liam obeyed. The drink tasted of nothing. He sat back in his chair. Soon, the anxieties that beset him started to slip from his brain. He listened to the low crackle of the fire, and that sound and the colour of the flames seemed to fill the world for him. He was aware of the doctor spreading a rug over him, and a distant whispered conversation with the maid as she brought the tinkling tea-things. Outside there was the steady soughing of the rain. From the corner of his eye he could see the window. Beyond it, the sky was wild and dark. His eyelids drooped. Within another minute, he was asleep.

Mary had left the house as soon as she could before the agent's return. The gossip in the town was full of what Townsend had done, and though it appalled her, it did not surprise her, for she knew what Townsend had planned. Equally she had known that she was powerless to stop it.

But she might at least be able to give help when it was all over. Now she stood in the yard of the deserted Phelan farm, looking about her. She was too late. Where had everybody gone? The rain splashed and pattered on the stamped ground of the yard. Beyond its wall, around the side of the house, she saw the pile of stones that she knew marked a fresh grave. It must have been Liam who had buried his father. But where was Maeve?

Another sound caught her attention and, looking in the direction it had come from, she saw the dog, crouching bedraggled under a corner of the fallen roof for shelter. The animal looked at her with plaintive eyes and whimpered, stretching its forelegs, wagging its tail hopefully. Her heart ached. 'I can do nothing for you,' she said.

Leaving the farm, she ran down the valley. Perhaps

Liam would know what had happened. She reached his house and knocked on the door. She waited. She listened. Was that a person she heard inside, or just the sound of the fire settling in the hearth? She knocked again. But all she heard this time was silence. She did not think to call out. The rain was drenching her. She pulled her shawl further over her head and took the road in the direction of Brannocktown.

Inside the house, Maeve, cowering in a corner with the children, heard the footsteps recede gratefully.

Mary was halfway to Brannocktown when she saw the rider up on the road ahead of her, coming her way. The horse made great splashes with its hooves in the puddles as it came. It was a big horse and its rider was a big man. Something about them made her apprehensive. Then she saw that the man was spurring his mount, lashing its flank with a whip, and shouting to her. He was coming after her! She looked round futilely in panic for somewhere to hide. There was nothing, and the rain had made the rough ground, which stretched bare of cover for miles on either side of the road until it lost itself in the murk, into a boundless bog. She turned and started to run in the direction she'd come from.

But it was useless. Stumbling along, her breathing ragged, she heard the pounding of the hooves coming ever closer. Would he ride her down? Then she felt the horse above and beside her, big as a mountain, and the man reached down and grabbed her arm, hauling her up by it so that it hurt, finally slinging her across the saddle, where the pommel cut into her stomach. She'd caught a glimpse of his face. She knew the man. Martin Ferry.

They rode furiously towards Galready, but turned off before reaching the town and galloped across country until they came to a lane which eventually began to skirt a high stone wall that seemed to go on for miles. At last they arrived at a gate in it, with rusting and broken bars, which stood open. Through it Ferry guided the horse, and they continued through trees that swished them with their branches and showered them from dripping leaves, before coming into parkland and a broad, shallow valley, at the centre of which stood the grey and massive structure of Galready House. Ferry spurred the horse on until they arrived at a side door. Ferry dismounted, unlocked it, and then pulled Mary roughly from the saddle. She struggled but he held her by her upper arm in a viciously tight grip.

'Be still, you turncoat bitch.' He flung her through the door, kicking it shut behind him. She sprawled on to the flagstone floor of a scullery before he was over her again, dragging her to her feet. For a moment she thought he was going to hit her, but then there was someone else in the room, pushing him back.

'Leave her!'

Ferry turned round: 'For Christ's sake, Daniel!'

'Leave her.'

Ferry spat. 'You wanted to see her. Here she is. Let me know when you want me to throw her back in the sewer.'

He left the room, vanishing into the depths of the empty house, which echoed around his angry footsteps.

Mary got to her feet, looking at Daniel. He did not help her, and his eyes were without expression. 'I thought you were gone,' she said. 'Far away.'

He took a step towards her, holding her shoulders. 'You're soaked through. Come on.' He lifted her in his arms and carried her along a corridor and through another room that opened on to a great hall, along one side of which a gigantic staircase wound to the upper floor. Its entire length was hung with ancestral portraits – Hawksboroughs from the time the land was given to the family by Queen Elizabeth. What Mary saw was like the landscape of a dream – faded opulence, the like of which was beyond her imagination, ancient, crumbling tapestries, dustcovers turning pieces of furniture into recumbent ghosts in the sullen winter light. Daniel was climbing the staircase now. Walking along the landing, he arrived at an enormous gilded double-door, which stood ajar. He pushed it open, and Mary saw a room so large that its corners were hidden in shadow. Everywhere there were candles, standing in great pools of wax. Those around the bed, which dominated the room, were lit. A small fire was dwarfed by the gigantic fireplace, where marble nereids supported by titans twisted elegant bodies towards a giant coat-of-arms.

Daniel laid her on the bed and covered her with a rug. She was shivering violently now.

'Thank God it's you,' she said. 'I don't know what I would have done. Something terrible has happened. Sean, Con …'

'I know.'

'And your father …'

'I know. I've been told.'

She wanted to cry. 'I don't know where Maeve and the children have gone.'

He placed a reassuring hand on her arm. 'We'll find her. Don't worry.' He knelt by her and started to undress her. She was too weak to resist; she did not want to resist. 'I don't know how we'll get your clothes dry. We daren't have a big fire and we'll have to douse this one when it stops raining.'

'I can't stay.'

He undid the black velvet ribbon she wore at her throat. 'Yes you can.'

Later, when they were lying naked together in the bed, Mary, who hardly dared to allow herself to feel happy, noticed that Daniel was silently weeping. She turned to him, stroked his forehead and his hair, and kissed his eyes. He took her into his arms again and she pressed her body against his, seeking his lips with her own. He kissed her roughly, hungrily, pulling her down on to him with strong hands. She shook herself free of the linen sheets and mounted him gently, easing him into her and smiling as she heard him gasp with pleasure. She moved her body up and down on him, tracing patterns on his stomach with her fingernails, stooping to kiss him.

'I love you,' he said. His voice seemed to come from far away.

By the next morning the rain had stopped, but it

was a wet and wild day that she saw through the tall windows when she awoke. Daniel was still lying beside her. He was awake too, and staring at the ceiling, where some Italian decorative painter of the last century had been commissioned to depict a series of erotic scenes from antiquity. She followed his gaze to a heavily built, naked woman with panic in her eyes, who lay on a couch attempting to ward off with a dagger a determined man in Roman military uniform. A second scene showed the same woman, alone now, the dagger aimed at her own breast, a veil drawn across her face.

'It's the rape of Lucretia,' said Daniel. She did not notice the hardness in his voice at first. 'She was a nobleman's wife. Sextus, the son of the tyrant, Tarquin the Proud, came to her when she was alone in her chamber. He threatened that unless she gave herself to him he would kill her and then cut the throat of a slave and lay the body beside hers, making it appear that she had been caught in adultery with a servant. So she let him have his way with her. But afterwards, having informed her husband and her father by letter, she killed herself. There, you see, she draws the veil across her face to hide her shame.'

Mary looked at the painting. Daniel drew the corner of the sheet across her face below her eyes. She laughed.

'Why do you not hide your shame, Mary?'

The laughter died on her lips. 'My shame?'

'Did you not think to kill yourself?'

'What?'

'After the agent had had his way with you?'

She was horrified. What was she hearing? Hadn't Daniel told her that he loved her? 'What are you talking about?' She sat up, drawing away from him. Suddenly he snatched at the sheet, dragging it out from under Mary, toppling her out of the bed, sending her falling to the floor. He was standing over her, holding the bedlinen.

'I see no blood on these sheets. Should there not be blood, the first time?'

Mary got to her feet and picked up her clothes. Feverishly, she started to dress herself. Her clothes were cold and damp. They would not go on easily. For no reason, the thought of the abandoned dog on the farm came into her mind.

'Aren't I right?' Daniel continued remorselessly. 'Should you not bleed the first time? Is that not right?' He shook the sheet at her angrily.

Mary shuddered. How could she explain to him why she had taken the job with Townsend? She had not known Townsend would turn out to be a monster. But Daniel had not helped her; and now he seemed to be as much of a brute as the agent. 'You don't love me,' she said.

He laughed at her.

'Your brothers are in jail,' she continued, 'your father is dead, and you are laughing. Nothing is real for you. It's all poems and songs and stories.'

Daniel crossed the room swiftly to his clothes and from among them drew a pistol. 'Is this real enough for you?' He came over to her and held her, pushing the muzzle of the gun against her throat. 'Is it? Ha!'

He threw her aside.

She looked at him with horror. 'I loved you. And you have used me.'

'It is Townsend who has used you.' She turned to go, but he grabbed her, pulling her back. He held her close to him. 'Mary, the time has come. Unlock the door for me tonight and I will kill your lover as he sleeps.'

She wrenched herself free and, trembling with disgust and fear, ran from the room. Daniel followed her and watched her from the landing as she hurried down the stairs. At their foot, Ferry blocked her way.

'Let her go,' said Daniel.

Ferry stood aside. The two men stood looking at each other, listening to the sounds of her departure echoing through the house.

'You're a fool,' said Ferry.

Daniel returned to the bedroom and dressed, watching Mary run across the park as he did so. It had started to rain again. Twice she fell over. He went and sat on the edge of the bed, burying his face in his hands. When he raised his eyes, he saw Mary's black velvet ribbon on the floor. He picked it up and packed it with his things.

Back on the landing, he looked again at the Hawksborough portraits. Ferry stood in the hall watching him. Daniel drew his knife. As he descended, he cut through the face of every painted Hawksborough he could reach.

Ferry watched him, laughing.

Townsend had not slept all night, his complacency

giving way to anger and then anxiety as the hours passed and Mary did not return. He cursed himself for not treating her with more sensitivity. He would explain everything to her, make it up to her somehow. Damn it, why should the girl have become his conscience? He was only doing his job! He had to do his job! He did not want to destroy people's lives.

His head felt woolly and light from lack of sleep and too much brandy. At last he went upstairs to wash and he was standing by his bedroom window, looking down on the gates where the police guards stood, when he saw her walking down the street from town. She walked heavily and clumsily. Her clothes were tattered and muddy, her hair lank and tousled. He saw the guards look at her curiously. There was a pause before they let her in. She was hidden by the gates and the garden wall. Then he saw her again, coming down the drive to the front door.

The relief he felt at seeing her safe took him by surprise.

At the door of the house, Mary paused. It was still not too late to turn back; but once she had crossed the threshold, something told her that she would have taken a step she could never retrace. It seemed to her that she had no friends. Daniel - whom she knew she still loved, because otherwise how could it hurt so? – had changed into a cold, unreasonable and even foolish man. He was lost to her, she knew, and perhaps he was lost to himself. Townsend was the enemy: hadn't he brought ruin on everyone who was dear to her? And yet she knew that she aroused in him instincts which would serve to protect her. Didn't she have a right to exploit that? Her arm ached from the bruise where Ferry had held her. She put a hand to her stomach, and it seemed to her that she could still feel the ghost of Daniel's embrace. Why had he told her that he loved her? Was that not as cruel as anything Townsend had done? She turned the doorknob and went in.

Liam looked at the altar furniture. The idea of selling it had come into his mind the day he witnessed his family's eviction; but it was not such an easy plan to come to terms with. He would have to make his decision alone: there was no time to consult his bishop, who in any case would almost certainly withhold his permission. He leant on the altar and closed his eyes in prayer; but it was as if he knew what God's answer would be before He gave it.

'You cannot eat silver and gold,' he said to himself, opening his eyes again. Sighing deeply, but with new purpose in his movements, he fetched a wooden case and began to pack it carefully. Into it went the candlesticks, the ciborium and the chalice. Then he saddled his horse and strapped the case to its back. If only, he thought as he rode on into Brannocktown, there was a better man to do business with than Coulter.

In the shop, Coulter inspected the articles Liam had brought, laying them carefully out on his counter. He looked wryly at the priest. 'I'm still waiting to be driven out of here with a scourge of ropes,' he said. 'It seems instead that Christ comes to trade with this particular publican and sinner.'

'Do not take His name in vain.'

Coulter tapped his teeth. 'It's good stuff you've brought me, Father; but where will I find a buyer?'

'You'll find one,' replied Liam, grimly.

'What? For things that belong to the Church? I'm a businessman, Father, not a receiver of stolen goods.'

Ignoring the jibe, Liam handed the storekeeper a list. 'This is what I want in exchange.'

Coulter took the list and looked through it. 'Hmn. Well, I have no candles, no bacon, no eggs and no cheese. The other items I can provide.'

'And will you?' said Liam. 'Provide?'

Coulter picked up one of the candlesticks. He weighed it in his hand and looked at the priest. He grinned.

When Liam arrived back at his house he was in a better frame of mind. His horse was loaded with the food he'd bought from Coulter. There were bags of meal and a box of dried salt fish, as well as some hard biscuit, sugar and tea. A basket containing three resigned chickens hung from his saddle-bow.

Some of the food he would distribute to the most needy of his parishioners, some he would give to Maeve and her children – he knew he could not keep her at his house forever, and if she had to live rough on the upland, at least he wanted to be sure she had some measure of sustenance. Coulter, he knew, had driven a very hard bargain, but the storekeeper was in a strong position – for, strictly speaking, Liam *had* stolen his church's silver. Nevertheless, some food was better than nothing, and if he was not able to perform a miracle with loaves and fishes, he could at least do the next best thing.

In a little while, the children were sitting at his table, eating happily. How very quickly they responded to a little comfort. Maeve was unable to eat, but she watched Joseph and Molly with a kind of weary pride, and spooned some broth into Hannah's mouth. After a time, however, she stood up and moved away to the door. Liam saw that she was crying silently and did not want the children to notice. He went and stood by her.

'Is it always a sin to take your own life?' she asked him.

'God gave us life. Only God has the power to take it away.'

'Some would say your father was a martyr.'

'They would be wrong.'

Maeve looked at him. 'I can't bear to think of Sean rotting in that prison. How can such terrible things have happened to us so fast?' She crossed her arms over her breast. 'This is likely to be our Christmas dinner. Thank you, Liam. I was thinking earlier today, if we could get through until the spring, my vegetables would be ready. Then I remembered that the garden I planted is no longer mine, and that in any case Townsend's men trampled it and tore it up.' She paused. 'If Sean is transported, I will kill myself.'

'Don't say that.'

'I will kill myself, and I will kill the children too.'

She was so desperate that he did not know what to

say to her. 'That is sinful talk, my child. We must have faith and pray for our afflicted brothers. We must pray for them, and pray that God will be merciful. All our oppressors are but the instruments of His will.'

Maeve looked at him and he was helpless in the face of what he saw in her eyes.

Christmas came and went unnoticed as the day set for the trial approached, but when it came, it seemed to have arrived all too soon. At least when there is uncertainty, we can allow ourselves to be comforted by that false friend we call hope.

Sean and Con stood in the dock as Magistrate Brady prepared to pronounce sentence. In the gallery, to one side, Liam, Maeve and the children looked on in anguish. Hannah had been left in the care of a kindly neighbour.

Sean was aware of his wife's presence and aware of her eyes on him, but he could not look at his family – it pained him too much. He had felt ill since he had been in prison, too – he'd felt feverish and suffered headaches, which was unusual for him. He'd known that Con had been in the cell next to his, and from time to time he'd heard Con's voice in the night, speaking to him through the wall; but he had not felt able to answer. They had given everything to stay on their farm, and still it was not enough. He was aghast at the injustice of it. Increasingly, he thought of his father and mother – how hard and how thanklessly they had worked – for what? And now it seemed that a similar fate awaited their children. He hoped that Daniel had got away. He hoped that Liam would leave this place. He did not know what he dared hope for his own wife and children, or indeed for Con and himself. Was there any point in hope at all? He had even picked up some kind of lice in the cell.

From the bench, Brady was speaking:

'I have heard the evidence against you and found you guilty as charged.' He paused to glare solemnly at the men. 'If I choose to be lenient, it is because I was witness to the events of that day, and know that you have already suffered the loss of your home and your father.'

Clinging to the word 'lenient', Maeve held her breath. 'Conor Phelan. Sean Phelan. You will walk the treadmill in Lifford Jail for six months.' Brady nodded to the police escort. 'Take them away.'

There was a ripple in the court – if the people had had more energy, there might have been uproar. In her relief, Maeve struggled across the room to get to Sean before they took him back to the cells. She stretched out her arms to him, calling his name. Oh, how ill he looked – how thin! Behind her, Liam struggled to protect Joseph and Molly from the press of humanity around them.

At last Sean looked at her. She had hoped the light sentence would have gladdened him, but his eyes remained glazed and tired. It was almost as if he had nothing to say to her. Then the policeman behind him gave him a shove, and he descended from the dock, out of sight. But Conor turned to her as he was taken away.

'Be strong, Maeve,' he called. 'Be strong!'

By now the court was clearing. Suddenly someone touched Maeve's arm, and she spun round to see Harkin, a livid mask of purple skin surrounding his eyes. Behind him stood Curran. They looked at her coldly.

'You were given notice to quit the estate, Maeve Phelan. You must go, and go now.'

Curran moved up to her, taking her arm.

'If you won't go freely, you'll be forcibly removed,' said Harkin.

Liam had reached her. 'Don't touch her,' he warned Curran. But the bailiffs ignored him, pushing Maeve towards the door. Liam took Harkin by the coat collar and pulled him away. 'Take your hands off her!'

'Don't, Father,' said Maeve wearily. 'It'll only make things worse.'

Curran had turned on Liam and the three men were struggling with each other. In a moment, the police had intervened, pinning Liam's arms behind his back, as Harkin and Curran drove Maeve and the children from the courthouse and into the street.

'Damn you!' shouted the priest. 'Damn you all!'

They released him soon afterwards. He made his way back to his house alone. Once there, he did not go into the house, but opened the door of the little chapel. He looked at the bare altar. Gritting his teeth to force back his tears, he knelt before it and held his arms wide, in the posture of Our Lord on the Cross. He lifted his head and stared at the wall.

He did not know how much time passed before the people came. The sky had darkened outside, he knew that from the changing light in the chapel, and he could hear his horse stamping and whinnying for its hay. The muscles of his arms were screaming and tears were in his eyes from the effort, but he would not lower them. It was time he felt some of the pain he was unable to spare his flock.

'Father?' said a hesitant voice behind him. 'Are you all right?'

He turned to see five of his parishioners, two old women, a middle-aged man and two younger women – all turned into wraiths by hunger. He lowered his arms painfully and stood to face them. 'What do you want?'

'God bless you, Father,' said one of the women. 'We've come to hear Mass.'

He looked at them. 'There will be no Mass,' he told them in tones of granite. 'Go home. Go home, all of you. Board yourselves in and die in silence.' He closed his eyes. He tried to imagine the pain of the nails in Christ's feet and hands. 'Go home!'

The bewildered remains of his congregation crossed themselves and left him in the silence. Outside, the remorseless rain once more began to fall.

Mary stood at the window of her room, looking out at the joyless view. The land seemed to shrink and wither under the rain. It was approaching the Feast of Three Kings, the year's midnight. There had been little reason to celebrate New Year. She had been forbidden to attend the trial by Townsend, and indeed she had had little desire to go, for she knew in what great disgrace many of the townspeople now held her. She longed to know the verdict, but had to be patient until Townsend returned from his office. She thought about him briefly. He had been furious that she had left the house, without his permission and without a police guard; but she knew that mixed with his anger had been gladness that she was not harmed. He had not even questioned her closely about where she had been. Perhaps he preferred not to know.

As she gazed emptily through the drizzle, she caught sight of three figures on the road near the gate, where they paused, seeming to hesitate. She rubbed the condensation from the window to get a better view. Suddenly excited, she recognised Maeve and her children. She ran from the room.

By the time she reached the gates, the guard there was trying to move her sister on. She pushed past him and flung her arms around Maeve. How thin she felt, and how cold. The children looked up like beaten dogs. The baby lay in a fold of her mother's shawl like a wax doll.

'Come in,' said Mary.

'I dare not. It's the agent's house.'

'I will answer for that. We have to get you and the children dry and warm.'

With the help of Mrs Brogan, she installed them in the kitchen and fetched blankets and towels, while Mrs Brogan dipped the ladle into a casserole of vegetable soup she had on the range and poured out three bowlfuls. She put on some milk to warm for the baby. Maeve looked about her, reviving in the warmth, wondering at the plenty she could see, and told her sister the result of the trial. Her voice was as lonely as the sea, and her lean frame shivered as she spoke. Mary was uncomfortable, aware of her own healthy plumpness. The wind had got up and whistled round the side of the house. She thought of Daniel, of what he had said to her, and of all the people even then crouching in ditches or clinging to the sides of hills because their homes had been taken from them by men who lived in houses such as this. Her own parents might still be suffering that fate, if God had not spared them by now; and her sister was on the threshold of it. She looked at the children eating. Joseph caught her eye and smiled shyly.

She heard the front door bang, and exchanged a look with Mrs Brogan. 'I'll go to him,' she said.

She found Townsend in his study. He had taken off his coat and thrown it on to a chair. A wet leather pouch lay on the desk, and from it he was taking a sheaf of papers.

'Ah, Mary. Take my coat and pour me a glass of brandy,' he said.

She hesitated. 'I wish to speak to you, sir.'

He looked up. 'What is it?'

She was nervous, now, that he would deny her. She was aware that she was still wet and bedraggled from the rain. 'My sister is alone now with the children,' she said. 'She has no home, no work ...' She broke off, looking at him. He returned her gaze but he said nothing to help her out. 'She's a good worker, sir. She can cook and clean.' She paused again. He continued to look at her, expectantly but not encouragingly. 'Could she not come here, sir?' she finished, floundering.

'Mary. I cannot turn a family out, only to take them into my own home.'

'You turned me out, and yet you took me into your home.'

'You are not a Phelan, Mary.'

Mary could not understand his logic. What would become of her sister if she were abandoned with the children in this freezing weather? She became desperate.

'She could stay in an outhouse, sir.' Mary got down on her knees. 'I beg you, sir.'

Townsend came from behind his desk to her, raising her up. 'Don't,' he said. He took her hands and sat her in a chair. 'I cannot take her in,' he said gently. 'But there may be another way I can help her.'

From the sheaf of papers in his pouch he drew one and handed it to Mary. Leaving her to read it, he went to the side-table and poured two tumblers of brandy. Mary looked up from the paper.

'Why is his Lordship offering his tenants free passage to America?'

'Simple economics,' replied Townsend. 'Lord Hawksborough is obliged to pay subsidy, through the poor-rate, for every tenant on the estate who cannot support himself. With the potato famine, the number of such people has grown out of all proportion. The poorhouse is full; it cannot take any more. Even with the relief works, every day a ragged army camps outside its gates. By a simple and single payment, his Lordship can rid himself of both tenant and obligation.'

'So it's not a question of charity?'

'It never is.'

'But what of tenants who've been evicted? The ones who have no place in the poorhouse or on the road? Do they have any rights to it?'

Townsend looked at her. 'The rules could be bent a little. I am not a man entirely without feeling.'

Would you help Maeve if it were not for me, Mary thought, but said nothing. Townsend handed her the brandy. She shook her head.

'Try a little. A sip. It will warm you.'

She did so, not without remembering the last time he had given her brandy.

'It is like this,' said Townsend. 'There are now more than a thousand paupers in the poorhouse. The smallest sum they can possibly cost is five pounds per head per annum. Thus the poor rates must amount to at least five thousand pounds a year. This year, next year, probably the year after. If *every one* of them, every man, woman and child now in the poorhouse, or even working on the road, accepted free passage to America, the cost would still not exceed five thousand pounds. Do you see? It is cheaper for his Lordship to provide free passage to America than to keep these people in the poorhouse. It will free the estate from pauperism and help all these people to a new and better life. If your sister desires to go, and applies to me, I will see that she is accommodated.'

Mary could not believe her ears. 'My sister goes to

America while her husband rots in prison?'

Townsend spread his hands. 'It is a short sentence. If Sean Phelan applies to me when he has served it, I will arrange free passage for him too.' He paused. 'You asked for help. This is all I can offer.'

'Can I speak with her, sir?'

Mrs Brogan had gone to serve Townsend's dinner. Mary sat with Maeve at the kitchen table and showed her the paper he had given her. She told her what he had said. For a long time Maeve said nothing. She was looking at Hannah, for whom they had made a makeshift crib with a shawl in a bread-crock. The baby was quiet, but her dark eyes were open.

'She used to change every day,' said Maeve at last. 'Now she just lies there. Her look never changes. She just looks empty.'

Mary took her sister's hand.

'I've never been more than twenty miles from Galready,' said Maeve. 'I've never been on the sea. Not even in a curragh.'

'I don't want you to go,' said Mary. 'God knows, I don't want you to go. But I had to tell you.' She looked at her sister. What did Maeve think of her? Of what she'd done? Did she, at least, understand?

Maeve considered what to do. Then she came to a decision. 'Would he give me a ticket to work on the road? If you asked him?'

'It's crippling work, Maeveen.'

Maeve squeezed her hand. 'Ask him for me. I have to work on the road, Mary. It's the only way to get by until Sean gets out; and I have to be here when Sean gets out. I have to be here so that he can find me.'

The prisoners for transport to Lifford were brought out at dawn. They were manacled as they left the cells in the police barracks at Brannocktown, and then handed over to the company of fusiliers whose job it would be to escort them to the jail. As Sean and his brother were shoved into line in their group, a big soldier with what looked like a hare-lip came over and looked hard at Conor.

'If it's not the stick-fighter,' said the soldier. He stood aside then to allow the prisoners to be bundled on to the back of a cart, where they were shackled to iron hoops.

'What did he mean, "stick-fighter"?' asked Sean.

Con shrugged fatalistically. 'I'm the one who did that to his face.'

Sean wanted to ask more, but at that moment he noticed the big Kerryman having a word with a bull-like sergeant major. Then the Kerryman came over and climbed into their cart with the sergeant major and the rest of their guards. He looked hard at Con again and smiled. There were no teeth in the front of his mouth. Of the three carts, theirs was the last. The sergeant major leant forward and said something to the driver. After they had left the town and were on the clifftop road, the cart slowed so that it lagged some way behind the others. At last, it drew to a halt. Con looked at the other soldiers. They had all been present on the day of the fight, when he'd split the Kerryman's face in two.

When the cart stopped, the soldiers got down. Con's shackle was unlocked. He was pulled from the cart. Without a word, the soldiers unlocked his manacles too. He glanced along the stretch of cliff. He knew where he was. The seabirds eggs would be undisturbed in the spring, he thought.

The soldiers were armed with sabres for escort duty. One of them drew his and handed it to Con, as the Kerryman unsheathed his own sword.

'All right, hoeboy,' he said. 'Let's see how you handle one of these.' Without waiting, he slashed at Con with his blade. Sean looked on in helpless agony.

Con stepped back quickly enough, but he felt the rush of air and heard the steel whine. He had no idea how to fight with a sword and simply managed, more by luck than judgement, to parry and fend off the sweeping blows that seemed to come at him from all sides at once. But he guessed that the Kerryman knew how great was his advantage, and quickly saw how this made him careless of his own guard. When his opponent's arm was wide, he dashed in and managed a head-butt which connected with the other man's nose. The soldier fell back with a cry.

Con heard Sean yelling to him, but he could not make out the words. Instead of pressing home a futile attack, he turned and ran as fast as he could for the edge of the cliff. The soldiers gaped, uncertain what to do; then one unslung his musket, cocked it and fired, but the powder was damp.

Con slid over the cliff. Sean cried out and tried to stand, but the shackle yanked him down.

For a moment nobody moved. Then the sergeant major yelled orders, and the soldiers advanced to the edge and looked over. The cliff had a steep hang and they could see nothing. Three hundred feet below, the winter sea lashed angrily at the rocks. Above it, hardy seabirds keened and mewed.

The sergeant major turned to three of his men. 'See if you can make your way down on to those rocks. Find the body before it's washed out to sea. We'll pick you up here on the way back.' He glanced at the Kerryman with distaste. 'Get him aboard. They ought to be able to patch him up in Lifford.' Without another word he mounted the cart with the rest of his men and soon it moved off. Sitting at the back, Sean kept his eyes on the place where he believed his brother had fallen to his death. It seemed that there could be no more pain stored up in heaven for him to take. He was beyond tears now. He shuddered and his muscles ached. His scalp and his beard itched. He kept his eyes on the clifftop until a turn in the road took it out of sight.

Under the edge of the cliff, Con clung for dear life. He had found half-inch footholds with his legs splayed, and his fingers dug into crevices that were scarcely deeper. He pressed his knees and face to the unforgiving rock and prayed that his diminished strength would yet be enough to keep him there until the danger had passed. The seabirds had seen him and circled not far away, screaming their fear and anger. He hoped that the soldiers were too much townsmen to read the sign. He hung on until his muscles wanted to burst, straining his ears against the infuriating bustle of the wind, but gaining no clue about where the soldiers had gone. At last he saw their bright red tunics and white crossbelts as they scoured the rocks and narrow shoreline far below him. Were there any more of them up above? Well, that was a risk he would have to take; if he held on any longer here, he would no longer have the strength to climb back up.

He braced his feet and, keeping his cheek flat to the stone, reached upward with one hand. When he had found a hold, he raised the opposite foot. Then he did the same with the other hand and foot until, his shirt tearing on the rock, he was able to grab a handful of the hardy grass that grew on the edge. He tugged it experimentally. If it came away, he would be done for. It did not, and soon he was hauling his body back on to the clifftop up to the waist. But then the outcrop supporting his left foot suddenly broke away and he slithered back with terrifying speed. He dug his fingers into the wet ground, tearing his nails, but he managed to halt his fall.

At last, his lungs bursting, knives in them, he lay on the top. There was no-one else there. But he did not allow himself to rest. He swivelled round on his stomach and looked down at the soldiers. They were looking at each other. Had they given up? Did they think his body truly washed out to sea? As he watched, he saw them make for the narrow path they'd found and begin their ascent.

In a moment Con was on his feet, running as best he could towards the shelter of the hills.

NINE

Liam sat by the fireplace in his house, his elbows on his knees and his head on his hands. He had allowed the fire to go out and he had not eaten. He knew that it was morning, but he had no idea of the exact time, nor of how long he had sat there. He had not prayed, though he had tried to.

He didn't react even though he heard the trap draw up. There was a brusque knock at the door and Dr Davis entered without waiting to be asked. Liam looked up at him. The doctor was angry. In his hand he carried a copy of *The Times*.

'Have you seen this?' he said, without greeting the priest. 'The London-bloody-Times has published our report. The leader makes interesting reading.' He spread the page: '"The report by Dr Davis and Father Phelan is certainly a *cri de coeur*, eloquent, impassioned – and almost wholly mendacious. A year does not pass without the Irish people complaining of starvation. It is our opinion that they have cried Wolf once too often. Once too often has the Irish wolf bitten the hand that feeds it ..."' He broke off furiously and handed Liam the page. It was only then that he saw the state his friend was in.

'I'm sorry,' he said. 'I'm sorry. I shouldn't have come here.'

'You're always welcome,' said Liam, making an effort.

After a moment's hesitation, Davis crumpled the paper, and, lighting it with his tinder-box, used it to get a fire going in the grate. Liam watched the flames spring up. Davis turned to him.

'Is there any news of Conor?'

Liam shook his head. 'I know they've called off the search. It has been three days now. They are convinced that his body must have been taken out to sea with the tide. They're going to look further down the coast to see if it washes up there.'

'What do you think?'

Liam shook his head. 'The waters are come into my soul. I sink in deep mire, where there is no standing.' He paused. There was fear in his eyes when he next spoke to the doctor. 'I cannot take Mass.'

'Why not?'

'I do not believe the great God of heaven will come down on the altar in this Aceldama. My heart is full of vengeance. I pray that I may wash my feet in the blood of my enemies.'

Dr Davis was silent for a while. Then he said, 'Father Liam, I want you to come to the fever hospital with me. I need your help there.'

It was dusk as Maeve returned to the scalpeen she had made for herself and the children up on the moor – a rough shelter of roof timbers and thatch

272

built in the ruins of a tumbled house. Here she and the children had lived since Mr Townsend had given her a ticket to work on the road, where she and Joseph now spent each long day fetching stones from the quarry, while Molly sat with Hannah in a group of other children by a peat fire – one of many – within sight of the labourers. Among the children, many had hair falling out in clumps, though oddly it grew thickly on their faces, so that they looked like overgrown monkeys squatting on the ground, or the wizened pygmies she'd once seen a picture of in an old illustrated journal.

It was crippling work they had to do on a stomach that was never far from empty, but she managed to keep herself and the children going on handfuls of oats bought at exorbitant prices from the shanty-town dealers, themselves supplied by Coulter. She eked this supply out with the food Liam had bought for her. Things could be worse, she told herself. At least her children were not as ill as some of the others. An iron will to live, not to be defeated, had entered her soul.

What concerned her chiefly was the cough Joseph had developed. She heard it again now as he and Molly helped her gather kindling for their fire. They had a heap placed ready in their rudimentary hearth when suddenly she became aware of a figure approaching them stealthily in the gathering darkness. Quickly she bundled the children into the scalpeen and grabbed a thick piece of wood to use as a club. She turned and stood her ground in the entrance. Whoever it was must have seen her. The figure continued its advance. All at once her nerve broke and with a scream she lunged forward, swinging her club. She felt the blow fall on the man's shoulder as he caught her hands and pulled her to face him.

'Maeveen, Maeveen, it's me, it's Conor.'

'Conor?'

Relief washed over her like the tide and she embraced him, half-fainting. There in the failing light they clung to each other like shipwrecked sailors to a spar, gasping and catching their breath in sobs of happiness and release: there was still a friend left in the world, after all. From the entrance of the hovel, Joseph and Molly emerged gingerly, like scared animals. Con crouched beside them and hugged them both.

'I'll stay with you now,' he said.

Maeve wanted him to, far more than she'd expected, even in her extremity, but she said: 'No. You must go. They'll find you here.'

'*If* they're still looking for me. I won't be worth that much of the British army's time. But even if they were, I'd stay. I'll take care of you until Sean is released.'

He lit the fire. Maeve could see how hungry he was, but he refused all food, saying that he would get some tomorrow, now that he'd found a home to provide for, making her smile for the first time since the ill-fated siege. As the night brought its chill, the five of them huddled together in a cosy heap inside the scalpeen. Her arms round Hannah, she rested in his arms. She looked down at Joseph and Molly, pressing close to the adults for warmth. Conor's embrace was big enough for them all. She closed her eyes.

In her room at the agent's house, Mary awoke feeling sick. She climbed out of bed carefully, as every movement increased the nausea, and washed her face in the corner basin. She felt no better. This was the third morning in the past week that this had happened to her. She left her room and made her way soundlessly along the corridor. She wanted to get to the kitchen and vomit, and clear up before Mrs Brogan or Townsend rose – Mrs Brogan would surely suspect what was up immediately.

On the first landing she encountered the agent, already dressed and apparently ready to go out. He looked at her in surprise.

'Mary?'

'Sir.' She willed him to go away. If she had to speak more she would be sick there and then.

'You are very pale. Are you unwell?' He approached her. Lately his desire for her had commuted itself into a kind of fatherly concern. If it hadn't seemed so ridiculous, she would have sworn he was trying to make a good impression on her.

'I'm a little tired, is all sir,' she said, brushing past him and continuing hurriedly down the stairs. He watched her go.

Two fevers trod on the coat-tails of the hunger. The black fever, which darkened the face of its victims, and the yellow, which boiled the blood and twisted the muscles into knots.

'We ought to keep them apart, I think; but how can we? Where would be the room?' Dr Davis said to Liam as they walked down the ward of twenty beds, in which thirty sick people of either sex lay in various stages of disease, some on mattresses on the floor. Two women employed as sisters squirted disinfectant on to the plaster walls and around the edges of the beds. In the face of such suffering, Liam had pulled himself together. Under Davis's direction, he was distributing water to the sick – an unending job, for the victims of the two plagues suffered from inordinate thirst. Both men and the two nurses wore handkerchiefs over their faces, for the entire ward was filled with the most loathsome stench – a virulent smell of decay. Despite the cold weather, the windows and doors were kept open, as there was a theory that ventilation reduced the effects of the fevers.

'But there's more to it,' Davis told Liam as they washed their hands and faces vigorously afterwards in Davis's room. 'The diseases come with the winter – when the people huddle together against the cold, and when families invite people in to stay from the road. If we were less hospitable, the illness would find it harder to spread.'

'What causes them?'

'We don't know. There are theories. But one thing is for sure: they thrive on human contact.'

'Aren't you taking a great risk yourself, then?'

The doctor shrugged and smiled. 'Of course, but what can I do?'

It was on his second visit to the ward that Liam saw his nephew standing indecisively by the entrance. Quickly he moved the boy away, down the corridor. 'Joseph! What are you doing here?'

The boy's eyes were wide with importance. 'I'll have to whisper.' Which he did, on tiptoe.

When he'd finished, Liam straightened and stroked the boy's head. His hair was thin and fine, his cheeks sunken. 'Tell your mammy I will go to Lifford. I will see your daddy and tell him Conor is safe.'

Joseph nodded.

'And give your Uncle Conor a message from me. Tell him: It's a miracle. Do you understand?'

'Yes, Father.'

By the fifth time it happened, Mary could no longer deny to herself what was wrong. She had been too proud to explain to Daniel on the night they had made love that it had indeed been her first time, that she had no more idea than he why she had not bled – but now she would be a marked woman. Pregnant, without a husband to protect her, she would be shunned by one and all; and it would be worse after the birth of the child, if she lived to give birth. It would be bad enough if people knew who the real father was – but that they never would, and everyone would think it was Townsend, which would make matters a hundred times worse.

She had to do something. There were remedies. She would try one.

One morning she rose before dawn and left the house silently, climbing the wall at the back of the house to avoid the police guard. She walked up the hill to a coppice where a group of gaunt, stunted trees clung stubbornly to a patch of earth just deep enough to sustain them. A shrub grew there with red berries. Approaching it almost fearfully, she willed herself to pick handfuls and cram them into her mouth. They tasted sour and burned her stomach. But she continued to eat them, until all the fruit was gone.

She managed to get back to the house before she collapsed.

Townsend stood next to Dr Davis at the bedside. Mary lay unconscious on her back, her limbs stiff. Cold sweat stood in beads on her brow. Davis bent over her, placing his fingers on the side of her throat. When he spoke, it was almost to himself:

'Her pulse is very fast. She's sweating, but her temperature is not raised.'

He looked puzzled. Then he stooped again, opening her mouth gently as it yielded to his pressure. Inside, he could see that it was stained red. He explored around her gums with his index finger. When he withdrew it, he noticed some minute yellow seeds and a trace of fruit skin on its tip. He sighed.

'What is it?' Townsend asked anxiously. 'What's wrong with her?'

Davis gave him a look of distaste, which surprised him, but otherwise ignored him, placing his hand, to the agent's further surprise, under her dress against her abdomen, which he palpated. Then he placed the side of his hand against her breast and pushed.

Afterwards, he moved away from the bed to the window. His look was grim.

'She has eaten something.'

'She has no need to scavenge in the woods,' said the agent.

'No. She has deliberately eaten something to harm herself – or perhaps it was the baby she meant to harm.' Davis gave Townsend a hard look.

'The baby?' Townsend was utterly taken aback, but his manner did nothing to allay the doctor's suspicion or reduce his aversion.

'I'll return in the morning,' said Davis. 'She won't die, and I don't think she'll lose the child. She's a strong girl. Not many would survive what she's done to herself.'

'What can I do?'

'Now? Just keep her quiet. Give her water if she asks for it but nothing else. The poison must be allowed to work its way out of her system.'

Left alone with Mary, Townsend drew up a chair to the bedside. With his handkerchief he mopped her brow. Later, for he would not leave her, he sent Mrs Brogan to give one of the police at his gate a message to take to his office. There was little to be done now anyway, except wait out the winter, and hope that as many as possible would take advantage of Lord Hawksborough's offer of free passage to the New World. He smiled grimly to himself. Perhaps he should apply too. He'd heard that the Government in London was proposing to replace the relief works with soup kitchens, but that the scheme was encountering difficulties. He only hoped he'd be gone before it fell to him to sort out those difficulties in this parish. He stroked Mary's hair. Such feelings of tenderness were unfamiliar to him. He supposed he'd felt like this when he'd nursed his wife, after their only child had been stillborn. How old was Mary? She might have been his daughter.

At nightfall Mrs Brogan brought him some soup, but he neglected it. He had also sent for a basin of water and a cloth, and with it he cleaned Mary's face. Towards nine o'clock she stirred, then opened her eyes. She looked at him, cradling her belly. He spoke gently:

'Mary. Mary, listen to me. You will stay here, with me. You will be safe here. No harm will ever come to you, or to your baby.'

Her face did not change but he saw tears fill her eyes. She reached for his hand and held it. She closed her eyes again. Townsend felt that he had just been paid the greatest compliment of his life.

At the gates of the jail in Lifford, Liam was encountering the same problems he'd faced when trying to see his brothers in Brannocktown.

'I'm sorry, Father,' the guard was saying. 'Prisoners are not allowed visitors.'

'I am not a visitor, I am a priest.'

The man looked embarrassed. 'Even so.'

'Well, can I give you a letter for him?' asked Liam in exasperation.

'Prisoners are not allowed letters.'

'I'll wait here. I must see him. Not only am I his priest, but his brother. You must speak to someone in authority. I will wait here.'

The guard walked away without another word. Liam gathered his cloak about him. The street by the jail was deserted. The wind howled down it. The place might have been built of iron.

It was a long time before anyone returned to the gate, and Liam, though no thought of leaving entered his head, had begun to give up hope. But at last two warders, one with a sergeant's stripes on his cuff, appeared on the other side of the grille and came walking purposefully towards him.

'Father Liam Phelan?' said the sergeant. He had a sad, old face that was not without sympathy.

'Yes.'

'It is good that you've come. Follow me.'

They unlocked the gate and Liam walked behind them across a rain-washed yard to a side door in a wall that looked like a mountain. On the other side of it was a corridor lit by the sickly glow of gas-lamps placed at the miserly distance of twelve feet apart. Along it they went, passing many doors that had once been painted a dark, glossy green. In each door was a little spyhole, its brass coverlet shut. Then the doors stopped and across the corridor was a yellow barred gate. This, too, was unlocked for Liam to pass through.

The lights were brighter here and the cell doors spaced more widely apart. At the fifth door they halted, and the sergeant produced a set of keys.

'Cover your face, Father. He's ill,' said the sergeant. As soon as the door opened, Liam recognised the smell.

Sean was on his own in the room. He did not see

his brother at first. Liam stood and watched as the door closed behind him. Sean had lost all his strength and the flesh on his bare arms was loose where the muscle had been. He sat, with his head back, on a pull-down bed, and he was gazing up at the tiny window high above him, through which a little resentful grey light came. His jaw was slack. They had shaved his head against lice but, despite the cold in the cell, it glistened with sweat.

Liam walked over to him, put an arm round him, wiped his forehead with a corner of his cloak. In a dark corner away from them, something rustled in the straw and was gone. Sean turned his head to his brother but there was no recognition in his eyes. Liam reached under his cloak and produced a flask. He put it to Sean's lips and helped him to drink. After a moment, his brother came to himself.

'Liam?' he asked, uncertainly.

'The fever is passing,' said Liam, with a confidence he did not feel. 'It's passing. Drink this.'

'Am I still in prison?'

Liam looked at his brother's legs and feet. They were bruised and battered from the treadmill. There were great callouses on his hands, too. 'They have put you in an isolation ward. You have been unwell. Drink some more. It will do you good.'

Sean drank. He sat up. Liam withdrew the flask. Too much whiskey now might be bad for him, Dr Davis had warned. Bad for him! What could be worse than this?

'How is Maeve?' asked Sean, in an old man's voice. 'How are my little ones?'

'They are well. Conor is with them.'

'Conor is dead.'

'No. He escaped. He is looking after them for you.' Liam paused. 'You will be free of this place soon.'

Suddenly, Sean stared hard into the gloom by the door. 'But she is here! You have brought Maeve with you!'

Involuntarily, Liam looked towards the door himself. 'Where is she now? Has she gone?' Sean's eyes searched the room wildly. Liam wiped his brother's face with a wet corner of his cloak, but he could not stop the violent sweating that drenched him. Sean's skin was as yellow as parchment. 'They give you muck to eat here,' he said suddenly. 'It twists your whole body from the centre of your gut.'

'Sean. Rest.' Liam listened to the silence around them. Had the guards gone away? He had not heard a footfall. Should he call for help?

'I was waiting for you, brother,' said Sean. 'I was waiting for someone to say goodbye to.'

'Don't …'

'Where is she? Where's Maeve?'

'She is with the children.'

'Ah.' But suddenly Sean cried out: 'The children!'

Liam stroked his face. What kind of terrible pietà was this?

'Maeveen,' said Sean, taking comfort in her name. 'She is here. We are all here.'

Sean had closed his eyes. Now he opened them again. He looked at Liam like a child. Liam took his hand.

'Con is here. And Joseph, and Molly, and Hannah,

and father and mother, and Daniel. We are all here.'

They both knew what was coming. Sean tried to raise himself up.

'Hold me. It's cold.'

Liam took him in his arms. 'I am holding you.'

Sean nestled there like a child.

'I am holding you, brother.'

Sean was still.

'I am holding you,' said Liam into the silence of the cell.

Death stalked the land.

Con was wading in the freezing water of the bright little river above the scalpeen. While Maeve and the children were away working on the road, he did his best to forage for food. There was virtually nothing to be had – the people were so hungry they had even eaten moles. But it took skill to catch a fish.

He had been hunting so long that he could no longer feel his feet as they sought to get a grip on the slippery stone beneath them. It was hard enough, when you saw the little silvery devils, to be still as a heron and then pounce in time to grab them before they drove through your hands like mercury; but he would not go home without one for each of them at least. He'd been at it two hours and he'd caught three.

He was poised over a fourth when he heard the horses. Quickly he strode through the water to the shelter of the bank and crouched there, darting his head out to see the black shakos and the red tunics as the men rode by. Where were they going? Would they find the scalpeen? Were they still looking for him? He grinned. The land was in such a state there was no broadsheet out on him. Would these men know him if they saw him? His clothes were cut for a man twice his size – the man he'd been. But that was a long time ago: three months at least – or was it four?

After the last sound of their hooves was not even an echo, he moved, wriggling his toes and shaking his legs to get his circulation going again. Then he had luck, and ten minutes later two more slender fish had joined their companions on the green bank. That would do. Whistling through his teeth with the cold, he gathered them up into his pocket and made his way down the hillside for home. Once there, he made up a fire. It was too late in the day for another patrol to come by now. When there was a merry glow, he gutted the fish with his knife and placed inside them wild garlic leaves. Skewering them on shrub-twigs, he placed a layer of grass on the fire, then the fish on the grass, then more grass on top. Then he mounded earth around the fire to make an oven for the fish, fanning the thick smoke away from his face and the scalpeen. It was so cold that the frost of morning had not gone. Soon he heard footsteps that he recognised. Maeve and the children were returning. His heart ached for them. He would have done all their work for them if he could. And what work! What for? There was talk now that it would come to an end, and that the English would send soup to keep what was left of them alive instead. Well, that'd be bad news for that bastard

Coulter, at least.

Maeve unwrapped Hannah from her shawl and laid her down carefully in a makeshift crib that Con had fashioned out of grasses and shrub-twigs, piling the shawl on top of her and putting her in the scalpeen. Hannah was half the size she should have been, but she was a wiry little thing, her eyes were bright and her grip hard. Molly had the same spare leanness as her mother; but she looked out at the world seriously, and there was little of the child left in her, two months short of her sixth birthday.

It was Joseph who broke her heart. He was so white that he might have been made out of alabaster. The cough was worse and his skin was like paper. But he still carried stones every day, and his face lit up when he saw Con and recognised the oven-fire he'd made.

'What've you found?' said Maeve. She was exhausted, and all the more grateful therefore to see the sparkle in his eye.

'Five fishes.'

'Oh, have you now? Well, all we need next is two loaves and a miracle.'

Con looked serious as he broke open the oven and gingerly extracted the fish, breaking off to clown for a moment at their heat to make Molly and Joseph laugh. And they did laugh – despite everything, they laughed. Laughter, strange as it may seem, is one of the last things to go.

'It was two fishes,' said Con gravely. 'In the miracle. The boy had five loaves and two small fishes.'

Maeve looked at him, caught the twinkle back in his eye, and began to laugh. She laughed as fully and as richly as if she had been back on the farm again in the good days, when she'd first come there as a bride and Con had known that there could never be another woman in the world for him. He joined in, laughing as merrily as he could without forgetting how stiff and sore he was. Molly looked at them and giggled because of the laughter, reassured by it, interrupting her eating.

Then Joseph, who had been sitting silently by, vomited his food and lay down in the grass, shivering as violently as if he were having a fit. Con and Maeve darted a glance at each other. Quickly, Conor gathered the boy in his arms and carried him into the scalpeen, where he laid him on a bed of bracken. He took his tattered jacket off and laid it tenderly over him, but there was no stopping Joseph's shivering.

'I'll fetch the doctor,' said Con.

In a moment, he had gone. Maeve leant over her son, stroking his brow with a nervous hand, as if she were afraid of breaking him. 'What is it my precious, my love?' she asked. Sitting by her, Molly started to cry frightened tears.

Con found the doctor in the fever hospital. By the time he got there, night had fallen. He had skirted the police barracks, which he could not avoid, with extreme care.

When Davis saw him appear on the ward where he was making his final rounds, he was shocked.

'For God's sake, Conor. What are you doing here?'

In as few words as possible, Conor explained.

Listening to his description of Joseph's symptoms, Davis's face grew grim. He knew only too well what the boy had contracted.

When he spoke, it was with difficulty. 'Look, Con. I cannot come with you. There is nothing I can do. The fever will run its course. It may take a week. Then Joseph may recover – but you must know that he might well relapse. He may be very close to death already. All you can do – and I could do no more myself – is keep him comfortable. Let him have plenty of water; but do not touch him, and do not touch his bedding. Keep away from him. It is the cruellest thing, but impress this on Maeve for her own good and for the good of the other children. We do not know what causes the illness, but it is through human contact that it spreads. I am sorry.'

By the time Con got back to the uplands, a bright moon was up over the hills, and the silvery grey light in which it bathed the earth and the sea which twinkled beyond it made Con think that perhaps one day there would be beauty in the world again. But he put the thought aside brusquely. Such ideas were a luxury in times like these. Cautiously, for night patrols were not unknown, he made his way back to the scalpeen, which clutched the moor like a hand ahead of him. There was a dim light from the oil-lamp Liam had let Maeve have and which was only used in emergencies. Before he reached the entrance, he heard a thin voice, like a ghost's, crying for water.

'He can't drink enough,' said Maeve as Con crawled in.

'I don't know if I dare give him more, his stomach's so swollen. Did you find the doctor?'

'You must come away from him, Maeve,' said Con.

'What?'

'We mustn't be near him.' He looked to where Molly was sleeping close by with the baby. 'Fetch them away over here. I'll give him water and watch over him, but we mustn't touch him.'

Maeve looked at him with eyes that burned and were uncomprehending. 'You cannot expect me to do that. Not touch him?'

Con pulled her away before she could collect herself. Then he passed the other children to her. They barely stirred in their sleep. He placed himself between her and Joseph. Roused from his delirium by the disturbance, the little boy opened his eyes and blinked them in the lamplight.

'Mammy?'

Maeve clawed at Con, but he held her fast. 'Let me hold him. I'm his mother. Let me hold him.'

'Mammy? It burns.' Joseph thrashed on his bed. The bracken was wet with his sweat. He had thrown Con's coat aside. But his breath froze in the night air.

They watched him for five hours. The sky was turning pale when he died.

Maeve was silent for a long time, but her eyes had never left her little boy. Now, in a low, dry voice, she began slowly to keen. Molly woke up and clung to Con. He put an arm round her, glanced at Hannah, still sleeping in her crib, and listened:

'My son, my first-born. When you came into this world they said you wouldn't live. But I nursed you.

I wrapped you in swaddling clothes and I held you to my breast and I nursed you. I tended you day and night, and my milk came, and you sucked, and you grew. They said you wouldn't live but I nursed you. Forgive me. Forgive me for letting you die. Forgive me for not holding you to my breast now. Forgive me, my son, my first born.'

Days passed, but to Maeve they were all the same day. The day that Con had tumbled the scalpeen over Joseph's little ruined body and set fire to the thatch. Watching the pyre. Knowing they could not live there any more, for the sickness was in there. Con's promise to build another home for them. Then down to the roadworks because empty bellies cannot take time to mourn. And the bandaged faces and hands of the stonebreakers. And the flying chip that cut Molly's cheek so badly that she would have a scar there for life; and the kreel of stones that dug into her back, so that across her spine there was nothing but one dark bruise. And then – when did it happen? – Mr Brewster of the Board of Works riding up one day to tell them that the works were to close at the end of the month, and that they would have soup kitchens to feed them instead. And the bitter, iron cold. And the works ended but the soup kitchens did not come: there had been a mix-up, they were not ready, the funds were not available. So that Maeve found herself down on the beach with a thousand others, scratching through the sand for a new generation of sand-eels, a new crop of seaweed.

It might have been five days or a thousand after

Joseph's death that she saw the big grave up on the dunes above the beach. The wagons had come out from Lifford, people said, some with quicklime in sacks and some bundled high with twisted corpses. Men had got work flinging them into the pit that'd been dug, rags over their faces, hauling the skeletons – for they were scarcely more – from the carts to the ditch. There was a sweet, dry smell in the air. It was not wholly unpleasant but it suffocated you if you breathed it in for too long.

She saw a priest silhouetted against the sky. They'd set a body down by him and he was stooping over it. She struggled up the slope towards him. It was Liam. The face of the corpse was turned towards her. It had fallen in upon itself but she could still see whose it was. The pain that racked her seemed to tear her apart. Liam went to her, held her.

'Sean!' she cried, as two men bent, threw him into the darkness, shovelled the white lime after him. 'Sean, my beloved!'

The emigration scheme was going well. February 1847 was the harshest month so far that winter and, as the road relief work was wound up, people began to queue outside the agent's office to put their names down. Townsend moved to the larger outer room on the days allocated to emigration business, and he and McBride were kept busy from early morning until late afternoon marking names down and issuing tickets. For each day of taking names, there was another of paperwork, settling the accounts; but against all the unpaid arrears written off forever,

Townsend knew that his employer could count on another one-to-five acres of unencumbered cattle pasture.

He looked up sharply as he heard the next-in-line give her name to McBride. McBride was giving her no friendly look, for he and the bailiffs knew all about the favoured treatment the agent had handed out to the Dolan sisters.

'Maeve Phelan, what is your business here?' he asked, deliberately obstructive. Maeve, holding Molly by the hand and with Hannah swaddled in a fold of shawl on her back, looked for a moment as if she would flee. Then she caught Townsend's eye and her expression became proud.

'McBride,' said the agent. 'Prepare tickets for Mrs Phelan and her two daughters.'

Maeve swallowed. 'If you please, sir, there is another passenger going as well.'

'What do you mean?'

'Another would travel with us.'

'Who?'

'I cannot say. But he has also suffered injustice at your hands.'

McBride looked up at this, but Townsend ignored him. Let them gossip. He was an Englishman and no Irishman could remove him from his post. He would do what he could to make amends to this family; though it intrigued him to know who Maeve's fellow-traveller might be. There was one person, however, whose departure he could not permit.

'Daniel Phelan?'

'No, sir.'

Townsend considered her request. He was sure she was not lying. With a sigh, he pulled the thick rental ledger towards him, opened it to the entries made over the past two months, and ran a finger down the column of names until he found one belonging to a farmer who had died. McGinley. That would do.

He looked at Maeve meaningfully as he spoke: 'McBride, make out the tickets for Mr Patrick McGinley, his wife and two daughters, one for an infant.'

'Yes, sir,' said McBride, tonelessly.

'May I see my sister before I go?' asked Maeve.

Townsend took a plain piece of writing paper and wrote a few lines on it swiftly. Then he folded and sealed it. Giving it to her, he said, 'Present this to the sentries at my gate. They will let you through.'

'Collect your tickets the day after tomorrow,' McBride told her. 'Muster will be at Brannocktown Bridge at nine in the morning on Monday. Departure will be at ten, and if you are late you will have to reapply. Bring all the belongings you wish to take and be prepared for a long walk.' He sniffed, and shouted through the open door where the queue stood patiently in the street: 'Next!'

Maeve looked at Townsend. 'Thank you, sir.'

She made her way straight back down the main road to the agent's house. One or two people stopped to stare at her as she passed – this woman who seemed to have charmed the agent into showing mercy. Townsend had given his permission for Maeve and her family to live at her brother-in-law's house by the Catholic chapel in Galready town after he had heard the news of Sean's death in Lifford Jail, and although Maeve still did her now purposeless work on the road, Liam was able to provide enough food out of his own meagre supply to support her children.

Townsend did not know that, sheltering in the stable behind the priest's house, Con was awaiting the outcome of her application to emigrate. Maeve had talked it over with both her brothers-in-law; and now there was nothing to hold her in Ireland, emigration was the best means of escape. The year ahead would be grim even if there were no blight, for there had been almost no seed potatoes to plant, and much of the land lay unused and uncared-for, awaiting either new tenants or conversion by the landlord to new purposes. The countryside was void of people, and only the ruins of the low, one-storey farmhouses attested that human beings had ever lived here. Over their fallen roofs you could see where the creepers and the grasses had already begun their slow but steady task of burial.

Maeve had not expected to find the getting of the tickets so easy, but now, instead of the elation she thought she should feel, she was enveloped in an even greater depression. She could not rid her mind of thoughts of the farm in the good times, and of Sean when he was laughing and confident, full of plans for the farm, though in truth those plans were no more, when it came down to it, than a continuation of the tradition all his fathers had established. She thought, too, of James, and how he had adored Joseph. She thought of the suit she had made out of James's cut-down Sunday frieze, lost in the smashing of the farm along with so many other things that were part of her past. Except for the buttons – the glass buttons Sean had bought for her that market day, when she'd been so angry with him. She'd picked them up after he'd walked off, and sewn them into the lining of her skirt. She'd meant to string them together and wear them as a necklace to surprise him, but there had never been time, and now it was too late. For the sake of Molly she did not cry, but once she was in the kitchen of the agent's house, and Mrs Brogan had taken the children out to see the ducks skating on the frozen pond at the back, she wept in Mary's arms:

'He needed me. He was calling for me. He was calling for me and I wasn't there. I should have been there. He was my man and he's gone,' she said brokenly, through her sobs. 'And my little boy. He was calling for me too, and I did not go to him.'

'And if you had? If you'd died? What would have become of Molly and Hannah then? Sean and Joseph are in a better place now. They are at peace. They are together and they will watch over you. Whatever you do, they will always be with you.'

Maeve looked at Mary through her tears. 'I want them here with me now. I miss them. I am so alone. How will I manage?'

'Be strong. What else is there to do? Conor will stand by you. Come. The copper is on to boil.'

She bustled and prepared a tub for her sister to

bathe in front of the roaring kitchen fire, but when it was all ready Mrs Brogan returned with the children and they bathed them first. Hannah wailed at the water but Molly leapt and squealed with delight. Once they were done and had been whisked away, bundled in towels by Mrs Brogan, to be given bowls of warm milk, Maeve immersed herself in the water and allowed herself to be washed by her sister. Her face, hands and feet were black. She looked ten years older than her twenty-five years and her once glossy black hair was dry and thin. Mary wept as she bathed her, but Maeve was soothed by the water, and talked to her sister of her own trouble.

'Who is the father?'

'Daniel.'

'Oh.' Maeve looked at her. 'And when is it due?'

'In the summer.'

'What will you do?'

Mary was silent and Maeve did not press her. She climbed out of the tub and rubbed herself dry in front of the fire. Her skin glowed and already she looked better. Together they went upstairs to Mary's room and Mary produced an old frock of her own, clean and in good repair, which hung loose on Maeve but was a great improvement on the rags she had been wearing. Mrs Brogan had produced a mishmash of hand-me-downs for Molly to wear, including a pair of soft leather shoes which by a miracle fitted her perfectly, and a pair of woollen blankets for the baby.

'Well,' said Maeve when they were ready.

'Well,' said Mary.

The two sisters looked at one another. It was time to part.

'I'll see you before you go,' said Mary. But, in truth, she wondered if she would. She still wondered, too, what Maeve really thought of her, but she knew she would never dare ask her – in any case, it was too late to do so now. She bent to kiss Molly, gave Hannah a last hug, and then embraced her sister.

'It's all so strange,' said Maeve. 'So much has happened, and it's not even a year since we lit the bonfires.'

Con's appearance had changed much since his escape. He would not take any of Liam's food, though he did accept a little grain from the two sympathetic neighbours who knew that he was hiding out. He had lost all the weight he could afford to lose, and the dark, threadbare clerical suit Liam had given him made him seem even leaner. He had grown a beard, which changed his appearance so much that, even if anyone had still been looking for him, they would not have recognised him – and the fusiliers who would have been most likely to do so had been relieved by a fresh unit in the lines, at the end of their tour of duty.

Now he sat in Liam's parlour with Maeve and the children and listened as she told him the outcome of her day's work.

'Patrick McGinley?' he said. 'That's my name to travel under?'

'Yes.'

'With my wife and daughters?'

Maeve nodded.

'We'll be travelling as man and wife?'

'Yes!' said Maeve irritably. Conor was usually anything but slow. Now he seemed positively obtuse. Or was he driving at something?

'And when we get there?' Con said seriously. 'What will I be then?'

Maeve was silent.

'What will I be to you then?' he insisted.

She looked at him. 'My husband's brother.'

Con looked down. Was he ashamed of his impetuosity? She felt a wave of tenderness towards him and reached out her hand. 'I need you, Conor.'

His eyes met hers. He took her hand in his. 'I will go anywhere with you. Whatever it is you want me to be to you.'

Hannah, lying in a basket in the alcove by the fire, choked in her sleep and started to grizzle. Maeve got up and went to pick the baby up, soothing her in her arms. In a little while Hannah quietened down.

'I'd better go,' said Con. 'What time will Liam be back?'

'He's over at the fever hospital. There's no telling.'

'Tell him good-night.'

'I will.'

Con left silently. Maeve put Hannah back in her basket and turned to see Molly watching her with wide eyes.

'What is it, my darling?'

'I've got a new name.'

Maeve was bewildered for a moment, then she smiled. 'Yes, you have, and you must remember it.

We're going on a long journey and we'll all be using that name while we're travelling.' She knelt by her daughter. 'Can you tell me that name now?'

'Molly McGinley,' said the little girl.

'That's right. And you must make-believe that Conor is your daddy.'

'I want my real daddy.'

'He is with Joseph.'

'Why?'

'He went to take care of him. You wouldn't have Joseph all alone over there in heaven, would you?'

'No.' But Molly was unsure.

'We're still together.'

She brightened 'Yes. And Conor is my new daddy.'

Maeve hesitated. 'Yes.'

After Molly had gone to sleep, Maeve took out the glass beads she had rescued from her old skirt. She had found some string that would do in the table drawer.

Now she threaded the beads on to it. They winked in the lamplight, mirroring her tears.

There were upwards of a hundred people at the muster by Brannocktown Bridge. It was so cold that people stamped their feet and flapped their arms to keep warm, making the muster look from a distance like a colony of birds; but at least there was no wind. On a makeshift platform a sergeant stood, papers in his gloved hand, and near him the armed escort that was to accompany the emigrants on the hundred-mile march to Sligo stood ready. Liam moved among the crowd, consoling those bidding a tearful farewell, blessing those who were setting out on the great adventure. The predominant emotion was excitement. As one man said to another, 'After all, there can be no worse hell than the one we're now in.'

Above the mutter of the crowd the sergeant raised his voice, addressing them through a loud-hailer:

'Remember that on the march you must not stray or scatter. The armed escort is there to protect you. Stay together at all times until you are safely on board the ship. Now, have your tickets ready for inspection and form a line.'

The crowd shambled into some kind of order on the townward side of the bridge, and then began to shuffle across it in little groups, showing papers and tickets to the two soldiers who stood there. Liam stood close to Conor and Maeve, who were among those closest to the bridge. He knew he could not acknowledge them. There was no question of taking the slightest risk now that might spoil their chances.

'God bless you, safe journey to you,' said Liam to the people in general as they passed. But Molly caught his eye and, although he looked away immediately, she turned to her mother in confusion. Maeve pulled her on. They were close to the soldiers now. Molly looked up at one of them. She pointed to Conor and said loudly:

'This is my daddy.'

The soldier looked at her, then at Con. Con took her hand.

'I am Molly McGinley and this is my daddy.'

The soldier smiled and handed the tickets back. 'Good luck, mate,' he said to Con.

They crossed over to the other side of the bridge and began their walk. Liam watched until they were lost in the crowd.

Townsend was tired that night, but the sight of all those people leaving had given him fresh heart. He noticed, however, how low-spirited Mary was as she served his dinner, and thought he could guess the reason.

'Have you eaten this evening, Mary?'

'No, sir.'

Townsend hesitated, then he said: 'Would you care to join me?'

Mary looked doubtful. Mrs Brogan would be eating her supper in the kitchen. But Mrs Brogan had the rare quality of being incurious. 'I have no appetite, sir.'

'There's plenty of food. Lay another place, take off your apron and sit down.' He looked at her. 'Please.'

She did so, and allowed him to serve her soup, which she made some show of eating. He watched her for a moment, wineglass in hand, then he rose and crossed the room to the sideboard. He unlocked a drawer and from it withdrew a tin moneybox, which he placed with its key by her place. Then he sat down again and refilled his glass.

'I want you to have that,' he said. 'I have been thinking about it for some time. It is not a vast sum, but it will mean that you and your baby will be financially secure and …' again he hesitated, 'independent.'

Mary could not believe it. She looked at him quickly and understood the seriousness of his expression. Then she looked at the box, hardly daring to touch it at first. But she did, and unlocked it. It was full of banknotes. She took them out, held them in her hands, looked at him again.

'There should be a hundred pounds there,' said Townsend. There was almost a note of apology in his voice.

She did not know what to say, or what to think. 'We were evicted from our home because my father could not make up the *ten* pounds he owed. My parents are almost certainly dead.'

Townsend hung his head. After a moment he looked up at her. 'I care for you, Mary. I care for you more than you know. I made a fool of myself with you once, but I will not do so again. I do not want to see any more harm come to you, and I want to make some small investment in your future. I do not want you to associate me only with ruin.'

She looked at him. Then she folded the money carefully and held it in one hand. She stood up and left the room. For the first time, Townsend stood as she did. She had closed the door softly as she left and as he sat down again he looked at it, as if by so doing he could will her back. Would she keep the money? He hoped she would, and buy herself a better future with it. Perhaps one day this good deed would be weighed in the balance against all his bad ones, though he dared not hope either for her gratitude or her forgiveness. He left the table and crossed the hall to the drawing room, taking the brandy decanter from the tantalus and sitting with it by the fire. The house felt empty. It had always felt empty.

Daniel had been planning the attack with Ferry and Meagher in Coulter's back room for days now, while the police and the army had been busy getting the muster of emigrants ready for departure. Now they were ready to strike. Armed with short-barrelled pistols and knives, dressed in dark clothes and with blackened faces, they made their way stealthily up the road, keeping low and moving along the bank at its side, until they came to the agent's house. Both guards were at the gate, smoking pipes to distract themselves from the cold. There had been no Ribbon activity for some time and the men were obviously getting slack. Daniel felt a surge of grim triumph fill him. He and his men moved in quickly. The silent scuffle did not last ten seconds. Ferry and Meagher knew how to kill with a knife and they did it easily, without fuss, dragging the guards' bodies into the bushes by the side of the gate. Then the three men followed the wall around to the back of the house and scrambled over it.

'It's good he doesn't keep a dog,' whispered Ferry.

'He'll soon wish he had,' said Daniel.

They made their way across the lawn and arrived at a single-storey wing at the back, on to which Ferry and Meagher hoisted Daniel, who then climbed the roof up to the chimney stacks. He knew which flue led down to the drawing room – he had studied the house from a distance often enough with his spy-glass. Steadying himself, he withdrew a brown paper parcel from his pocket. Then he waited until he saw Ferry and Meagher go round to the front of the house.

Townsend was pouring himself another brandy when the fire settled and spluttered. Debris falling down the chimney, he thought, and leant forward for the poker. It was then that he saw the parcel lying on the burning turf. Instinctively, he knew what it must be. He threw the poker down with a cry and turned his back on the fire, making for the door. As he opened it, a deafening explosion from the grate blazed out and blew him into the hall. He turned to see furniture scattered and burning, the chair in which he had been sitting an obliterated wreck. He felt that his coat back and the hair on the back of his head were scorched. The room was full of smoke and seemed like a chamber in hell, but holding his sleeve across his face he dived back in. His revolver was in the drawer of the escritoire, which, being against the side wall at the far end of the parlour, had escaped damage. He reached it and retrieved the gun, then turned back immediately. The front door was being forced open with crowbars.

Daniel burst into the kitchen, where Mary stood up in horror to face him. He slammed the outer door behind him as he moved quickly through the room. He had drawn two pistols.

'Stay in here!' he shouted at her.

From the hall there came a sound of tearing wood as the front door gave. In another minute, Ferry and Meagher were in the hall. Townsend stayed just within the drawing room, out of sight. Ferry's attention was on the staircase. Mrs Brogan was hurrying down, having heard the explosion. She stopped when she saw Ferry, and he shot her in the face. The force of the ball knocked her backwards, then her body crumpled and rolled down the last steps of the flight to end up curled at its foot.

As Ferry spun round, Townsend emerged from the drawing room and shot him in the stomach. Then he swung his revolver on to Meagher and shot him too. Meagher was dead even before he'd lost his balance and fallen. But Daniel had come up from the kitchen and managed to shoot Townsend before the agent could turn. Townsend staggered and fell. Daniel stood over him.

'Don't,' screamed Mary. 'Don't!'

'Stay back!' shouted Daniel. For the split second his attention was distracted from Townsend, the agent had fired at him from where he lay, the bullet smashing his right arm. The pistol flew from his hand, but he still had a loaded gun in his left. Townsend lay there, bleeding heavily, trying to raise his revolver to get in a second shot. Daniel knelt down close to Townsend so that he could not miss, and shot the agent in the head. Then he collapsed.

Mary stood at the threshold of the front door, looking back at the carnage. The fire in the drawing-room flickered and cackled, but it did not spread. She would have done nothing if it had. Ferry rolled over on his back, groaning and coughing blood. Then he lay still. Daniel's head was pillowed against Townsend's chest, his hair matted with the agent's blood. Mary sank to her knees.

After an age she heard the sound of shouting from outside. Someone had heard the explosion and raised the alarm. McCafferty with a troop of police had ridden up. Dr Davis was with them.

Davis took her gently by the shoulder. 'Are you hit?'
She looked at him dumbly.

'We must get you away from here,' he said.

'One of them's still alive, doctor,' called one of the
constables. They were pulling Daniel to his feet.
'Murdering bastard.'

'Let me see to him,' said Davis.

'Time enough for that in the cells,' said McCafferty
as they dragged Daniel away.

By dawn the bodies were laid out on the front
lawn, while McCafferty and Brady consulted
about what to do with them. A letter would have
to be sent to Lord Hawksborough by the next
packet, but no-one knew of any relatives of
Townsend who would have to be informed. The
house looked mournful in the grey daylight, its
shattered front door and burnt-out parlour windows
like wounds. Liam had come there with Davis,
who'd been the one to tell him what had occurred
when he'd brought Mary to him in the middle
of the night. With the help of laudanum, she
was still sleeping peacefully in the care of Liam's
neighbours.

'God in heaven, what are we to do?' Liam said to
Davis as he surveyed the scene at the agent's house.

Davis shook his head silently. He had no answers
any more.

They had allowed Davis to set Daniel's shattered
arm, but it ached and throbbed, allowing Daniel's
mind no rest. He could not concentrate on anything

but the pain, and yet he felt he had much to think about. He sat in a corner of his cell at the police barracks and looked at the wall. At least he had killed the agent. They couldn't go on sending replacements forever. Sooner or later they would have to understand.

He turned as the door was unlocked to admit Liam. 'I told them that I did not want to see you, Father,' he said coldly.

'I know. I have brought someone else.'

'Who is it?'

'She has something to tell you. Something important.' Liam stood aside to let Mary enter the cell. Then he withdrew. He sat down outside and listened to the murmur of her voice through the wall.

When she had finished speaking, Daniel looked at her with remoteness in his eyes. 'How do I know the child is mine?'

He couldn't hurt her any more than he had already. 'Because it could not be anyone else's,' she said patiently. 'Why should I lie to you?'

'It won't make me say I am wrong. That I've been wrong to do what I've done.'

'But you are wrong.'

'No! O'Connell is wrong. "Human blood is no cement for the temple of liberty." Well, you get nothing in this life without a struggle, without a fight, and a bloody one at that.'

'What have you achieved by fighting?'

Daniel fell silent and looked away. But suddenly he turned back to Mary, continuing his argument as much to convince himself as to persuade her. 'All of Father Liam's beatitudes are a lie. "Blessed are the meek, for they shall inherit the earth. Blessed are the peacemakers, for they shall be called the sons of God." Lies to keep us meek and mild and in our place.'

'Words to give us hope.'

'Hope? What can a child of yours hope for?'

'A child of ours.'

Daniel faltered. 'A child of ours.'

'To have a home,' she said. 'Not to hunger. To be loved.'

'Yes, you would not think that was too much to ask for, would you?'

There was a pause. 'Do you not know how much you are loved?' said Mary.

Daniel looked away.

'By your brothers? By me?'

He was fighting back his tears.

'Let Father Liam give you absolution. Daniel. Open your heart again. Daniel.'

But Daniel refused to look at her.

By the end of the month he had been tried and found guilty. The day of the execution was fixed, and the public gallows made ready. Liam, whom Daniel had admitted, and to whom he had opened his heart, sat with his brother in the cell. The condemned man was quiet.

'Hail Mary, full of grace, the Lord is with thee. Blessed art thou among women, and blessed is the Fruit of thy womb, Jesus. Pray for us sinners, now and at the hour of our death. Amen.' Liam prayed. He held his brother's hand.

They heard the footsteps approach. The key on its rattling chain. The lock undone. They stood together and walked out into the dawn.

A dozen police stood by the gallows, but no crowd had gathered to watch the hanging. Daniel mounted the gallows and a policeman placed a black hood over his head. Through a slit in it, Liam anointed his brother's forehead:

'*Per istam sanctum Unctionem indulgeat tibi Dominus quidquid delquisiti. Amen.*'

Liam stepped to one side. They placed the noose over Daniel's head and pulled it tight. The man at the trap lever looked at McCafferty.

Daniel began to tremble violently. 'God save Ireland!' he shouted.

McCafferty nodded.

'Go forth from this world in the name of the Father, and of the Son, and of the Holy Ghost. Amen.' Liam prayed to himself.

Daniel's body twisted on the rope's end, fighting for life. Then, at last, he was still.

When Liam returned to his house, Mary had already packed. She would leave for Dublin that afternoon and take the boat for Liverpool from there.

He did not tell her about the execution and she did not ask. Indeed, they talked little while they waited for the wagon that would take her to Letterkenny, where she would pick up the stage-coach that would carry her the long distance south-east across the country to the capital.

When it arrived, she kissed him on the cheek and mounted the box-seat by the driver. It was still cold, but there was a faint promise of spring in the air and the sun was out, sparkling on the sea. Liam watched her go. It seemed to him that he was spending too much time these days saying goodbye to people.

But he stayed in Galready. There was work to do at the fever hospital, and the people needed a priest. He found himself able to take Mass again, without merely going through the motions, and that was a joy to him.

In the late Summer he had a letter from Mary. He had not wanted to be alone when he opened it and had taken it along to Dr Davis's house. His fingers trembled as he broke the seal.

'What does she write?' asked Davis, watching his face.

'She has a son,' said Liam.